M000035140

1.30p

LOST CAUSE

Also by Richard Greensted

Coming to Terms

LOST CAUSE

Richard Greensted

HEADLINE
FEATURE

Copyright © 1996 Richard Greensted

The right of Richard Greensted to be identified as the Author of
the Work has been asserted by him in accordance with the
Copyright, Designs and Patents Act 1988.

First published in 1996
by HEADLINE BOOK PUBLISHING

A HEADLINE FEATURE hardback

10 9 8 7 6 5 4 3 2 1

All rights reserved. No part of this publication may be
reproduced, stored in a retrieval system, or transmitted
in any form or by any means without the prior written
permission of the publisher, nor be otherwise circulated
in any form of binding or cover other than that in which
it is published and without a similar condition being
imposed on the subsequent purchaser.

All characters in this publication are fictitious
and any resemblance to real persons, living or dead,
is purely coincidental.

British Library Cataloguing in Publication Data

Greensted, Richard
Lost Cause
1. English fiction – 20th century
I. Title
823.9'14 [F]

ISBN 0-7472-1565-0

Typeset by
CBS, Felixstowe, Suffolk

Printed and bound in Great Britain by
Mackays of Chatham PLC, Chatham, Kent

HEADLINE BOOK PUBLISHING
A division of Hodder Headline PLC
338 Euston Road
London NW1 3BH

For Jane

PART ONE

ONE

'Exactly when did you last see your boy?'

Will picked at the cuticle on his thumb until it bled. The room was thick with the smell of human excretions and secretions, as if other visitors here might disguise their fear or shame with them. Lieutenant Jablonowski sat opposite him at the battered metal desk, twirling a pencil between his fingers as he waited for an answer.

'As I've already told you, we went to the store at six-thirty. I know that because I looked at the station clock as we were crossing the concourse. Our train was due to leave at six-fifty, so I knew we had plenty of time to get Tom a drink. We were in the store for three, maybe five minutes.' The echo of Will's English accent reminded him of how foreign he now felt in New York, and the thought alarmed him.

Jablonowski wrote something on his pad. 'And did you see anyone in the store you might recognise again?'

'I'm not certain,' Will said. 'It was busy, and I was concentrating on Tom.' He was trying to hold back the anger and frustration, desperately aware that he should keep his head. Jablonowski tossed his pencil on to the pad and leant back in his chair, putting his hands behind his neck. His shirt was stained with accumulated layers

3

of sweat, and his face was creased by all the batterings of a thousand confessions and denials that he'd heard in this room.

'OK, Mr Easterbrook. Your kid's disappeared. Maybe he's run off and is lost in the train station, maybe not. If he's in the station, we'll find him. If he's someplace else, well' – he shrugged and puffed out some air – 'it'll be tougher to locate him.' Will waited for more encouraging words, but none came.

'Tom wouldn't have run off, I'm sure of that,' Will said.

'Well, yes, I'm sure you are. But plenty of things might've confused him. Say, for instance, the guy in front of you was wearing the same pants. Your kid might have had his eyes on those, and followed them out of the store. By the time he knew it wasn't his dad, he might be lost. Happens all the time.'

'I accept that there are a number of theories,' Will snapped, 'but can we just concentrate on the idea that Tom was taken? What would happen then?' He felt his voice cracking as he faced up to this, and started picking at another cuticle.

'Have you phoned home?' Jablonowski asked, breaking the momentum of Will's questions.

'There's no one there,' Will replied. 'My wife, Clare, is in England with her parents.'

'OK.' Jablonowski leant forward across the desk. 'This town is full of crazies, Mr Easterbrook. Everyone's got an angle. Maybe they're sick, and don't know what they're doing. They've got your kid, but they don't know why. That's option one. Option two is, he's just gotten himself lost. You say your boy wouldn't run off on his own. OK, I'll buy that. But we could be looking at something else –

4

the possibility that your son was taken on purpose. Could be professionals, could be someone who was so desperate to have a kid of their own they just took him as an impulse thing. Either way, he'd be long gone by now. And that's our problem.' His jaundiced eyes looked watery, as if the conclusion distressed him. He looked at his watch. 'Your boy's been gone for what – two hours? If he's lost, one of our guys will pick him up real quick. But if he's taken' – he shook his head – 'he could be on an airplane by now, going to Christ knows where.'

'Do you watch the airports?'

'For sure, but these guys might be professionals. They'll have shaved his head in the rest room, put a wig on him maybe, changed his clothes so that he looks like a girl, maybe even given him a shot to calm him down. He'd be unrecognisable.'

'So how do we find him?'

'That's the problem, Mr Easterbrook. We can go through all the motions, issue posters, even put his photo on milk cartons, but the danger is that he's not even in the country.' He paused and looked at Will, lowering his head and his voice. 'I'm telling you all this now because it'll save some grief later. We have maybe a thousand cases just like yours, and all those parents think that we have some magic up our sleeves to get their kids back. But we don't – sure as hell, we'll do the best we can, but that may not be enough. We'll need a lot of luck. I don't want to get your hopes up.'

Will rubbed his eyebrows gently with his fingertips, partly to hide the tears that were forming. A vision of Tom danced cruelly before him: he was crying, shivering, bruised, in a squalid room with no furniture, shouting for his mum and dad. Will swallowed back the misery of that image, and looked up at Jablonowski.

'What can I do? Is there something, anything, I can do?' This man, this tired, overworked officer of the law was the only rope he had to hang on to, and he wanted to hear the smallest word of hope.

'There's a number you can call,' he said. 'Kind of a support group, for people in your situation. They have a nationwide network, all looking for kids who've gone missing. It's a long shot, but I guess it's your best bet right now.' He pulled open his desk drawer and scrabbled around until he found a card, the details of which he wrote down on a scrap of paper. He handed it to Will. 'Call them, see what they have to say. We'll keep on looking, of course, but they might be able to help too.' His writing was barely legible: *Family Matters, Inc., 1 800 499 2000.*

'Thanks. I'll do that. But what happens now?'

'We've circulated his photo and details to all the precincts in the city, and they'll be looking out for him. We plug the information into our national computer, so that every cop in the country should be aware he's disappeared. Maybe we'll get lucky, and he'll be found safe and sound. It does happen – just not as often as we'd all like. Right now, I guess your best option is to go home and get some sleep. We have your number, and we'll call if there's any news. There's nothing more you can do here.'

The advice, kindly given, was impossible to follow: the thought of sleeping whilst Tom was out there somewhere, frightened and alone, was inconceivable. Will closed his eyes tightly and tried to smile at him. 'Thanks,' he said weakly. 'Shall I call in tomorrow?'

'If you like,' he said, hardly encouragingly. 'But honestly, first news we get, you'll hear about it.' The interview was over, and Jablonowski had no wish to prolong it. He got up and walked to the door of his office. Will followed him, shook his hand and left the building, out into the cold night air. Suddenly Manhattan had become a threatening place, darker than before; the people on the street all seemed menacing, forbidding, hiding something that they would never let him know. He stood on the sidewalk and cried, huge sobs juddering through him. With what little voice he had left inside him, he shouted 'Tom! Tom!'

Grand Central was a foreign country, a state within a state, where the laws of existence differed from the world outside. Will was not certain how he got there but, once inside, he knew he couldn't leave. He shambled between groups of travellers, seemingly the only single person amongst a flood of happy families as they rushed to catch their trains and eat a final doughnut. Saturday night in the city, and everyone was invigorated by the throbbing energy of Manhattan, running from cab rank to bagel store to platform in an unrehearsed ballet of joyous movement. He shuffled uncertainly, having walked into a performance that he could barely understand, clutching a photo of Tom, still mumbling his name like some spiritual mantra. At the foot of a bank of escalators, a black woman, wretched with anxiety and gaunt through hunger, sat on the floor with her child, holding a scrap of cardboard that said simply *Please Help*. Will pulled out a twenty-dollar bill and handed it to her; she was so weary she could hardly take it.

'I'm sorry, but have you seen this boy?' he asked,

showing her the photo. Her large dark eyes studied it and then looked up at him as he crouched before her.

'No,' she said in a cracked voice, shaking her head.

'Thanks anyway,' he said. The nearness of the child, who stared blankly at the floor, had a powerful, enervating effect: he didn't want to get up and leave, feeling some strange magnetic pull towards this pathetic tableau. He dragged himself away, walking mechanically towards the deli where he had lost Tom; it was busier now, and there was a man serving at the till. With a misplaced sense of decorum, Will joined the queue and waited until he was in front of the man, thrusting the photo at him.

'I lost my son here earlier today,' he said pathetically. 'I don't suppose you've seen him?' The man looked at the photo, then at the queue behind Will, weighing up the options of being helpful or telling him to get lost. He grimaced.

'Sorry man, I can't help you,' he said, and took the shopping of the woman behind Will. He walked round the deli again, looking under shelf units and even opening a cold cabinet in desperation. The echo of Tom's recent presence rang in his ears, but nothing more. He left the store and walked back out on to the concourse, following a haphazard path around the terminus and accosting passers-by with his plaintive requests for information. Some simply ignored him, others looked at the photo then shook their heads sadly, briefly distracted from their own world. Will went to the cab rank outside, asked every driver, every person in the queue, until a policeman came up to him.

'What's your problem?' he barked at him.

'I'm sorry, officer, but I lost my son here earlier today

and I'm looking for him. Perhaps you heard about it.' He showed him the photo.

'You say you lost him, huh? You filed a report?'

'Yes, you're supposed to be looking for him.' Will was angry that he seemed to know nothing about it.

'OK. I'll check it out. Meanwhile, you just leave these folks alone, all right?'

'Look, I've lost my child, and I don't know what the hell's happened to him. I think I have a right to look for him.'

'Maybe so, but not if you're harassing other people,' he said. 'Now move along.' He put his hands on his hips in a gesture of authority; Will wanted to punch him, to attack him until he saw his point of view, but he slunk away instead, feeling a cold stare on his back.

He lost track of time and reason, wandering in large circles around the station as the flow of passengers decreased to a minor trickle, until he reached the waiting area, a large barren space set to one side of the concourse, with long wooden benches on which several winos and tramps were untidily arranged in various resting positions. He slumped down on an empty bench, and the cessation of movement, for the first time since he'd left Jablonowski, brought the full force of the tragedy back to him. Weeping, he closed his eyes and held out his hand, aching to feel the touch of Tom's soft skin against it. 'Tom,' he whispered.

He was distracted by the sound of vomiting, a dry heaving that betrayed an empty stomach; next to him, a man was crouched over his knees, retching furiously. Will got up and tried to stretch, arms and legs stiff after the short break of movement. The man beside him turned his head and grinned at him grotesquely, a line of spittle tracing down his dirty beard, then returned to his efforts to evacuate the contents of his gut on to the floor. Will's stomach turned, partly in revulsion, partly in hunger. He checked his watch: three-thirty a.m.

As he dragged himself around the station, searching each nook and cranny for signs of a little hand or foot or scarf or hat, his head spun like a top that was just about to lose its momentum, and he crashed to the floor near the information booth. His body told him to lie there, to close his eyes and shut out the horrors, but his heart forced him to pick himself up, steady himself against the booth, focus on the departures board and try to introduce some reason into his thinking. He dug his hands into his pockets and felt the small note that Jablonowski had given him. He pulled it out and looked at it: reactively, as if in a trance induced by the sight of it, he walked to a phone and called the number. It barely rang before someone answered.

'Hi. Family Matters, Julie speaking. How may I help you?' Will hadn't considered what to say, and it came out in a torrent.

'Hallo. My name's Will Easterbrook. I've lost my son, Tom, and I don't know what to do. The police said you could help.'

'OK, Will, can you give me some details? Where, when and how did this happen?' Julie's voice was sweet and calm, a professional carer.

'At Grand Central, about six o'clock in the evening. We were in a deli, and I lost him when I went to pay. The police seem to think he may have been taken.' His voice was cracking.

'Uh-huh. And how old is your boy?'

10

'Three. This was meant to be his birthday treat.'

'Where are you now?'

'I'm still at Grand Central.'

'Fine. You really need to come in and see us, Will. Can you do that?'

'Yes, yes of course. Where are you?' The offer of action and movement was strangely invigorating.

'We're on Second and Thirty-third, right above the Japanese restaurant. You're in walking distance.' The feeling in his legs suggested that she was wrong, but he didn't dispute it.

'Should I come now?' he asked.

'That'll be fine, Will. Ask for me, and we can talk. Do you have a photo of Tom?'

'Yes I do,' he said.

'Well, we'll see you in a little while then. Is there anything else you want to tell me now?'

'No, that's all. Thanks – I'll be there shortly.' Will put the phone back on the cradle and sighed deeply. Someone else had expressed an interest, however objective, in his plight, and that pumped fresh adrenalin from hidden resources into his system. But he needed to call the police again, in spite of the advice Jablonowski had given. He almost knew there would be nothing to report, and the call confirmed it. A duty officer told him that there were no further developments, and that they had his home number should there be any news.

He walked out to the cab rank, but no taxis were there so he headed south, the city towering above him, the spires of the skyscrapers appearing to join together to form a forbidding canopy that barred the light and hindered escape. Intimidating to an adult, the effect of this would

11

surely frighten a small child to death; he flushed the thought from his soul, but it stalked him all the way.

TWO

Ralph stood at the top of the stairs, dressed only in a pair of Aertex underpants that might once have been white. His body, though not fat, seemed to hang in weary resignation at the dual effects of gravity and age.

'Have you seen my socks?' he bellowed down the stairwell. Clare came out of the kitchen and looked up at the figure of her father, his hair still wet from the bath.

'They're in your hand,' she said, as if to a child. Ralph looked down and smiled, nodded, then went back into the bathroom. Clare returned to the kitchen to finish loading the dishwasher – a machine that was never used unless she came to visit. Her father's interruption had broken her train of thought, and now she tried to pick it up once more. They would have to leave by ten-thirty if they wanted to be at the hospital by midday; she dreaded taking Ralph with her, but dreaded more the thought of leaving him by himself. When she had arrived, he was building a fire on the floor of his studio – 'It gets so damned cold up here,' he had said – and the kitchen bore all the signs of his eccentricity, as the family had come to refer to it: a hammer for opening tins, traces of fried porridge in a pan, and an egg cracked straight on to the hob. As usual, Ralph had seemed capable only of opening a bottle of whisky and drinking it; all other domestic duties were beyond him.

The creeping lethargy she felt was gradually invading every joint, reminding her of the growing pains she'd felt as a child, when her mother had wrapped scarves around her knees to take away the aches. Clare's first efforts at sewing had been a pair of knee-warmers for her father, fashioned out of the old bedroom curtains; it never crossed her mind that he might not suffer from the same pain as she did. And, somewhere in this house, those knee-warmers were stored, along with many other things that her mother couldn't discard. Clare faltered at the thought; her industry abated as she remembered the boxes of photographs, the drawers stuffed full of old teddies and dolls, first dresses and shoes neatly wrapped in scented paper and filed away for ever. Did her mother ever pull them out in quiet moments, feel the nap of that velvet cape she'd made for Clare, sort the photos into chronological order? She didn't know, and that alone upset her. Now she knew so little of what they did, how they lived, and whether they were happy. With Dad like this . . . she stopped the thought before it grew too painful.

Clare switched the machine on and let the noise of the circulating water hypnotise her. She leant against the work-surface and closed her eyes, trying to clear her mind and concentrate on the things that had to be done. In a moment she would go upstairs and see what Ralph was up to; he might have put on the clothes she'd laid out for him, or he might be dressed in something totally unsuitable – he was particularly fond of a khaki shirt with matching shorts that he'd bought to go on a trip to Africa when she was a little girl. She could hear him above the

14

whirr of the dishwasher, and the anxiety she felt reminded her of Tom. It was as if she were looking after her own son, never completely relaxed when he was out of sight, a long period of silence normally signifying that he was doing something naughty. With her father it was much the same: without someone watching over him, he was almost certainly getting himself into trouble.

She pulled herself straight and felt her stomach, a little surprised that no wave of nausea accompanied the movement. She wrote some words down on a scrap of paper – polish, Jif, Dettol, Finish – and put the list in the back pocket of her jeans. A stupid idea crossed her mind: she thought of the supermarket trolleys you could put a toddler in, and wondered if she could fit her father into one. It would be so much easier than letting him roam free along the aisles, picking up armfuls of useless items. In the pantry she had found eight pounds of rice and six packets of sanitary towels. Shopping with Ralph would be extremely wearing.

He appeared in the kitchen, smiling and whistling, dressed exactly as she had wanted. Relief spread across her face: maybe this was going to be one of his good days. She walked over to him and put her arms around him, enjoying the closeness and the smell of him.

'So,' he said brightly as they pulled apart, 'what's the plan for today?' She remained unruffled by this question, even though she had told him earlier exactly what they had to do.

'As soon as I'm done here we'll go to the hospital and see Mum,' she said.

'Hospital?' he asked, looking perplexed.

'Yes, Dad, Mum's in hospital, remember?' His

eyebrows twitched downwards as he considered this.

'But I thought she'd gone to see Bea,' he said after a while.

'No. She was going to, you're right, but she never made it. She had a stroke.' He seemed no clearer in his mind about this course of events.

'Oh,' he said, nodding. 'Is she all right? We should really go and see her.'

'That's what we're going to do,' Clare replied encouragingly, as if he had just had a very good idea and she was delighted with him.

'Well, what are we waiting for? Let's go.' Clare looked around the kitchen and decided that the mess could wait. Collecting their coats, she guided him out of the back door and into the car.

'We'll have to do a little bit of shopping on the way home,' Clare said as she pulled out of the drive.

'Yes – we need rice,' Ralph said.

'Do you have a partner?' Julie asked.

Partnerships assume unlimited liability, right down to their last button. Partners are equal, unless otherwise specified, and have an equal call on the assets of the partnership. Was Tom a partner in the family? Did he have rights and obligations, duties and perquisites, or was he merely an employee of the partnership that Clare and Will had forged? How had he been treated: as an equal, or a minion? What should he expect from them now, as part of the care package assembled for him? Will's blood froze as he tried to envisage calling Clare and telling her the news.

'Yes. She's out of the country, visiting her mother.'

'Have you contacted her?'

'Not yet. I didn't want to worry her, in case . . . well, if it was a false alarm.' He shrugged apologetically at this selfish statement.

'I think you should call her,' Julie said quietly. 'She'll need to know.'

'Of course,' Will replied. 'I haven't really sorted things out very well yet.'

'That's understandable, Will. That's why we're here, to try and get things straight.' Julie was petite, pretty and neat, with a small voice that belied her calm and strength. Her manner was entirely appropriate to her job, and he wanted to hug her, not from some sexual urge but just to feel the closeness of another body, warm and comforting with the fragrance of acceptance and compassion.

On the wall behind her there were rows of photographs tacked up, children of all ages and colours smiling or studiously serious, each with a label stuck to the bottom which gave their details. All these faces seemed to stare at Will, seemed to be asking him directly if he could help restore the balance of their lives. Julie saw him studying them.

'I call that Heartache Gallery,' she said. 'If I ever get tired or feisty, I look at those pictures and they make me realise what I'm here for. All those kids just want their mom and pop.'

'What do you do all day? I mean, how do you actually go about it?'

'Well, we have thirty-two offices around the country. They're all doing the same as us, looking out for kids who've disappeared. We have details of everyone who's been reported missing, and we have teams of volunteers

17

who search the streets. But we do much more than that –
we counsel parents, and siblings, on how to face up to
this terrible thing that's happened in their lives.'

'And what's your success rate? How many of these do
you find?' he asked, motioning to the wall of photos.

'It varies. Some weeks we do real well and pick up a
lot; other weeks . . .' She shook her head and raised her
eyebrows. 'But we never give up hope, and neither should
you.'

'What happens to them? Is there a single main reason
for them going?'

'I wish,' she said. 'Sometimes, with the older kids,
they're in a bad situation, and the only way out is to run
away. With younger kids, like Tom, I'm afraid it's not that
simple.'

'The police said there's a trade in small children. Is
that right?'

'Sadly it is. You have to understand the despair of
couples that can't have children. They'll do anything to
get a child of their own. People, bad people, feed on that
despair. Loads of babies come into this country illegally
from South America, but there's a real premium market
for fair-skinned children. The government isn't doing
much to help – the adoption laws are so tough, there's
too much demand and not enough supply.'

'So what do you think has happened to Tom?'

'I don't know, Will, and it would be counter-productive
to speculate. There are so many things that might have
occurred. But we'll find out, in time. Right now, we just
have to hope for a lucky break.' No magic cure, no easy
solution; although this was what he expected, Will's heart
cracked at the thought of waiting, of time slipping by while

18

Tom remained tacked to their wall, his little life boiled down to three typewritten lines on a label.

'What should I do?' He felt so helpless and inadequate asking this, knowing her answer already.

'It really is better if you go home and rest,' she said. 'There's nothing more you can do for now. If Tom turns up, you need to be where we can reach you, and that's at home.' He nodded slowly, tears not far away. 'Don't be too hard on yourself, Will. Blaming yourself won't make it any easier.' She leant across and squeezed his hand, but hers was not the touch he wanted.

Clare had not known what to expect. She had the natural fear of hospitals that lives with every healthy person, and she was frightened at the prospect of seeing her mother attached to tubes and monitors, wires and drips pumping life into her. But Peggy was sitting in a wood and plastic armchair, the type you only ever see in institutions, fully clothed and working on a tapestry. When she looked up at Ralph and Clare her left eye was lazy; the lower lid was rolled back to reveal the scarlet tissue beneath it, and both eyes were watery. She put the tapestry on her lap, and held out her arms slowly.

'I won't get up,' Peggy said. 'It takes too much time.' Clare hugged her awkwardly as Ralph stood behind them, clutching the bunch of flowers they'd bought on the way.

'Well, I didn't expect you to be looking so chipper,' Clare said. 'You're a fraud.'

'Exactly what I think,' Peggy said. 'I've said I want to go home, but they won't let me.' Clare sat on the edge of the bed, but Ralph remained where he was, looking

19

around him as if concerned that they were in the wrong place.

'So how are you feeling?' Clare asked.

'Fine. I can't sleep here, of course, and the food is diabolical, but everyone's been very nice and kind. Bea came in – she brought the tapestry, said it's very therapeutic.'

'What do the doctors say?'

'A warning. A message from the system, apparently, but nothing more. They say that I should make a full recovery, but I will need some physiotherapy. I just want to get home; I'm so bored here.'

'I'd do exactly what they tell you, Mum. They do know what they're doing.' Clare tried to sound authoritative, unsuccessfully.

'I think they'll kick me out soon anyway,' Peggy said. 'They need the beds. Another ward just closed down.' Clare and Peggy both turned their heads when Ralph finally spoke.

'Listen, Peg, my old love, I'd get out of here pronto. It's full of people who look decidedly unwell. You might catch something.'

'That's right,' Peggy said, smiling. 'You'll look after me, won't you?' She turned and smiled at Clare, who leant over and touched her arm.

'Mum, I'm going to speak to social services, see if we can get you some home help,' Clare said quietly. 'Just until you're back on your feet.'

'That's very sweet of you, dear, but it's quite unnecessary. I'll be fine. Now, tell me all your news. How's that lovely boy?'

'Tom is wonderful. He's started at kindergarten and is

loving it. Will was taking him to see *Sesame Street* in Manhattan yesterday – he was so excited, he was practically bursting.'

'You should be there,' Peggy said. 'It's so silly, making all this fuss and flying over. And how's Will? How's his job going?'

'Oh, frantically busy as usual – jetting all over the place. Our next-door neighbour, Marla, is looking after Tom for him whilst I'm away, so there's no need to worry. I can stay as long as necessary.'

'It's him you need to look after,' Peggy whispered to Clare as she nodded at Ralph. 'How's he coping?' Clare shook her head and raised her eyebrows.

'Good and bad,' she said. 'Nothing I can't handle. But you can't be expected to look after him as well; you'll need help.'

'After forty-five years of it,' Peggy said, 'I think I can manage.'

'Well, we'd better be going, old girl,' Ralph said. 'Got to get the shopping done, and then I thought I might start on the hall.' The hall redecoration had been a project that Ralph had threatened to execute for more years than any of them could remember.

'That'll be wonderful, Ralph – something to look forward to,' Peggy said. Clare got up and hugged her again, and kissed her on both cheeks.

'I'll try to pop back tonight,' she said.

'Don't worry about me,' Peggy replied. 'Just do what you can.' Clare felt tears coming and turned away quickly.

'Come on, Dad, let's go and do that shopping.' She grabbed Ralph by the arm before he had a chance to wander off, looked back at Peggy and gave a small wave.

21

'See you later,' she whispered. She needed to get Ralph out of the hospital grounds before they apprehended him and locked him up in a rubber room.

THREE

The house smelt different – sterilised, disinfected, as if
there had been a conspiracy to conceal any trace of Tom
in the air – and the silence was more profound, more
intense and more empty than Will had ever known before.
Outside, the morning was crisp and clear, with frost still
crunching underfoot despite the brilliance of the sun. Will
stood at the front door, leaving it open, and called Tom's
name, continuing to call it as he went into every room,
looking behind furniture and curtains, crawling on his
belly to see under chairs and sofas, opening cupboards
and drawers, parting the clothes in wardrobes, pulling
back duvets, opening laundry baskets and emptying them
on to the floor. By the time he reached Tom's bedroom
he was crying desperately, still reciting the name and
frantically rearranging the tidiness in an effort to convince
himself that he would find something, some sign of his
presence or life force.

Scanning Tom's room, and seeing the toys that his little
hands had only recently touched, the pillow his light head
had lain on, the shoes Will had decided he should not
wear to Manhattan, the bag of nappies that he still used at
night, was the final agony, the rusty dagger that was twisted
remorselessly in his heart, and he collapsed on the bed,

inhaling the sweet perfume of Tom's aura in which the bedclothes were steeped. Will covered his face with the pillow and lay inert, immobilised by grief and weariness.

'Hi. Anyone home?'Will heard a voice from downstairs. A pair of heels clacked against the tiles of the hallway. 'Hallo?' He pulled himself up, wiped his eyes and went to the door of Tom's room. At the foot of the stairs stood Marla, their friend and neighbour. 'Will? What's up?'

He was clutching the banister, lacking the confidence to stand unsupported. She looked up at him.

'Will, what is it? What's happened?' He walked slowly down the stairs, manfully but vainly trying to hold back a fresh wave of tears; as he reached Marla, he almost fell into her arms, her soft embrace wrapping around him like a mother's. She stroked his back and head with her hand, then pulled her face away to look at him. 'Where were you guys? I thought you were meant to get back last night.'

'Something's happened, Marla,' he said falteringly. 'Tom's gone.'

'What do you mean, he's gone? How? Where?' The pitch of her voice rose as she spoke.

'We were at Grand Central, and I let go of Tom, and he just . . . disappeared. I've been looking for him all night.' Marla spent some time assimilating this news, all the while stroking his hair and holding on to him. At last she responded.

'What did the police say?'

'They think he might have been kidnapped. They're looking for him.' Will's speech was punctuated by sobs and sniffs, and Marla pulled a tissue from her sleeve and gave it to him.

'Oh, Will, that's terrible,' she said. 'Come and sit down, and I'll make some coffee.' She led him into the sitting room, put him on a sofa, and went into the kitchen. Will sat as she had left him, not wanting to move for fear that further pain would result. When she came back she was carrying a tray of cups and a cafetière which she placed on the coffee table. She sat down beside him and put her hand on his.

'Do you want to talk?' she asked softly.

'Nothing much to say,' Will said.

'Does Clare know?'

'I haven't had the courage to call her. I only just got back.'

'Do you have her number? I'll call her right now – she must know, Will.' Her prompt action was reassuring: someone was prepared to do something positive whilst he remained redundant. She went to the phone and he called out the number as she dialled. After an eternity, she spoke.

'Hi, Clare, it's Marla.' There was a subdued brightness to her tone. 'Listen, babe, I've got Will here with me, and there's some bad news. Little Tom's gone missing – seems he got separated from Will at Grand Central. I think you'd best come back. Will really needs you here.' There was a pause as Marla listened, then she spoke again. 'No, Will's resting right now. He was up all night looking for Tom, and with the police and all. Just give me a call here – I'll stay with him – and we'll come and fetch you from the airport.' She listened some more, nodded her head, then spoke. 'Yeah, that's fine.' It was obvious to Will that Clare was asking a lot of questions, and equally obvious that Marla had no intention of answering them. 'Listen, don't worry, I'm sure everything's going to be fine. I'll take care of things here. You just get yourself back safely, OK?' Marla put the phone down, looked at Will and smiled.

'How did she take it?'

'She had a lot of questions, but I didn't have so many answers,' she said. 'Hey, you've got to get some sleep. Go on upstairs, and I'll stay here.' She came up to him and put her hands on his head, her abdomen against his face. 'Poor Will,' she said.

'Poor Tom,' he replied into her body, and the tears began to sink into her clothes.

Ralph was dozing in front of the television. Clare watched him as he slept, so harmless, so peaceful, so utterly oblivious to the horrors that now engulfed her. She knew she should be active, making plans and arrangements, organising his life so that she could get on with her own. She wondered if he would understand the news if she told him, and thought it unlikely: in his confused world, where nothing assumed any order of priority or significance, he would take the information and store it randomly, perhaps to be recalled at a later moment, perhaps to be lost for ever in the labyrinth of his twisted mind. There were no tears in her eyes; the call from Marla had sucked everything from her, drying her up and shrivelling the senses, so that she stood now in suspension, unable to function or act. Like loose ropes around her, the news simply restricted movement.

Standing with her hands on the back of an armchair, she tried to clear her mind and focus on the present. Activity might distract her from the horror of Marla's news and the pain that awaited her in New York. In the sanctuary of this house, where so much of her life had taken place, so many dreams and nightmares realised, Clare still struggled to take control and accept her role as guardian and protector of her family. With her father in the room, she wanted to ask his advice; needed him, or someone, to take control and tell her what to do. Instinctively she wanted to call Will, get more information in an attempt to arrange the facts so that they might make more sense. What Marla had not said seemed so much more important than what she had, and she was incapable of visualising the event without those details that would deliver the full blow of the news. This gap in her knowledge had suspended her in a vacuum between action and grief.

With heavy effort Clare pushed herself upright and turned to the telephone. But the number she dialled was not Will's; she decided to delay an instant response for fear that it would consume her every thought and action, and she needed a delay until she had the time to deal with it, wanting to clear the space around her that was crowded with Ralph and Peggy. She waited as it rang, watching the top of Ralph's head as he slumbered.

'Hallo, Dr Cassidy? It's Clare Easterbrook, Ralph and Peggy Waldron's daughter.'

'Hallo, Clare, long time no see. How are you? How's the Big Apple?' Dr Cassidy was the same age as Ralph, and had attended the family since they had moved to St Ives.

'Fine. I'm terribly sorry to call you at home, but I need to speak to you rather urgently.' He muttered his understanding and Clare continued. 'Something's cropped up in the States and I've got to go back. I'm rather concerned about Mum and Dad coping on their own, and I wanted your advice.'

'What's the situation with your mother?' Cassidy asked.

'I saw her this morning and she seems well enough – just very weak and tired. But actually, I'm more worried about my father. Have you seen him recently?'

'No – should I have?'

'I don't know. But he's acting oddly. Sometimes he's lucid, sometimes not.' Clare checked Ralph's head to make sure he was still sleeping as she betrayed him. 'Anyway, I really don't think he's capable of looking after Mum when she comes home, and I wondered if there's anything we can do to help them – you know, like a home help or something.' She could hear him sigh.

'Well, my dear, it sounds as if I need to come and see your father. Once I've examined him I can make a report to social services, and they'll come and assess him to see if he qualifies for home care. But it all takes a bit of time.' Time, space – these were commodities that Clare did not have in stock, and the thought of sitting on her hands whilst social workers filed endless reports and used every delaying tactic they could find to resist spending money chilled her.

'When could you come?' she asked hopefully.

'I'll be over as soon as I can,' he said, fulfilling her hope. 'I'd hate to see Ralph and Peggy stranded.'

On the video of Will's subconscious a nasty film was running: he was standing in a huge field, in bright sunshine, and his feet were tangled in thick mats of grass and straw. Every time he tried to move the tendrils tightened around his ankles, and he screamed silently into the still air. At the edge of the horizon Will could see a minuscule figure that might have been a child or an adult, running back and forth and utterly heedless to his plight. The figure threatened to disappear completely, and Will held his arms above his head to try and wave, but the grass anchors beneath him restricted his movements and upset his balance. The struggle exhausted him but he knew he could not lie down and rest in case he lost sight of the figure, who seemed to represent his only hope of escape.

Will woke to find himself completely soaked with sweat. For the briefest moment he thought that he had dreamt it all, and he jumped off the bed and ran across the landing to Tom's room, hoping to find him on the floor surrounded by his toys. The bed still bore the indentation of Will's body, and he felt foolish, a heavy lump appearing in his throat to validate the feeling. Entering Tom's room, and seeing a thousand signals of his absence, brought the full fury of events back to him, and he ran into the bathroom to turn on the cold tap and wash the horror away.

Marla came in behind him, and he felt her hand on his back. 'How're you doing?' she asked.

'Pretty grim,' he managed to croak.

'Hey, a lady called Julie called. Sounded real concerned. She's left a number.' Will turned off the tap and dried himself.

'Did she have any news?' he asked anxiously.

'Didn't say. She wants you to call her, though.'

It was impossible for Will to believe that Julie might have anything to tell him, but reason had long since departed. He went to the phone in the bedroom and called the number she had given him. As he waited for her to answer he looked at his watch: it was four-thirty in the afternoon. Outside, darkness was already falling, and the black coldness of the dusk reminded him of the image of Tom alone, tired and scared.

Julie's tone was unchanged when she answered – calm, low and reassuring – and she sounded pleased to hear from him.

'Any news?' he asked.

'Nothing yet, Will, but it's early days. I was really calling just to see how you're dealing with things, and to remind you that I'm always at the end of the phone. I know it's difficult to sit tight, but it's the best thing you can do.'

'I appreciate that. There must be something I could be doing.' He knew there wasn't.

'Just stay where you're reachable, and if you think of anything, any detail at all that might help, call and let us know. That's about it.' She was well practised in this routine of comforting the uncomfortable.

'OK, I'll try and take your advice.'

'It might be a good idea,' she concluded, 'to bring your partner along to see us, if she wants to. Might make her feel that there is someone else worrying about Tom. Anyways, that's up to you.'

'Thanks, Julie. Stay in touch.'

Marla was making a big sandwich in the kitchen – salami, tomato, Swiss cheese, lettuce and mayonnaise – but the sight of it turned his stomach. She seemed to know it would.

'You've got to keep your strength up,' she said in a tone of admonition.

'I can't face it, Marla.' She stopped work on the sandwich, and looked at him.

'Look, stop me if this is too painful, but I was thinking. Jay knows this really good private investigator. Perhaps you should give her a call, see if she has any angles that you haven't considered.'

'Why not?' he said after some random thought. 'Anything that'll help.'

'Good for you. I'll get her number, and you can call her. Who knows?' She shrugged and smiled at him, a good, kind smile that laid her thoughts bare and touched him to the core.

FOUR

There were several numbers in his head. He knew that they were all important, that they all had some significance in his life; but his mind was not working properly, and they danced about and got jumbled together. He looked ahead of him as his sight returned, and he could make out the silhouette of a man's head. It hurt a little when he turned to look beside him: in the darkness of the car it was difficult to make out who was sitting next to him, but he didn't recognise the shape or form of the person.

His trousers were damp, cold and uncomfortable. They felt strange, a different material than usual: his hands were resting on his thighs, and he moved them to test the sensation. Instinctively one hand moved to where his pocket should be but he found no opening, and he searched for a while in the dark before finding the slit and pushing his fingers in. The pocket was empty, which alarmed him.

'Well now, will you look at this?' a woman's voice said in the blackness. 'Our little prince has woken up. How are you feeling, honey?' The voice sounded kind, but unrecognisable, and he stayed silent. A soft hand stroked his cheek and he sat very still.

'Lost his tongue, huh?' the silhouette said from the

33

front of the car. 'Guess he's still a bit tired.'

'Are you hungry, angel? You want to stop somewhere and get something to eat?' Tom listened: he was very hungry, and thirsty, but he dared not speak. Although the voices were friendly, they remained unidentifiable. 'Do you like cheeseburgers?' the woman continued. 'With fries and a milkshake?'

'Yes,' Tom said huskily.

'Well, good. Chuck, why don't you stop soon and we'll take a break? Seems the little man needs nourishment.'

This was encouraging news for Tom and he felt a little more confident. He felt the arms of the car seat he was strapped into, and looked out of the window. The night was punctuated by the flash of lights in the distance and he tried to focus on the brightness of them. He felt very tired, but something told him to stay awake.

Before long they had pulled into the parking lot of a diner; his door was opened by the man and he was unstrapped and gently pulled out of his seat. The man's arms were big and strong, and he held Tom firmly against his torso. Tom's arms hung limply by his sides as they walked to the diner. Inside the neon lights burned his eyes and he squinted to protect them. He was put down on a big plastic bench seat and the man sat beside him, blocking his exit. The woman sat opposite them and Tom tried to sneak a look at her: she had blonde, almost white hair, and very little make-up. Her face was spare, haunted, and her eyes darted from left to right. She seemed to jump a little when the waitress came over with a jug of iced water.

'Well hi,' the waitress said. 'What can I get for you tonight?' Tom listened as the man ordered food and drinks;

he watched as the woman lit a cigarette and was fascinated by the swirling spiral of smoke that rose to the ceiling. His attention was diverted by the woman's voice.

'Guess you're a little confused,' she said, and Tom looked at his feet swinging beneath the table. 'I'm Betsy, and this is Chuck. We're going to be looking after you for a little while, honey. Your mom and pop asked us to, seeing as they have some problems they've got to take care of.' Tom couldn't determine exactly what this meant, but he got the general message. He thought briefly of Marla: she always looked after him when Mum and Dad asked her to. She must be busy, he thought.

'Hey, listen,' the man said brightly. 'We're going to play a little game. We're going to pretend that we're on a secret mission, that no one must ever know what we're doing. Top secret, right? And you're a special man, so we'll need to give you a special name. What do you say if we call you Ricky – Ricky Callahan, special agent. Sound good?' Tom liked the idea of a game, but he was surprised that these two grown-ups wanted to play. He thought about the name, and he thought about his name. But he was too tired to argue. He nodded, still looking downwards.

'Great,' said the woman. 'So from now on, you're Ricky Callahan. We'll always call you that. And you can call us Chuck and Betsy, OK? Those aren't our real names, of course. We're secret agents too.'

The food arrived, and Tom's cheeseburger was put in front of him. A huge pile of fries sat on the side of the plate and he reached out to pick one up. It was hot and he dropped it.

'Careful, honey. They're real hot,' Betsy said. She sounded just like Mom, and that reassured him. He tried to pick up the tall glass of milkshake and Chuck helped him to steady it. Tom sucked some through the straw, then put the glass down, again with Chuck's help.

'Isn't this great?' Betsy said. 'I bet you've never been to a diner this late, have you, Ricky?' So it was late: that was exciting. He looked around the diner; there were only one or two other people eating, and he thought that everyone else must be in bed. He picked up the cheeseburger and bit into it. 'I bet you can't finish all that,' Betsy said.

'Well, I don't know about that,' Chuck said. 'Looks like he's a big man with a big appetite. I think he'll do it.' Tom was amazed. These people were just like his parents; they said the same things, and made the same fuss. He relaxed a little as he ate. He noticed that Betsy hardly touched her food: she must be on a diet, just like Mummy.

By the time the meal was finished, Tom felt much better. Everything the grown-ups said was either about him or to him. They were nice people, he concluded. Chuck wiped his mouth very carefully with a paper napkin; he was a big man, much bigger than Daddy, with huge forearms covered in sandy hair. But he was gentle.

'Now, you want to use the bathroom before we get going?' Betsy asked Tom. He shook his head before thinking about it. 'You sure, honey? We've got a long journey ahead of us.' He shook his head again: it was a routine he'd followed a thousand times with his parents. It was really strange, how similar everything was. But, as they got back into the car, Tom remembered those numbers again. He knew they had something to do with Mum and Dad and Grandpa, but he was too exhausted

36

to think what. No sooner had they set off again than he was asleep.

Marla stood in her own kitchen, torn apart by the quandary she'd faced. She wanted to be with Will and Clare, helping them in their hour of need, but she knew she'd be intruding on some private moments of grief. On the journey back from the airport, neither had spoken more than a couple of brief sentences. They sat in the back of the car and Marla had to bite her tongue a dozen times as she thought of something comforting to say and then changed her mind.

The doorbell rang, and Marla moved quickly to open it. On the step stood Clare, red-eyed and shoulders drooping. 'Got some wine?' she said quietly to Marla.

'Sure, come in,' Marla said, and they went through the hall and into the kitchen. Clare slumped on to a chair at the large round table and Marla brought out glasses and a bottle from the fridge. 'So how's it going?' Clare looked at her blankly. 'Dumb question, I guess.'

'Will's asleep. He took something pretty powerful to help him. But I can't do it. I can't sleep whilst Tom's out there somewhere.' Clare waved an arm towards the window. 'Jesus, it just can't happen, can it? He can't just have disappeared. Where's he gone?' She sobbed, and Marla put a hand on her back and rubbed it.

'You know the oddest thing?' Clare said, sniffing and drying her eyes with the back of her hand. 'I want to blame someone. I want someone to be responsible for all this. But I can't blame Will. It wasn't his fault. The number of times Tom could have been snatched, when we left him for a minute in the car or at the shops, it was bound to happen. Will was just unlucky it happened to him. But whoever took Tom, that's who I want to blame, and I don't know where to start.'

'The first priority is getting Tom back,' Marla said. 'And I know you will, sooner or later.'

'I wish,' Clare said. 'But where the hell do we start?' The despair overwhelmed her again, and this time the sobs shook her whole body. Marla chewed the inside of her cheek in anguish, unable to find anything suitable to say. She had never been so close to someone else's grief without having the necessary skills to lessen it, and the feeling was worse because Clare had always been a model of common sense and calm: nothing ever put her out of her stride or changed her even temper. Clare's collapse was all the worse to Marla for this.

The sobbing finally subsided, and Clare drank some wine and smiled weakly at Marla. 'Sorry. I shouldn't be doing this to you. But—'

'Don't be so silly,' Marla interrupted. 'That's what I'm here for. And we're going to work it out, together.' She pulled a chair up next to Clare, sat on it and hugged her awkwardly. 'Tom will be back sooner than that,' she said, snapping her fingers. 'This is all some crazy nightmare that'll be over real soon.' Clare nodded as she rested her head against Marla's bosom. It was a comfortable feeling, and it made her think of Tom and the same comfort he would take from cuddles with her, a mutual comfort that was now denied to both of them. Where was he to do his crying, and where could he find his support?

FIVE

Lotus Ridge stood in one hundred and fifty acres of woods next to Lake Waccabuc in Westchester County. There were seven houses, all finished slightly differently but based on the same interior layout; behind the development there was a communal swimming pool and tennis court. Only four of the houses were occupied: Clare and Will lived in one, with Marla and Jay as their neighbours, with the other two taken by an Australian businessman who was never there, and a family of five. The houses were set around a cul-de-sac, well away from the road that led eventually to New York City, some sixty miles away.

At first Clare had not been enthusiastic about living there, in spite of the astounding natural beauty and the wonderful design of the house. She'd wanted to be somewhere more lively, nearer to civilisation, but she gave in to Will, who reasoned that he would need to return to this sanctuary after the rigours of a working day in Manhattan. She had grown to love the area and the people in it, who were friendly and open, always ready to help and talk. Will's job – he was in charge of the corporate debt recovery division for a large American bank – took him away from home one or two nights every week, and

Clare had worked hard to build a circle of friends; in this Tom had been helpful, acting as a catalyst for conversation and introductions. The children of the other family on the estate were much older, but they treated him like one of their own, looking after him at the pool and taking him out for bike rides.

Three days had passed since Tom's disappearance, and there had been no news. Will had been told to take as much time off as he needed, but every day he would go to Manhattan by train, down to Grand Central for a comprehensive search of the station. Clare watched him go with resignation: she could scarcely blame him for his compulsion, even though she felt it unlikely that anything would result from his trips. He would return bleary-eyed and sullen, and they would sit opposite each other in their large sitting room, with nothing to say and no need or desire to enunciate their grief. They ate mechanically and slept fitfully, whilst the frustration gnawed away at them. Jablonowski called them once, a routine call that might have been scripted for him; Julie called whenever she could, updating them on her work and offering extra sympathy if they needed it.

The fourth morning was no different; Will got up at five-thirty, showered and dressed, made breakfast and brought it up to Clare in bed. They sat silently together, both wishing they could be alone with their thoughts but unable to articulate this in case it offended the other. By nine o'clock they were ready for their caller; they sat on the window-seat in the kitchen that overlooked the drive and waited. At ten past a battered car appeared and parked in front of the house. A woman got out, then leant back in to pull out her case and jacket. She slammed the door,

40

pushed her fingers through her thick red hair, then came to the front door which opened before she had a chance to ring the bell.

'Hi. Mr Easterbrook? Sorry I'm a little late – you guys are certainly secluded here.' She shook hands with Will and moved inside without waiting to be asked. Will's initial reaction was one of surprise: she was no more than five-foot-two, and was dressed in a blue wool trouser suit with a crimson blouse. Her hair was wild, tumbling to her shoulders in soft red curls, and she wore little make-up. She was not what he had expected, but then he had not entirely known what to expect.

Clare came into the hall to greet her. 'Hi. I'm Rocket Stubblefield. My folks had a sense of humour, I guess.' They shook hands briefly, then Clare led her into the sitting room with Will following them. They all sat down and Clare motioned to the cafetière on the table.

'Coffee?' she asked Rocket.

'Please,' she replied enthusiastically. 'Black, no sugar – I hope it's not decaf. I thrive on caffeine.' Clare poured three cups and Rocket picked hers up immediately and sipped at it. 'That's better,' she said. 'Now, let's get down to business. Mind if I smoke?' Clare and Will both shrugged, and Rocket pulled a pack of cigarettes from her case and lit one. 'So – what? – it's been three days since little Tom went AWOL, right?'

'That's right,' Clare said quietly.

'OK. That pretty much rules out the possibility that he wandered off and got lost. The cops would have picked him up by now.'

'So you're saying he was snatched deliberately?' Will asked.

'Can't say,' Rocket replied. 'But it does seem to be the most likely option, doesn't it?'

'Before we go any further,' Clare said, 'can you just tell us a little bit about what you do, and how you operate?'

'Sure. I find people. I get used by all sorts, banks and stores and businesses that have got debtors who've skipped their payments. I bring them back. Kind of like a modern-day bounty-hunter, I guess you'd say.'

'And how do you do that exactly?' Clare asked.

'If I told you that, you wouldn't need to use me,' Rocket said, laughing. 'But let's just say I have a load of contacts, and they keep me in touch with what's going on. There's a lot of sweat involved, and a little bit of luck. Mostly what I do is completely legal.'

'Have you ever heard of Family Matters?' Will said.

'Yeah, I've heard of them,' Rocket said disdainfully. 'A bunch of well-meaning amateurs. But they're so high-profile that they scare people off – people who might talk to me. They're kind of like a nice aunt – a shoulder to cry on, but totally useless when it comes down to it. Why? You thinking of using them?' Clare and Will looked at each other. 'Uh-oh,' Rocket continued. 'Have I put my foot in my mouth again?'

'No, no,' Will said, putting his hands up. 'We're just exploring every avenue.'

'Yeah, and that's understandable,' Rocket said. 'But take it from me, if we're going to find your boy, we need to be really professional. Look, why don't we start by you telling me a little more about what exactly happened.'

'I took Tom to see a show at Madison Square Gardens,' Will started. 'We left there at about six o'clock, and got a cab over to Grand Central. We went to the deli to get some drinks and I queued to pay for them. I thought Tom was right by me. When I looked round, he'd gone. That's all there is to it.'

'Who knew you were going?' The question surprised both Will and Clare, and they paused whilst they considered the reasons for it.

'A neighbour of ours,' Will said, shaking his head. 'No one else that I can remember. Why?'

'You'd be surprised,' Rocket said. 'Quite a few of these things are done by people you know, people who know your movements and when they'll have an opportunity. Is the neighbour Marla – Jay's wife? You trust her? She doesn't have any kids, does she?'

'That's ludicrous,' Will said. 'She is completely trustworthy. End of discussion.' He was irritated and wanted to let her know it.

'Fine,' Rocket said, apparently unconcerned. 'We'll work on the basis that he went off with someone he doesn't know.'

'Have you ever handled one of these cases before – that is, child kidnapping?' Clare asked.

'Couple of years back I found a kid who'd been taken – by her uncle. His wife had lost a baby in childbirth, and he was all cut up about it. Took a few weeks to get it sorted out.'

'So – assuming we want to use you,' Will said, 'what would you do first?'

'Well, we're looking at two options here. The first is that the kidnapping was organised and planned, that you were watched and followed and Tom was taken when the time was right. That's what I'm hoping is the case.'

'And the other option?' Clare asked.

'Yeah, the other option,' Rocket sighed. 'Someone saw your kid and thought to themselves: "Wouldn't it be neat to have him?", just like they were shopping. And they took him.'

'Why is the first alternative preferable?' Clare said, watching Will, who was looking desperate.

'Because it's organised, and organisation leaves tracks. Many more people are involved, and someone might get careless or talk out of turn. And some of the gangs who do this are well known, even to the police. But the other . . .' Rocket shrugged and pulled on her cigarette.

There was silence as Will and Clare assimilated her information. Rocket got up and walked over to a small circular table in the corner: she picked up a framed photograph from it.

'This Tom? He's a beautiful kid.'

'Oh, of course, you'll need a photo of him,' Clare said, jumping up and going to a chest of drawers.

'Only if you want me to work on your case.' Rocket walked over to Clare. 'Can we talk alone for just a moment?' she said quietly. Clare nodded and they went into the kitchen. Will remained seated, head down in contemplation of the full horror that lay before him.

'Listen,' Rocket said, 'it's none of my business, I know, but you folks should really think about counselling. You're good people, and you think you can pull through this together, but believe me, it doesn't always work like that. It eats away at you, and you take it out on each other without even knowing it's happening to you.'

'Thanks. We'll think about it.'

'Do that. I don't mind if you decide you don't want to use me, but you should get some help. You've got to look at the worst-case scenario – what if he never comes back? What will you do then?'

'I've thought about that,' Clare said. 'Will won't accept the possibility, which is right, but I know what you're saying and it's on my mind. I also have another reason to think about the future.'

Rocket looked at her carefully, then put her hand on Clare's abdomen. 'How many weeks?' she asked.

'Nine.'

'And you haven't told him?'

'I only found out when I was in England. I haven't had a chance.'

'Sounds like you and your husband have got some talking to do,' Rocket said. 'I'd better leave you to it.'

'Look, thanks for coming over. I'd like to use you, but I'll have to discuss it with Will. We'll be in touch, OK?'

'Sure. No problem.' They went back into the sitting room and Rocket picked up her case from the sofa. Will was in the same position, but looked up as she stood in front of him. She held out her hand. 'Nice meeting you, Mr Easterbrook. I'm really sorry this has happened to you, and I want to help if you'll let me.'

He nodded and tried a little smile. 'Thanks,' he said. Rocket left, and Will and Clare returned to the heavy silence that engulfed the house.

When Tom woke up he found Betsy sitting in a chair next to his bed. He tried to remember who she was, and where he was. The room was unfamiliar, but it looked special: there were mobiles hanging from the ceiling, and the walls were decorated with cartoon characters that he recognised from videos. There was a big box of toys in the corner,

45

and lots of books in a wooden bookshelf near the head of the bed.

Betsy had something in her hand: he reached out automatically for it and she gave it to him. It was a scrap of material, a yellow square of a blanket he'd had in his cot as a baby. The material was worn through the constant rubbing against his nose and mouth.

'I'm sorry, Ricky. I found it in your other trousers. I thought it might be special for you.' He clutched it in his fist and plugged his thumb into his mouth. Everything seemed clearer and better with his comforter close to him. 'Now what do you like for breakfast? We have Cheerios, or French toast, or waffles and syrup, or eggs. What would you like?'

'Where's Mummy?' Tom said. Betsy leaned over and stroked his head.

'Mummy's very busy, and she's asked me and Chuck to look after you for a while. Tell you what, shall we call her later?'

'Yes,' Tom said, the prospect cheering him. He couldn't understand why Mummy hadn't said goodbye.

'We'll do that right after breakfast. Now, let's get you up and dressed. We've got a busy day ahead, and we don't want to miss it.'

'What are we doing?' Tom asked.

'You'll just have to wait and find out,' Betsy teased him. 'Come on, sleepyhead, let's get this show on the road.' Tom moved slowly out of bed and let Betsy take his pyjamas off and dress him. He was looking forward to talking to Mummy.

SIX

Will slept on the edge. Physically he hung over the side of the bed, arm dangling and leg crooked; mentally he never plunged into the depths of the subconscious, always sleeping like a dog, ready to jump up and take action at the slightest noise or provocation. He was always awake at first light, and was incapable of lying inert: he would get up and get prepared, whether preparation was needed or not.

He was neither fit nor unfit; he played a little tennis and some golf, but spent no time on his health. His life, and his opinion of it, were uncomplicated by considerations of physical or mental well-being and contentment; he merely existed, taking pleasure or pain in his stride, questioning nothing and rarely worrying about the direction he might or should be taking. This to Clare was frustrating and attractive in equal measure; she liked Will's casual approach to events, the way he let the river of life carry him along where it would, but this same kismet, this unchallenged acceptance of fate, annoyed her too, as she wondered where they were heading and how they could shape their dual destiny. He never had a plan; he never made a decision, even about the most ordinary of things, if he could delegate it to her. He seemed to pursue the line of least resistance, and she sometimes wondered if that had been his primary, perhaps his sole, motivation for marrying her: it was easy, it sorted out some problems for him and satisfied her, and there was nothing more to it than that.

By turns Clare thought him weak and strong: he accepted the probable as inevitable without putting up a fight, but he also accepted associated troubles with equanimity. Or had done: now, as she sat in the bathroom and retched, her tears a product of the effort and her grief, she saw a different side to Will. The loss of Tom had scratched a little of the surface, and underneath she could see the vaguest traces of resolve, as if at last Will had found a cause that he believed in, a crusade that he could follow. He was sullen and withdrawn, and this itself was new; Will never normally brooded on the past, shrugging it off without looking either back or forward, but he was doing both in reaction to Tom's disappearance. He kept his thoughts to himself, but she could see the change and, perversely, it encouraged her.

She was considering this when Will came in. Clare was perched on the side of the bath and he interpreted the scene incorrectly. 'Sleep is a pretty rare commodity at the moment,' he said quietly as he washed his hands at the basin. He was always washing his hands, a habit he'd picked up from the time Tom was born. At first he wouldn't even pick Tom up unless he'd washed them thoroughly; he would come home from work and would head straight for the kitchen sink. Clare watched him now and remembered a small incident.

'Do you remember those bottles?' she asked. He shook his head and looked at her reflection in the mirror above

48

the basin, frowning. 'The steriliser?' Then he smiled, more in embarrassment than amusement. Like all good parents, they had religiously sterilised all the feeding bottles for Tom and anything else that might come into contact with his busy mouth. One evening, just before Tom's night-time feed, Clare had come into the kitchen and found Will taking the bottles and teats out of the sterilising bucket and rinsing each of them in turn under the tap. He'd explained that he thought Tom wouldn't like the taste of the steriliser; Clare wondered how Tom had managed to survive. It was now a standing joke between them, and something that they would tell Tom when . . .

The thought riveted Clare, and she knew that exactly the same had happened to Will. He turned to look at her, shaking the water off his hands.

'What are we going to do, Will?' she said, without making it a question he had to answer. She rarely asked him real questions, but normally delivered answers.

'We're going to get him back,' he replied, surprising her with the quiet determination in his voice. 'Whatever it takes, however much we have to sacrifice, we have to get him back. Otherwise what's the point?'

It was the first time since she'd known him that he'd ever said anything like this, that he'd ever raised the question of the meaning of their existence. He'd never seemed to care before: they had each other, they had a life, for better or worse, and they must just get on with it. Even when Tom arrived he'd taken it in his stride, happy and devoted as a father but failing to display some greater level of awareness of the complexities and challenges of living. He took the arrival of Tom as another inevitability and folded it into his portfolio of experiences without a

49

further thought about the ramifications. It was not for her to challenge this, just as she didn't wish now to diminish the resolution he had revealed. She had her doubts, as she was sure he did, but they couldn't acknowledge these.

'Are we going to use Rocket?' she asked, to circumnavigate the awkwardness of the situation.

'What did you think of her?' he asked typically, a question for a question.

'I liked her,' Clare said, enough latitude in her tone so that Will could challenge it if necessary.

'I think I did as well. She was a little different, a little unconventional, but I expect that's a good thing in cases like this. I don't know. What's the alternative?' He shrugged and stared at his feet.

'I agree with you,' Clare said cleverly. 'We've got to take every opportunity we can to find him. We can't do anything. I don't even want to leave the house in case someone calls. At least Rocket would be out there looking. That must be better than nothing.'

'Why don't you call her in the morning?' Will said. 'Get her started.'

She nodded and rubbed her hands along her thighs. This was the moment to tell him, to break the news, to get it out of the way but, more from pity than fear, she found her courage fading. She honestly couldn't judge how he'd react; she didn't know herself how to react. Was she happy, scared, disappointed, or a little of each? She realised how much their lives had changed in the last three days, how the incident had even affected her understanding of herself and Will and their relationship.

Clare straightened her back as if strengthening herself.

She knew it had to be said, much as she dreaded what might follow. 'Will, there's something else we need to discuss.' He smiled and nodded at her to demonstrate his attention. 'I'm pregnant.'

She watched his face as it went blank; she remembered how he had taken the news the first time, as they sat in a pub one evening, and how long he had taken to accept the fact before his face broke into a gormless grin that he was unable to alter for the rest of the night. She remembered how he had stroked her belly gently and squeezed her hand, his naked delight so frank and innocent. She waited now as his mind struggled to grasp this information, hoping desperately that the same emotional series would eventually ensue.

'Are you sure?' he asked huskily.

'Very. I saw Dr Cassidy when I was back home.' She didn't want to ask how he felt; that would be pushing too hard.

He shook his head in a small movement of disbelief. 'Jesus,' he murmured.

'We never do things by halves, do we?' she said, trying to lighten the mood.

'When?'

'I'm about nine weeks gone.'

'So what do we do now?' Will asked, still quiet and flat.

'I was rather hoping you'd have the answer to that.'

'Well, it's obviously great news,' he said unconvincingly, 'but it's come at rather a bad time, wouldn't you say?'

'We just have to get on with life, I suppose. What else can we do?' Clare looked into his eyes and saw nothing. Will seemed trapped in a vortex of confusion and doubt, and there was nothing she could do or say to rescue him.

51

'Things will have to change, I'm sure, but I don't want us to get diverted,' he said. 'We have to concentrate all our efforts on Tom. You agree, don't you?'

'For now, yes. But we're going to have to think about the baby's future too. That's going to be just as important.'

'Yes,' he sighed, and then he fell silent again, an ominous quiet that unsettled Clare. She wanted to break it quickly.

'Do you want some tea?' she asked, and he briefly smiled.

'The English solution to every problem,' he said. 'Yes I do, and I'll make it. You go back to bed.' He leaned forward and touched her hair softly, then left the bathroom. Clare's stomach churned again, but this time she knew the pain was not from the little dependent life inside her. The sensation was from herself, and no less sickening for it.

There were three golden rules by which Rocket Stubblefield ran her life: she never took a man back to her place, she never worked for anyone she didn't like, and she never let the first two rules get in the way if circumstances dictated otherwise. On each birthday she believed that her life was starting to go downhill, but every year seemed to get better: money was always tight, but she'd learned to live with that long ago, and she had a steady stream of clients and a healthy social life. She'd tried marriage once, but it didn't agree with her, and she was now fully committed to a life of independence and self-reliance. She liked the feeling of danger that it gave her, the feeling that something or someone was always around the corner waiting to catch her unawares, and she always behaved as if she were half expecting the unexpected.

Rocket sat in her office, one room crammed full of files, dust and cast-off furniture, and flicked through a folder she'd been sent by one of her customers. Fourteen naughty boys had skipped away without settling their debts, and she was tasked with tracing them. But her full attention had deserted her as she thought of little Tom and those nice Easterbrooks; in this she surprised herself, as she'd never thought of herself as remotely compassionate or caring. She liked to be perceived as hardbitten and professional, a tough lady who took no prisoners. Her routine assignments gave her much scope to work on this image: she thought nothing of kicking in doors of motel rooms in the search for skippers, as she called them, and had often used physical persuasion, like a well-aimed foot in the groin, to convince her prey to surrender.

The Easterbrook case was different: the target was innocent, a perpetrator of no crime but still causing untold sadness, and wanting, she guessed, to be found and returned. She knew that the odds of success were long at best, and she also knew that the Easterbrooks had to be told this; the bleeding hearts at Family Matters wouldn't break it to them, holding out hope where none was justified, promising efforts that never quite materialised. But if nobody tried, if no one believed that he could be found, then what was there left in life? The prospect excited her normally cynical mind; her promise of action, if not of results, would make some dent in the Easterbrooks' grief, even if that was the most they could hope for.

Mrs Easterbrook had rung that morning and given her the brief. Already she'd made a few calls to various low-life contacts who regularly dealt in anything and everything that could be bought and sold, including humans. There was a general murmur that a boy had been taken, but everyone denied firsthand knowledge, even when she offered incentives or blackmail. No one, it appeared, was involved at a professional level, the consensus being that this was an opportunistic snatch. That closed down a lot of alternative lines of inquiry, and Rocket needed to think through her tactics. She always thought best when she sat in the bar across the street, a Seven and Seven in front of her – Seven Roses bourbon with a hint of Seven-Up – and several inside her. She tossed the folder to the floor, grabbed her bag and sauntered out of the building and over to the bar.

Manny the barman greeted her with his most engaging grunt and poured her drink without bidding. She lit a cigarette and took a sip before sitting on a barstool and looking round. There were a couple of customers hidden away in dark corners, but the long wooden bar was otherwise empty.

'Got a new case then?' Manny asked, wiping a glass with a cloth that Rocket knew had not been clean for several weeks.

'How perceptive you are,' she said. 'How do you do it?'

'Years of training at barman's school,' Manny replied. 'Plus it's only ten-thirty and you're already knocking them back. That only happens if you've got something on your mind.'

'Is that the time?' Rocket said, feigning surprise. 'God, I'll be late for my golf lesson.'

'Yeah, right,' Manny said. 'I can just see you and the

ladies from the country club hitting it off real well.' He tossed the cloth over his shoulder and continued laughing as he walked down to the other end of the bar.

Rocket sipped at her drink again and rubbed her forehead. She tried to put herself in the position of whoever it was who'd taken Tom: what would they do, where would they go, how would they explain his sudden arrival? She thought of the options, each of them blocking her progress. They could have gone abroad but, with the need for a passport, that seemed unlikely. More probable, she reasoned, they'd go back home, wherever that might be, and explain to any neighbours that they were looking after Tom for some relatives or friends. But Tom had an accent: he was not an American, and that would be obvious – unless, of course, they were holed up in some redneck part of the country where his accent could be explained as very New England. The locals probably wouldn't know the difference.

Would they risk taking a plane, even on an internal flight? She knew that she wouldn't; she would drive, avoiding public transport, but not too far, not with a little one in the back. He'd get tired and fidgety, and would need a lot of stops, increasing the likelihood that someone would spot them and report it. Her guess, by the time the second Seven and Seven appeared magically, was that Tom wasn't too far away from New York. That didn't help her too much, but it made her feel better anyway – now she only needed to concentrate her search on about fourteen states. ·

She revisited the initial problem: if Tom had been taken from Grand Central, then it followed that the people who took him saw Manhattan as the best local centre for such an opportunity. That would mean they were nearer to New York than to any other big city: otherwise they needn't have bothered to come here. Perhaps it was just coincidence that it happened at a train station, but she started thinking about the coincidence, and decided that, on balance, it was likely that the kidnappers – and she'd assumed there was more than one – came and left by train, timing the snatch to fit in with a train departure back to their intended destination. Grand Central served the counties and states north of the city, so that's where she felt they might have gone.

But if not? And anyway, what good did that information do her, even if it were correct? She took her third Seven and Seven and decided that some serious research was required: she'd go to the library this afternoon and dig up all the stories she could find on previous cases, trying to establish some pattern to behaviour, to see if there was any common key to apparently unrelated incidents. Research was what she hated most, and she ordered a strip steak sandwich with fries and pickles to fortify her for the ordeal ahead. As she ate her thoughts returned to Clare and Will: they'd be sitting by the phone, paralysed by their own uselessness, and she would have to deliver something to help them. A strangely invigorating feeling rose in her, and she both feared and enjoyed it. Perhaps she had a value after all, she thought: but then she pulled herself together and counselled herself not to be so damn sentimental. A job is just a job – someone pays you and you get a result.

SEVEN

Ralph was a painter – or rather, he had been a painter. When the family had moved to St Ives he was prolific, with a reputation as an artist of minor contemporary importance. Will had always treated his work with suspicion, believing that Ralph's neo-Impressionist style was merely a cover for the fact that he didn't have a total grasp of the basics of art, but his paintings sold well and the money kept them comfortable.

When Clare left home Ralph's output diminished to a trickle, and then stopped altogether. He would disappear for long periods to his studio, sometimes sitting there with the radio on and doing nothing, sometimes scribbling on a pad and then rejecting the results. The studio became his sanctuary, a place to which he would escape whenever it seemed that real life was likely to intrude. Peggy had always accepted this as part of the deal, knowing that his grasp, and tolerance, of reality was limited; she ran their lives, and let him exist in an insulated environment where he was safe from the dangers he perceived.

The family had always hovered on the cusp of normality as a result: until they reached St Ives, they had lived in fourteen different houses and flats and three different countries. Peggy would get a home established, Clare would settle into a school, and then Ralph would decree that he felt constricted, that he needed fresh inspiration, and they would dutifully follow him to the next station. To the outside world Ralph was a mild and gentle eccentric; to his family, he was an unpredictable and volatile figure, likely to explode if he didn't get his way and retaining many of the more hideous aspects of childhood.

The light of St Ives seemed finally to calm him: his rages subsided and his temper improved, but his work faltered. In his paintings there was little to suggest any underlying anger or bitterness: mostly he produced landscapes, watery scenes in muted colours which offended no one and were barely distinguishable from one another. But whatever motivated his work, it left him in St Ives.

Clare watched this change with mixed emotions: she had suffered from his caprices, and looked back on her childhood as semi-happy, the times she spent with her mother providing the few bright memories. He had never contributed as a father, neither praising nor scolding her, and he appeared almost indifferent to her development and well-being. Though her principles were built on firmer foundations, Peggy was equally but differently frustrating as a parent, passing on few hints as to how Clare should prepare herself for life. Peggy perceived her role, if it were perceived at all, as that of physical provider rather than spiritual guide: she cooked the meals and dispensed cuddles and sympathy as required, but never dared to tread more uncertain ground. Emotionally, Clare was left to fend for herself.

Clare had concluded that the reproductive instinct was

never stronger than it had been with her parents, that the act of conception was purely a natural reaction and one that, once concluded, need never be considered again. She never saw a sign that told her her parents had really wanted her, that her arrival and presence fulfilled a need within them, and she struggled with this void. She didn't consider herself as having been short-changed on love or affection, but there was something missing, some deeper bond that simply failed to tie them all together. They were a unit, as three matches in a box is a unit, each with their individual tips of incendiary material but otherwise unconnected.

To Will this family was fascinating: his own experience was conventional and dull in comparison. He rarely saw his younger brother, who worked in Singapore, and his mother and father had died within six months of each other several years before. His had been an uneventful childhood, with none of the upheavals that had affected Clare. Although he recognised the characteristics that troubled her, he didn't try to analyse them or provide an alternative. Perversely Clare liked him all the more for this, appreciating the way in which he simply got on with life and took her on at face value, assuming that she had the same range and depth of feelings as everyone else, including himself. He was not overly attracted or repelled by the manner in which her parents had looked after her, even though he was interested in her background and often described her formative years as bohemian, without really knowing what that meant. He assumed, with scant regard for circumstances, that Clare was already assimilated into the real world, that the way in which she'd lived her life would not unduly alter her attitudes or morals, and this helped her. If he accepted her as normal, then maybe she was.

If there were scar tissue within Clare, she hid it well. She certainly strived to be normal, to conform to standards that, as a child, she'd never really been introduced to; she'd married a banker, lived in a halls-adjoining Edwardian house in Wimbledon, had a baby and bought her clothes from Peter Jones. Her conformity was confirmed once they went to the States, where her new friends marvelled at her Englishness: she blossomed in a foreign land where everyone accepted her as a paradigm of a certain type of behaviour. She was never happier than when she was three thousand miles away from home, her mind and manners uncluttered by the debris of her upbringing.

Peggy was proud of Clare, not because she had managed to survive and prosper, but because her ambitions for her had been so limited that anything she did was a welcome bonus. Peggy didn't feel that Clare had been treated differently to any other child: she knew that Ralph was distant at best, but believed that this was only natural and would have little or no impact on Clare's character. Peggy liked Will without ever understanding him, knowing that he was devoted to Clare and seeing a pragmatism in him that was refreshing and comforting. He never appeared to be at a loss, always dealing with life in the same calm and sensible way: perhaps, somewhere within her psyche, Peggy saw in Will the type of man she would have preferred to spend her life with, but she never admitted that to herself.

On their own in the house, Peggy and Ralph rumbled along together without ever feeling the need to be too close. Ralph festered in his studio most days, his mind taking increasingly bizarre turns as he sat alone and tried half-heartedly to find inspiration: he would drink from lunchtime onwards, always the same amount so that, by the time he came downstairs for supper, he was numb but not incoherent. Supper, as they called it, got earlier and earlier: the dishes would be cleared away and clean by seven-thirty, and they'd normally be in bed by nine. Their lives were really over; they'd made the contribution they were going to make and now waited for their recall.

Clare had told Peggy about Tom's disappearance before she left, and the episode only served to reinforce the distance between them. Peggy had been concerned but was clearly at a loss to know how to react. She asked some banal questions, and Clare repeated what she knew and what she suspected; she sat by Peggy's bed and held her hand, but there was no special sense that her mother would provide the comfort she craved. Peggy promised to tell Ralph: when she did, he took the news silently and displayed no particular interest or sorrow. Peggy was not surprised by this, so rarely did he demonstrate any logical reaction to anything. But she knew, deep inside, that they were failing Clare in some major way, and that she didn't have the necessary tools to fix the problem.

Typically Peggy had discharged herself from hospital. Bea came to pick her up and drove her home. She expected, and received, no fuss from Ralph, who seemed happy enough to see her but went about his routine as if she'd never been away. Her first evening home Dr Cassidy came to call, ostensibly to check on her but also to report on his previous examination of Ralph when Clare had called him over.

'What I have to tell you will come as no surprise,' he said to her. Ralph had disappeared upstairs as soon as he could, and they sat alone in the musty sitting room. 'Ralph has senile dementia. It's progressive – unstoppable, I'm afraid, and really untreatable. He'll be lucid at times but, increasingly, there will be periods where he just isn't with it at all.'

'How will I notice?' Peggy asked, trying to make a joke of it. 'He's always been like that.'

'The problem is, Peggy, that you're going to be less able to deal with it. I know you think that your stroke was just an interruption of normal service, but it doesn't quite work like that. You're not getting any younger, and you're going to have to be more careful. Looking after Ralph will become more onerous – physically he's as fit as a fiddle, but that won't help you with the mental side. I just have to warn you that life is likely to be very tough from now on.'

'We can manage,' Peggy said, dismissing his warning with a little smile.

'I hope you can, because it's going to be very difficult to get you any additional help. Social services might do something, although I doubt it – you and Ralph don't really qualify as a priority.'

'We don't need them,' Peggy admonished him. 'We're fine – always have been, and always will be. Really.' She said this last word almost as if she were trying to convince herself as much as him.

'I'd be much happier if you were closer to relatives or friends. You're terribly isolated here – if there were a problem . . .' Dr Cassidy let his pause speak for him, but Peggy didn't seem to hear it.

'Tell me one thing. Who's going to die first – him or me?'

'I can't answer that, Peggy. I really have no idea. You could last a long time, you know, if you take care and look after yourself properly. Your heart's strong, and the stroke is a warning. Pay attention to it, and you'll go on for ever.'

She nodded and drew breath, then seemed to hesitate. Finally she made up her mind to speak. 'I can say this to you because I know it won't go any further,' she said. 'I need to outlast Ralph. That's not malicious. It's just something I want to do. Life hasn't always been very easy living with him, and I think I deserve a bit of time to myself. There are lots of things I still want to do, but they can't be done whilst he's alive. I love him dearly, but I do long for a break. And I don't want him as a burden on anyone else – if I died and left him on his own, he couldn't survive, not without a lot of help. So you shouldn't worry about me – I'm going to take very good care of myself, just to make sure I don't go before he does.'

Cassidy didn't know what to say, so he pursed his lips and nodded. He felt some sympathy for her – Ralph was rapidly going downhill and was already very trying – but he couldn't hold out the promise that her wishes would be satisfied. Nature wasn't that benign. He got up to leave.

'Just take it easy,' he said weakly. 'Rest as much as you can, and get friends to help.' He walked towards the door. 'By the way, how's Clare? I gather she had some big crisis she had to fly back to. Is everything all right?'

'I haven't heard,' Peggy said. 'I'm sure she'll call if there's any news.' But Peggy knew that Clare was unlikely to share her troubles with her; they didn't have that kind of relationship.

63

* * *

Tom sat very quietly on a bench, his legs swinging slowly as he sucked his thumb and rubbed his face with the special scrap of blanket. Betsy sat next to him. Tom was still thinking about those numbers, numbers which had become much more important since Betsy had asked him for them.

'Ricky,' she had said to him, 'I've been a very silly old woman. I've lost your mommy's phone number. Can you remember what it is?'

Those numbers he had juggled in his head came back to him. He recalled the endless conversations with his parents, the games they'd played as they ate their lunch, when Dad would ask him his address, his phone number, and whom he would call if he were ever in trouble. It was fun, but a little difficult. His address started and finished with numbers, he knew that, but they were getting muddled up with the others. He wanted to show Betsy that he knew things like this: he remembered how pleased his dad was whenever he got them all right, and he was sure that Betsy would be just as impressed. As he sat on the bench he tried to get everything in order. Finally he pulled his thumb out of his mouth and scrumpled the comforting material into a ball within his fist.

'Nine-one-four three-three-six one-seven-zero-six,' he said thoughtfully, not directly at Betsy but out into the air.

'That's ace, Ricky,' Betsy said. 'You are so smart. A little boy like you remembering a long number like that.' He was duly satisfied with the praise and relaxed a little.

'Can we call Mummy now?' he asked.

'We sure can. Just as soon as Chuck gets back.' She

took his hand and patted it. 'Do you want some cotton candy while we wait?'

Clare was asleep. Will had gone down to Manhattan, and Marla was in the kitchen preparing a salad. The phone rang; Marla jumped a little, then raced over to it.

'Hallo?'

'Mummy, it's Tom.'

'Tom? Tom, this isn't Mummy, this is Marla. Where are you, baby?' Marla's heart was trying to burst through her ribcage. There was a pause on the line. Marla was torn; she wanted to shout for Clare, but didn't want to break the conversation with Tom, or frighten him.

'Marla,' Tom said at last. 'Where's Mummy?'

'I'll get her for you, Tom. She's just sleeping. Can you stay on the line, honey? Don't hang up and I'll run and get her. OK, Tom?' She could hear something in the background, but couldn't concentrate on that noise. 'Just stay there and Mummy will come on the phone.' She put the receiver down very gently, as if a sudden movement might cut the line, and ran upstairs to Clare. She shook her shoulders and Clare turned over and opened her eyes. 'Clare, Tom's on the phone.' Clare jumped and reached across for the phone by her bed. She picked it up and shouted at once, 'Tom. Tom, it's Mummy.' But the line was already dead.

EIGHT

Will listened to Susan Scattaligia, but hardly heard what she was saying. As his deputy, she was running the office in his absence, and he had gone in to get an update on the work that had piled up on his desk.

The phone on Susan's desk rang, breaking the drone of her monologue. She answered and then handed the receiver to Will.

'Will, it's me,' Clare said, and he immediately straightened his back. 'Tom's been on the phone. He spoke to Marla.'

'What do you mean?'

'I was asleep in the bedroom when he called. By the time Marla had come up to get me he'd hung up.'

'How did he sound? What did he say to Marla?'

'Nothing very much. He didn't say where he was, or who he was with. Just asked for me. Oh, Will . . .' He listened as she tried to hold back the tears, unable to find anything positive to say that might comfort her. He felt strangely deadened by the news, as if it were so unlikely, so outside the scope of his dreams and nightmares, that he was incapable of fitting it into his thinking.

'Have you called Rocket?' he asked at last.

'I left a message on her machine. Told her to call us at

67

home. I think you'd better come back.'

'Yes, of course,' Will said rather distractedly, aware of Susan watching him.

'Will? This is good news, right?'

'Yes, yes,' he replied unconvincingly. 'I'll see you soon.'

When he had left the office Will had not yet absorbed the information. His body seemed to work independently, as if there had been a power failure, and now it was operating on stand-by, with emergency generators keeping only the bare minimum of functions running. He walked aimlessly along Park Avenue towards Grand Central, seeing no one he passed on the sidewalk and hearing no traffic as it sped alongside him. The news was so unexpected that he had no way of dealing with it, no method of working out what it might mean or its ramifications.

Immured in this capsule of incomprehension, Will cut across the concourse of the station and got on a train. He had an image of little Tom sitting opposite him, his excitement barely contained as they travelled on their last journey together; he remembered holding Tom up to look out of the window, stroking his head as he slept for the last few minutes, but the memories came from another world, another life, something that had happened to someone else.

By the time he got home Rocket was already there. She sat on the sofa next to Clare, smoking and taking notes. Will went to Clare and hugged her tightly, then slumped in an armchair opposite them.

'So what happens now?' he asked. Rocket lit another cigarette.

'Are you rich?' she replied.

'No, not at all,' he said, shaking his head. 'Why do you ask?'

'I can't figure it out. This type of call is quite common – the kid speaks a little, to establish that they're alive and OK, then you get another call with the demand. You know, it's the old cliché – "we have your boy, he's doing fine, now give us the money if you want to see him again". They might have cut off the call because it was taking too long and they didn't want it traced. But if you don't have anything to give, it doesn't make sense.' She shook her head and drank some coffee. Will and Clare tried to avoid each other's eyes. 'The other alternative is the one I prefer.'

'What's that?' Will asked.

'Well, it may not give you too much comfort, but it may just be that the people who have Tom are genuinely sorry for what they did, that they have feelings and they want to let you know that Tom is all right.'

'How far does this remorse go? Will they give him back to us?'

'That's the sixty-four-thousand-dollar question, Mr Easterbrook. If they need Tom, for whatever twisted reason, then the answer is probably no. But it's a good sign that they've called, because it establishes that at least there's a little bit of doubt about what they've done. Tell me, is he a well-behaved child?'

'We think so, but he's like any lively three-year-old – he has his moments,' Will replied.

'If he were to become a real pain it would help,' Rocket said. 'I know that sounds callous, but it's true. He's obviously smart, remembering your number, and Marla said he sounded calm, no crying or anything. We just have to hope that he doesn't suit them, that they decide it was all a terrible mistake.'

'Why do you keep on saying "they"?'

'Because most likely it's a couple. I did a little research on previous cases, and the vast majority are couples who have either lost their own child or have never had any. My guess would be that we're dealing with at least two people.' Throughout this exchange Clare had remained silent, but now she spoke.

'What about the practicalities, Rocket? How could they explain the sudden appearance of a little boy with an English accent? And what would they do about school? Someone else must have seen something – they must have friends or neighbours who'll get suspicious.'

'It'd be so easy to invent a story. They could say they adopted him, or that he's the son of distant relatives from England. There'd be a hundred different ways of dealing with it. But you're right – we need a nosy neighbour who smells something odd and calls the police.'

'And in the meantime?'

Rocket looked at both of them, pausing as she measured her words. 'In the meantime, you wait. There's really nothing else you can do. I know how painful that's going to be, but I'll keep on digging, and the police will do what they can, and you just have to sit by that phone and hope like hell that he calls again.'

Peggy had a morning routine that she refused to change as a result of her stroke. The first – and quite often the only – domestic task of the day that Ralph fulfilled was to make a pot of tea. Each night he would set out the teapot, two cups of different sizes and a bowl of sugar lumps on the tray in the kitchen, and each morning he would rise at five o'clock and make the tea. Neither of them took sugar, but it was a habit of Ralph's that Peggy found too unimportant to query. By six Peggy would have had her first cup and would be ready to start the day, to embark upon the tedious and repetitive regime that had become her life since Clare had left home. She would put on a thick old dressing-gown and have breakfast with Ralph, a silence between them that marked neither contempt nor innate understanding, merely tiredness. She would wash, brush her thinning hair and make the bed. She would put the dishes in the sink and leave them for later, hating to waste the hot water on such an insignificant pile.

The morning of Tom's phone call, Peggy never drank her tea. She never put the crockery in the sink, nor nodded at Ralph as he disappeared upstairs to his studio. Ralph's schedule changed little, however; he delivered her tea to the bedside table, pecking her on the cheek as she lay inert on her back, and then shuffled towards the bathroom, whistling an indistinguishable tune between his teeth. He always left his clothes in the bathroom, retaining some obscure puritanical belief that he should not be watched by her as he dressed for the day. He went straight from the bathroom down the stairs and into the kitchen, seated himself at the table and waited.

With his limited concept of time, and his lack of a watch – an affectation that Will had noted with disdain – Ralph waited a long time. There were no hunger pangs to alert him to the minutes that passed, the delay that was so unusual. His appetite had diminished to such an extent that eating was more a ritual than a necessity, a break in the continuum of the day. His mind rambled as he sat

71

there, brief lucidity punctuating the private realm of his imagination; he was only mildly aware of something amiss when he saw that his cup was empty, and realised that Peggy was not there to refill it. He stirred himself and walked to the bottom of the stairs, pausing there as if uncertain of how to proceed in this unfamiliar scene. He called out – 'Peg?' – in a tone that suggested he did not expect a response, as if he were pretty sure that she was not there, and this was merely a confirmatory question that needed no reply.

When he received none he waited again, then returned to the kitchen, looking around him to see if she might have slipped in without his noticing. His mind disengaged again and he left the kitchen, pulled himself up the stairs and went into his studio, oblivious to the message that should have been sending warning signals. He sat at his drawing-board and stared at it, a blank piece of white cartridge paper clipped on to it, and he moved a pot of pencils from one side of it to the other. He sighed and was lost.

It was nearly eleven o'clock before he opened the studio door and wandered across the landing to the bathroom. As he passed the bedroom he saw Peggy lying in bed; the sight of her there piqued his interest, rather than his concern, and he went in to stand beside her. She looked strange, even to him as a casual observer: the base of each side of her face was heavily darkened, almost purple, whilst the rest of her skin was pale and waxy. He put out his hand and touched hers. It was very cold, but this recognisable sign was not immediately apparent to him. He took her hand and held it up against its weight, then dropped it. Slowly the understanding that he had lacked

came upon him, seeping into him from her lifeless flesh.
He stared at her with blank eyes.

'Oh, Peggy,' he said, almost as an admonishment.
'Where have you gone?'

NINE

Once again, Marla was stationed in their kitchen; once again, she was dabbing her eyes over someone else's misfortune. She had never met Peggy, nor Ralph, and the grief she felt was not for them but for Will and Clare. Selfishly she wondered how others might react when bad things happened to her, but her real crisis was a continuing one, invisible to others and never reaching a climax. The dramas of her neighbours helped to dull the pain for her, giving her a diversion from the discreet disappointments of her life.

Clare had gone; Dr Cassidy had called to tell her the news and she had agonised briefly over her priorities, but Will was insistent that she go to her father. He would stay behind and sit by the phone, awaiting a call that they anticipated with equal amounts of dread and hope. Marla was there for no particular reason, as if she were merely a levee between Will's sanity and total collapse.

Will was in the bedroom, on the phone to Ralph. The conversation was following a familiar pattern of misunderstanding.

'William.' Ralph said the name as if trying it out for the first time, a foreign name that he had trouble pronouncing.

'Your son-in-law. Clare's husband.'

'William,' he repeated more certainly.

'Yes. You've got it. I'm sorry to call so late, but I thought you'd like to know that Clare got off all right. She'll be down there early tomorrow morning.' There was no immediate reaction to this news, and Will struggled to fill the silence, worrying that he might have dropped off to sleep. 'Ralph, you know that if you need anything, anything at all, you only need to ask.'

'Yes,' Ralph grunted. He thought for a little while, then drew breath. 'There is something.'

'Yes?'

'You don't happen to know where Peg keeps the tin-opener, do you? I'm buggered if I can find it.'

'Have you looked in the kitchen drawer?'

'The kitchen drawer. Good idea. I'll go and take a look. Yes, thanks for that. Most helpful.' Will thought he might go off at that moment, leaving him hanging on whilst he searched. But he stayed put.

'Ralph, is everything OK there? Are you looking after yourself?'

'Fine, fine. House is bloody cold, but I've got a fire going.' Visions of a pile of blazing furniture stacked up in the middle of the sitting room flashed through Will's mind; Clare would arrive to find the smouldering remains of the house, and Ralph, and would blame him. He could hardly imagine that Ralph might be capable, sober or drunk, of starting a fire in the fireplace: that was too practical, too prosaic, for him.

'Well, remember to damp it down before you go to bed.' A painful thought occurred to Will as he said this. Giving these instructions to Tom would have been more successful; Ralph's inability, or unwillingness, to deal with the real world was worse than a toddler's.

'Oh, I won't be going to bed for some time,' he said vigorously. 'There's so much to do. The garden's a terrible mess, and the hall needs painting.'

'I wouldn't worry too much about that. If I were you, I'd get some rest.' This set him off.

'I can't rest. You probably don't know about it. Peggy isn't here. Had a heart attack. She's always been so strong, it came as something of a surprise, I can tell you. Left me on my own. But I think my daughter's coming to look after me, just until Peg comes back. I just hope' – there was a pause as he collected his hopes together – 'I just hope she knows where the tin-opener is.'

'She will, Ralph, I'm sure. You go and get some sleep, and Clare will be with you soon. Ralph, I have to go now. I'll call you tomorrow. Look after yourself.'

'Well, thanks for ringing,' he said brightly. 'Lovely to hear from you.' He sounded almost normal, which was equally worrying.

Ralph's apparent refusal to accept Peggy's death struck a chord with Will. He identified the same reluctance in his own attitude towards Tom's disappearance, scarcely believing that he was no longer in the house and in their care and control. As part of this there was also a subliminal horror of what life would be like without something they had always taken for granted; they had wanted a child and it had happened, Tom had easily become another of their possessions, and now he had been taken away without permission or consent. As Will sat on the bed these thoughts began to overwhelm him, replacing the sadness with something more profound, an emptiness that needed to be filled. It was like walking into a favourite room and finding that all the furniture had been removed. One's natural reaction would be to try and fill it up again and recreate the habitat. Even though he was not conscious of it, Will began to think in terms of reparation rather than despair.

He walked across to Tom's room and stared into it, leaning against the door jamb. He carried out an audit of the things he knew so well, the mobiles above the bed, the little shoes and slippers, the books and toys and pictures and posters, knowing that the vital element was missing, that this was a dead room where time had stopped. He expected tears, but none came. He wanted to cry, to purge himself and feel some sense of expiation. But the feeling within him was simply one of lack. He shut the door without going in and ran down the stairs, aware of a change in himself but unable to suppress it.

Sleep is a gift that knows no justice, bestowing or denying its favours to victims and criminals without discrimination. Though she felt tired in a way that made her marrow ache, Clare was unable to get comfortable enough even to doze. The baby was hardly showing, but she felt it as an enormous mass within her and this restricted her movement. Her feet throbbed, her head ached; she couldn't concentrate on the film, or the book she had brought for the journey. It seemed that her whole body had conspired to force her to think about her own circumstances, something she had carefully avoided until now.

Her pregnancy had complicated everything. The despair she felt at Tom's disappearance was blunted by the imminence of another life's arrival. As if closing the circle, nature had a way of conjoining beginnings and endings, like the old trees that died to make way for saplings. But the long advent of a new life terrified Clare in a way that defied rational thought, presenting fresh problems before the current ones had been resolved, and diverting her attention from the matters at hand. She tried to address the issue of her mother's death, and surprised herself with the detachment with which she was able to do it. There was no immediate grief – which she suspected might be the result of some inbuilt denial mechanism – simply a dazed nothingness into which the full swell of sadness and loss had been subsumed. Despite her best efforts, she couldn't find within herself any depth of concern for her father: he remained to her, in spite of everything, an awkward burden to be carried without grace or favour.

A little boy pottered up and down the aisle of the plane, clutching a plastic beaker of juice and a grubby toy. He took his time, as if aware that he couldn't escape and should therefore make the best of the situation. He looked at Clare and grinned teasingly, a certain smile that invited attention but advised caution. Clare smiled back and he looked away; perhaps, she thought, his radar tells him that I'm not much fun. He moved on to seek out more promising company, and she was left to herself. She wondered about Tom's radar, the sense that children have but adults lose, knowing like a dog when something isn't right. Did Tom's hackles rise when these people approached him? Did he resist or scream? Did he call out for Dad? The thought of Tom's small voice, maybe muffled by a hand, finally pierced the skin of Clare's detachment, releasing all the accumulated sorrow and pain; she sat very still, her face a mask, as the tears poured down her cheeks.

Tom lay asleep on a couch, curled up and sucking his thumb. He was still wearing the baseball hat that Chuck had bought him at the fair. Betsy sat beside him with her hand laid lightly on his thigh, as if she might restrain him if he tried to jump up.

'He's a good boy,' she said to Chuck.

'The very best we could've hoped for,' Chuck agreed as he flipped the top on a can of beer.

'I wish he might have spoken with his mom. That would've made him feel a whole lot better.' Betsy stroked the little thigh as she spoke. 'But I didn't like the set-up. It sounded like they were trying to get a trace on the call. We can't be too careful.'

'We could try again.'

'Better to leave it now,' Betsy said. 'We want to get it out of his head.'

'Right. Start of a new life. Kick over the traces. So when do we leave?' Chuck swigged at his beer and wiped his mouth with the back of his hand.

'First thing in the morning, just like we planned.'

'I still think it'd be safer at night.'

'No way. Travelling at night would only arouse suspicion. Better to hide in plain sight. Just a normal family outing, nothing out of the ordinary. That's the way to do it, Chuck.'

He nodded slowly and kept quiet. Then he got up and walked over to a sideboard; he paused in front of a photograph, a picture of a beaming boy with a pile of presents in front of him. Chuck picked it up and studied it, then looked across at Betsy, who was watching him closely.

'Where is he, I wonder? Where did he go?' Chuck said, more to himself than Betsy.

'We don't know that. We've been through this a thousand times. He's not coming back, Chuck. Gone for ever. But now we have Ricky here, and that'll do just fine for me – and you too, I shouldn't wonder.'

'Yeah, I guess, but what happens if he tries to call us when we're gone? What then?'

'He hasn't called for five years, Chuck. That's a long shot, and you know it. He's not going to reappear out of the blue. So let's worry about this little mite, and make damn sure the same thing doesn't happen again.'

Chuck put the photo down and went back to his chair. Betsy noticed the uncertainty of movement, the body language that betrayed his unease.

'What is it, hon? What's eating you?'

'Betsy, are we evil people? I mean, are we doing something bad here?'

She had waited for this question, and she was well prepared. 'Look at this little guy. Does he look like he's suffering? He's having the time of his life. He has all our attention, and everything he needs. I reckon we're doing right by him, don't you? Does it look to you as if we're being evil?'

'No, but what about his folks? Won't they be sick with worry?'

'Sure, for a while, but they'll get to where they don't think so much about him, have another kid – maybe they already have others – and before they know it he'll just be a distant memory. It'll seem to them like he hardly ever existed.'

'But we haven't forgotten ours, Betsy. He's not a distant memory to us.'

'That's your problem, Chuck. You need to do that. Flush it out, erase it from your mind. It's ancient history, and it won't do nobody any good to linger on it. That's what I've done.'

Chuck wanted to say more, but couldn't find the words to combat her. He sipped his beer and sighed. 'Guess you're right – as always.' He gave her a watery smile.

'Now then, there's gas in the car, we have all the food ready, and we're all packed. We need to get this guy into bed and then we'll be all set. And you need to get off your fat butt and start planning our route.'

'When are you going to do his hair?'

'First thing,' Betsy said firmly. 'Tomorrow we'll all be different. It's a new life for the three of us, and boy, are we going to enjoy it.'

TEN

In the absence of any better ideas, Rocket had gone to sit with Will. He had expressed little surprise, or even regret, at her lack of progress, and they sat together and drank coffee. Will was smoking one of Rocket's cigarettes.

'Was it a shock, about your mother-in-law?' Rocket asked, more out of good form than from any particular interest. In spite of her profession, she was allergic to other people's tragedies and their discussion.

'I think so,' he replied dreamily. 'She'd had a minor stroke, but seemed to be recovering. She's the lucky one, though. We've now got to live with the consequences.'

'How's Clare's father taking it?'

'Just as you'd expect. I think the fashionable term is "in denial". When I spoke to him he hadn't really grasped it – although that's been the story of his life, always in denial. We might put that on his tombstone.'

'So what do you think you'll do?'

'No idea. I'm leaving that side of things to Clare. She'll have a plan, no doubt, and we'll just follow that.' Will said this without any trace of bitterness, merely relief. Rocket looked at him more closely; he had seemed to her to be a regular guy, simply knocked sideways by events, but now she reconsidered her initial assessment, and decided there was something more to him. It wasn't depth, she thought, but the resignation with which he dealt with his misfortunes suggested that he was built in a different way to most other men. Her experience had been that they always wanted to have control, even if they were pathologically incapable of dealing with it if they got it; but he appeared willing to let things take their course and simply follow where they led. Maybe, she thought, that was the British way. An inappropriate thought came to her, but she entertained it anyway: did British men like to be on top in the sack? Before she had time to pursue the thought further, he was speaking again.

'In the normal course of events, we might decide to go back to London, I suppose. But with everything that's going on here, that's not practical. We need to get all this sorted out first.' The way he said this emboldened Rocket; she felt that he wanted to tell her exactly how he felt things might be resolved, and whether he had already given up hope of finding Tom. She struggled a little before finding the right way to broach the subject.

'I know it's tough, but I really believe that Tom is safe and well,' she began. 'I think that call confirms it. They wanted to set your minds at rest, however clumsily.' She waited for some sign from Will that he agreed, some flicker of emotion that would tell her more about his condition.

'I want to agree with you. I cannot conceive of anyone wanting to hurt him, or cause him harm. But there are lots of very sick people out there, and I can't stop thinking about them. That's my private nightmare and, even though we've not discussed it, I'm sure it's Clare's too. You just can't ignore that.' He shook his head and took another of her cigarettes, a move that Rocket thought was intended to divert attention from any pain he might display. After taking a large drag, he continued. 'You know, as a parent, you're always saying to yourself, and anyone else who'll listen, that all you want for your children is that they're happy and safe. It doesn't matter what they achieve, as long as they're content. But that's patently untrue. We all force our own aspirations on our children, desperately trying to compensate for our own disappointments and lack of achievement. From the minute they're born, we're wondering what they'll become, and how we can help them to make it. The pressure's always there – when will they sit up, when will they walk, when will they say their first word, when will they read? It's like a competition – you know, the one who dies with most money wins. And there's not a thing you can do to stop it. Or there wasn't, until Tom disappeared. But now – well, it all seems pretty irrelevant, doesn't it?'

'Natural is the word that springs to mind,' Rocket said.

'Do you think so? Is it natural to want to shape your child in your image – not even your image, but a better, burnished version of it? Is that the point of procreation? God, if it is this world is pretty sick. Shouldn't we be saying that we've created another human being, and they should just develop as nature allows them? Do we have to keep on imposing our values, our preconceptions, on future generations? I don't like the sound of that too much – and I'm as much to blame as the next man.'

'So what do you want for Tom?'

'In my heart, I really don't know. You have a child – your choice of course, not his – and then you spend your life telling him how to behave. You don't act as a mentor as much as a puppet-master. Now Tom's not with us, and we don't have the luxury of bullying him into our way of doing things, it's hard to work out what he really needs from anyone. If he's warm, and safe, and loved, and well fed, isn't that enough?'

'But isn't your role to improve the lot of man? Isn't that every parent's dream – to give their children something better than they had?'

'I'm not so sure. Look at medicine. The next generation is going to live until they're well past a hundred. Is that an improvement, letting people struggle on into their dotage and make them ever more dependent on others? Three-score years and ten seems fine to me.' For the first time, Rocket saw some animation in Will, a sign that he cared about something and had thought it through. She wondered if this was a recent phenomenon.

'Does your wife agree with you?' she asked tentatively.

'We've never really discussed it as such, but I think she does. I remember us talking about the fact that a child is the biggest investment you ever make – financially and emotionally – and they don't even give you a manual. You just muddle along as best you can.'

'I thought the Bible was meant to be a manual,' Rocket suggested. Will laughed at this, then stopped suddenly.

'Sorry – I didn't mean to laugh, but it just sounded so odd. In England we'd never say something like that – religion's a subject that's best avoided. It's rather like having halitosis or being an alcoholic. Speaking of which, would you like a drink?' He got up and went towards the kitchen. 'I have bourbon, gin, vodka, wine and beer.' Rocket asked for a beer and waited. When Will returned he seemed to have tightened up again, retreating from his truth session. He smiled at her sheepishly, then sat silently.

86

She took some long drinks from the bottle of beer and then tried to relaunch the discussion.

'Look, I think it's only fair to tell you that the likelihood of findingTom decreases by the day. Some cases, a missing person is found immediately, but the longer they're away, the less chance there is of picking them up. You and Mrs Easterbrook have to be prepared for that.' His reaction surprised her.

'I know. I've gone through it a thousand times, and I can't see how we could find him unless someone wanted him to be found. You'd need such an incredible amount of luck, and that's been in pretty short supply recently. But we won't give up – or, at least, I won't give up until Clare tells me to.'

'That's good. And I'll help you all I can, although I can't promise very much.'

Will paused as he thought about what to say next. 'It's a strange business being a father,' he said finally. 'Most of us are never really tested. We're never asked the difficult questions about the bond between us and our children. We don't have that maternal instinct that's nurtured in the womb. It's only when something like this happens that we discover what we're really made of. And I'll tell you this, it's one hell of a challenge. It's as if someone's given you a massive injection of adrenalin. It does funny things to you, and you can't control your reactions despite all your efforts.'

'What are you getting at?'

'I want revenge. I want retribution. Whoever took my son will have to answer to me. I don't have much faith in the legal system meting out the proper justice, and I want to make sure they get what they deserve. That's how strong my love for Tom is. I want those bastards to suffer for what they've done – and if I'm the one who has to do something about it, then I will. That's what all this has done to me.'

Rocket was taken aback by the passion with which he said this: he really meant it. She shivered a little at the realisation of what he might be capable of. Before she had a chance to discuss it further, the phone rang and they both stiffened. Will picked it up, then looked across at Rocket and mouthed: 'It's Clare.' Their mutual deflation was almost palpable.

Aron Dack was on the early shift at the Hungry Horse diner, a scruffy stopover on the Jersey turnpike forty miles south of New York. He was clearing tables and doing the washing-up. His head and guts throbbed from the excesses of the previous night's drinking session, and he moved slowly between tables, oblivious to the customers as they tucked into piles of steaming food. He had managed to hold down coffee and juice, but solids were still out of the question. He barely noticed the couple and their kid as they walked into the diner and sat at a table he'd just cleared. He was more concerned with how he'd explain to Julie that he hadn't called her last night, as he'd promised he would. Women were complicated animals, and Aron wasn't sure he could deal with them. Her job at Family Matters meant she worked odd hours; she was sometimes there all night, and they weren't connecting properly.

It wasn't really until he went to remove their plates that he took a closer interest in the three of them. Even through the fog of his hangover, Aron sensed something slightly wrong about this group: the kid was very young to be theirs, and he didn't seem to be communicating with them. The couple were a little edgy, looking up anxiously every time someone approached their table. But when he heard the boy speak, he knew it was an odd set-up; the accent wasn't right at all, completely different to the adults', and Aron lingered at the next table to see if he could pick up any information.

'So, Ricky, are you excited about your vacation?' the woman said.

'Where are we going? To the beach?' the boy replied in that foreign accent.

'That's right, buster – the beach,' the man said. Aron finished his work at the next table and wandered back to the kitchen. As he dumped a huge pile of crockery into the sink he thought about this exchange and tried to figure it out. They must be heading south to hit the beach in the fall, he thought. He plunged his hands into the hot water and began scrubbing dishes, still trying to reconcile what he'd seen and heard, his brain stubbornly unwilling to function effectively. Then he stopped his work, wiped his hands on his apron and went over to the wall phone. He started punching Julie's number, then stopped. Speaking to her now might not be such a good idea: there were explanations and apologies to be made, and he didn't feel up to it. He looked through the hatch to the dining area and saw the three of them still sitting there, chewed his lip for a while, then turned back and picked up the phone again. This time he completed the connection.

'It's me,' he said.

'Oh, the invisible date,' Julie said, making him cringe.

'Hey, sorry babe, just got tied up. But I'm calling now, right?'

'Right.' Then silence – the worst form of torture. Aron tried to ignore it.

'Listen, I've got a little situation here you might be interested in. There's a kid here with an old couple – they don't look like his parents, and he doesn't seem too enamoured with them. He's got an accent too. Might be from Australia or something.' Again there was silence, but this time he realised that it was a thinking silence.

'Could it be an English accent?' Julie asked at last.

'I guess so.'

'Tell me about the kid. What does he look like?'

'He looks like a kid, for God's sake. They all look the same to me.'

'Hair colour?'

'Doesn't have much hair at all – looks as if it's been shaved recently, I don't know.'

'Call the cops right now, Aron. Tell them what you just told me. I think it's one of mine. Hang up and dial 911. And stop those folks leaving. Hold the bill, spill juice on them, do anything to delay them. You understand?'

'Yeah, I understand. I'm right on it, babe.' He hung up and quickly dialled 911, bending at the waist to look out of the serving hatch again. The table was empty, and he slammed the phone back and ran into the dining area, scanning from left to right to spot them. As he reached the door he saw them getting into their car and he caught the eye of the woman. For a moment they stood staring at each other, then she said something to the man and they slammed their doors and pulled away quickly. Aron tried to memorise the number on the plates – New York, that was for sure – and watched as the car left the parking lot and sped southwards. He was rooted to the spot, unable to decide what to do next. He knew he faced yet another difficult conversation with Julie.

ELEVEN

There had never been a time when Clare had felt true compassion for her father; although he displayed all the characteristics of a victim, someone to whom life had dealt an unfair hand, she believed, in no particularly implicit way, that Ralph was simply too lazy to face up to his fate. In this, Clare felt, he had had a willing accomplice in her mother, who let him get away with his various whims without a second thought – or, if she had them, kept them well concealed. Clare had often speculated about how her mother might develop once Ralph died, about the interests that would blossom and the opinions that would suddenly appear, free from scrutiny and ridicule. Very occasionally, Peggy would give a hint of the depth to which these feelings ran: once she had admitted to Clare that she had a passion for jazz, that she longed to visit Ronnie Scott's and drink bourbon into the early hours. Clare's surprise at hearing this was soon replaced by misery; analysis of this almost shameful admission made her realise to what extent her father's will had dominated Peggy's life, the extent to which her mother would go to relegate her own desires and needs beneath his to keep the peace and fragile status quo. Ralph, of course, despised jazz as simply sound without form, and Peggy dutifully agreed.

Arriving at the house, Clare's energy returned in an enormous wave. A thousand matters needed her attention: her father was merely one of many priorities, and one to which she was inclined to give the minimum. He seemed on the edge of resentment, as if Peggy's death had somehow deprived him of his normal position at centre stage; if there were grief within him, it was not yet manifesting itself, and this only served to irritate Clare. She had called Dr Cassidy, speaking to him briefly about documentation and procedure; she had spoken to the bank, knowing that Peggy controlled the finances; and she had got three quotes from undertakers. Now she was in the bedroom, clearing out the wardrobe and chest of drawers in a time-filling exercise that owed nothing to tidiness and everything to keeping busy.

Sad, small piles of clothes grew around Clare as she pulled them from their shelves and hangers and dropped them to the floor; even in her appearance, she thought, Mum had taken only as much interest as Dad would allow her.

Ralph hovered uncertainly, neither wanting to help nor intending to be forgotten. He had been remarkably lucid since Clare's arrival, apparently grasping the new situation without necessarily being part of it. He had found some of Peggy's papers; he had even dug out a government booklet on how to deal with a death; but beyond this he was not prepared to go. He wandered from room to room, looking into each as if he might discover someone or something that had been forgotten, and returning to the bedroom as if it housed the lodestar of his existence. Eventually he tired of the routine and sat on the edge of the bed, sighing deeply and dramatically. Clare braced herself and turned to face him.

'Shall we have a drink?' she asked.

'What an excellent idea,' he replied, brightening at the prospect. They went downstairs to the kitchen and Clare poured two large glasses of Scotch as Ralph sat at the scarred table.

'How are you doing, Dad?'

'I suppose numb is the right word. You know, Mum was my life for a long time. In fact, I can't really remember a time without her.' He sounded coherent and rational, and Clare relaxed a little.

'She was a wonderful mother,' she said.

'Oh yes, absolutely. You know, she never raised her voice to you, never smacked you.' Clare knew this to be entirely untrue, but nodded. 'She and I used to sit and talk about you, how you were getting on at school and everything, well into the early hours of the morning, I can tell you.' He shook his head at the memory of it and Clare tried to imagine this unlikely scenario. 'We were a happy family, weren't we?'

Clare looked at her drink and struggled with a reply. 'Were you happy, Dad? I never really knew whether having Mum and me was a burden for you.'

'Well, of course, it isn't always easy being the provider and having dependants,' he said. 'But I think I did all right, all things considered.' He drank his Scotch and waited for affirmation from Clare. She reached out her hand and put it on top of his across the table.

'I think you and I are survivors. Whatever's thrown at us, we come through it somehow,' she said, more in hope than belief in this statement. 'Now we have to get through this, and it's not going to be easy. We'll both have to make some tough decisions.'

'That reminds me,' he said very firmly, suddenly animated. 'What about little Tom – any news?' She was shocked by this, like a sharp slap on the cheek. She knew Peggy had told him, but she never expected that he would digest the information and recall it later.

'Nothing yet.'

'That's too bad,' he said. 'He's a nice boy. I do hope he comes back.'

'So do I, Dad. So do I.' She didn't know what else to say; the gulf between them was so wide that she had no way of bridging it now, after so many years of benign neglect.

'When I spoke to him on the phone he seemed very sad,' Ralph said.

'What do you mean?' Clare was wary of pursuing this discussion, as it would inevitably lead into a blind alley.

'He called me just the other day. Yes, he was a very miserable little pup.' Ralph sounded coherent and, although Clare was wise to his ramblings, she was too interested to ignore him.

'He called you? When?' she asked.

He seemed to think hard about this, and eventually screwed up his face in frustration. 'Well, I'm not sure,' he said vaguely. 'Sometimes things get a bit muddled up here.' He tapped his forehead and smiled weakly.

'Sure, Dad.' She tried to think of some way to divert his attention; it was too painful to humour him on such a sensitive subject.

Then Ralph's eyes glazed over and he began to twitch a little. 'Well, I have to get going,' he said almost mechanically. 'Can't sit around here all day.' But he made no effort to move.

'Why don't you go and put your feet up in front of the fire? I'll bring your drink in, and you can read the paper.'

'No time for that,' he said distractedly. 'No time at all.' She didn't understand what he meant, and suspected he didn't either.

The four of them sat at a window table in the Hungry Horse – Rocket, Will, Julie and Lieutenant Jablonowski – with thick white coffee mugs in front of them. Jablonowski was chewing on a frosted jelly doughnut as he spoke.

'Of course, this doesn't prove diddly squat. In fact, there could be a thousand plausible reasons for this, none of which you folks are very keen on entertaining. And this guy Dack – well, he hardly seems very sure about what he saw, now does he?'

'I thought he was reasonably confident when we showed him Tom's photo,' Will said.

'No disrespect, Mr Easterbrook, but this guy seems a little flaky to me,' Jablonowski said. 'I'm not so sure I'd rely on his testimony.'

'If I could just say something here?' Julie asked. 'I know Aron – and yes, he can be flaky, as you say. But he's smart enough to know when something's up. He wouldn't have called me unless he had a pretty good reason, believe me. And if there's any chance that it is the kid, shouldn't we pursue it?'

'We are pursuing it. We're right on it. All I'm saying is, don't get your hopes up, that's all.' Jablonowski crammed the last of the doughnut into his mouth and swilled it down with a slurp of coffee.

97

Rocket was sitting next to Will, and she could feel his leg pumping frantically. She wanted to put her hand on his knee to calm him, but thought better of it. She offered her cigarettes around, then took one out and lit it.

'Where do you think they're heading?' she asked Jablonowski.

'If this guy Aron heard them right, then they're obviously heading much further south – Florida, perhaps,' he replied.

'By car?' Rocket exclaimed.

'Maybe, maybe not. It'd be smart to drive some of the way, then take a plane or train from somewhere else. Perhaps they're going to Philadelphia, or Washington. They just want to cover their tracks by using different transportation. That's what I'd do.'

'Why Florida?' Will asked, his leg still hammering under the table.

'They're an older couple, right? It makes sense to go somewhere nice and warm with the boy, to keep him happy and occupied. Maybe they have a condo down there – who knows? But that'd be my best guess, for what it's worth.' Jablonowski looked at his watch. 'Listen, I've got to shoot. First thing we hear, we'll let you know. If they call again, you let us know.'

'Fine. Thanks very much,' Will said, and Jablonowski left. Julie slid out after him and nodded to Will.

'Bring your wife in when she's ready, Will. We'd really like to meet her.' Will sent her a pale smile as she shook his hand. She ignored Rocket and left.

'So what has this achieved?' Will asked.

'For a start, it gives us hope. If it is little Tom, then that's good. They aren't being quite as careful as they should be, and the chances are that someone else will spot them. But the fact is, it's pretty certain he's alive and well and in good hands. Aron said they were being real nice to him, and he didn't look at all unhappy.'

'Something doesn't make sense to me,' Will said. 'Why are they only here by now? They could be thousands of miles away.'

'Yeah, I've thought of that too. I figure they took him back home first, wherever home is, and sat low before moving. They may have guessed that there'd be an immediate concentration of effort by the cops, and so they'd only move once that had died down a little. If they were coming from north of New York, somewhere upstate, that would tie in with the timing.'

'Sounds plausible,' Will replied. 'But what do we do in the meantime?'

'You wait, and I work. I have a friend down in Florida – if Tom is going that way, and he so much as sneezes, we'll know about it.'

They sat facing each other across a low table scarred with the burn marks of cigarettes and rings from coffee cups, one small and dusty lamp making a feeble attempt to light their space. Tom was curled up on the big bed, his hand clutching the scrap of yellow blanket, his breathing no more than a distant whisper. Rain drummed against the window, and occasionally they could hear the swish of tyres as another car pulled into the motel forecourt.

'Dumb, that's what it was, dumb,' Betsy said, to herself as much as to Chuck.

'He was hungry.'

'Then we should have given him some candy, or chips.

99

We never should have done that.' They fell silent again, the rain still driving insistently against the glass, as if it wanted to be inside with them. Betsy pulled herself up and walked over to the window, pulling back a curtain without really wishing to see outside, or be seen.

'Betsy?' Chuck spoke softly without turning to look at her. 'Can this be right? I mean, shouldn't we take him back?' He seemed to shrink in his chair as he asked these questions. But Betsy continued to stare out of the window, her breath making little patches of steam on the pane.

'Listen to the rain, Chuck. It's washing everything away. God's cleaning the planet, clearing a path for us and covering all our tracks. I think this was meant to be.'

'You think our Lord approves of what we're doing?'

'Sure do. This storm's a sign, Chuck. It's telling us that we're doing the right thing. God is guiding us in all this, make no mistake. It wasn't chance that we found little Ricky – it was preordained. All this is part of His plan, and we're just His executors.'

Chuck considered these remarks, delivered with a quiet force that had always eluded him. Betsy's convictions, carved out at an early age and steadily etched deeper, were palely reflected in him. The doubts he carried were normally overrun by her consistent power and, at times like this, he followed her with something close to awe, dazed by her certainty of purpose and sense of direction. She held the compass and the map; he was a mere Sherpa in their adventures.

Betsy came back to the table and sat on the arm of his chair. 'This is our chance, honey. We had it all taken away from us. What did we do to deserve that? Haven't we earned the right to a little bit of happiness? All that's happening now is that God is balancing the books, and it's our turn to be in credit. Little Ricky here is going to have the best that we can give him – he'll want for nothing, and that will be our contribution. We're going to have given back much more than we have taken, once they finalise the accounts. I know it's hard to see that now, but you've got to trust the Lord. He will guide us, Chuck – He will.'

Chuck took her hand and nodded, attempting with the physical contact to draw on some of her strength. Their eyes moved together across the room to Tom, peaceful and oblivious to the agonies that raged within Chuck.

'I'll tell you something else for nothing,' Betsy said more brightly. 'Today he didn't even ask about his mom and dad, not once. You see, he's already one of the family. Kids are like that – they can really adapt much better than we can. And if we show him that we're strong, that we can protect him and give him all he needs, he'll respond to that.' Chuck picked up the unspoken threat – don't let him see us weak and uncertain, she was saying.

'He sure is a neat boy,' Chuck said, moving them on to safer ground. 'And bright as a button.'

'That's for sure. All the time he's asking questions, like he's really keen to learn more. It's going to be a load of fun trying to keep up with him.' She patted Chuck's hand and they smiled at each other. 'I just know we're doing the right thing. This is going to be the most amazing time for us, and that little guy is going to make us very happy.'

'Guess you're right,' Chuck said.

'Aren't I always?'

TWELVE

'Evidently they held up a store in White Plains with handguns. They were black, of course. The cops chased them right up 684, finally caught them at the crossing out there.' The lady behind the deli counter pointed towards the window and, even though he was not part of the conversation, Will's head turned involuntarily to follow her finger. 'They shot the driver right through the head, and the car just spun off and came to rest in the ditch.'

'And you were here?' the other woman asked, clearly in awe.

'Sure was. We were just fixing the shelves when we heard the shots. Chip runs to the door and throws it open – real smart, huh? – and he sees the car spinning into the ditch. The driver's got his brains half hanging out, and the other guy stays real still. Within a minute, maybe less, there were police and paramedics everywhere. I tell you, it was scary all right. I'd never heard gunshots before.' The two women shook their heads in unison. 'Right here in Evansboro – makes you think, huh?'

Will continued to wait as the women thought, his mind half on the events that had just been relayed. Finally his turn came as the woman paid for her groceries and he stood at the counter.

'Hi, Mr Easterbrook. Say, I'm real sorry to hear about

103

little Tommy. You know if there's anything Chip and me can do, you just holler, OK?' Will did know that what she said was utterly sincere; he had learnt not to underestimate the reservoirs of kindness in American souls. When they made an offer of help, they really meant it, and this would be no different.

'That's kind of you, Sally. We think someone may have spotted Tom, so we're hoping for the best.' In divulging this information Will was making a shrewd calculation: Sally would have broadcast the news by lunchtime, and it would obviate the need for him to explain the current situation to everyone else he met. The local newspaper could not compete with Sally's news-gathering and dissemination network – the Fifth Division deli supplied much more than good ham and salads, acting as the modern village pump.

'Well, that's good. We're praying for you and him. Now what can I get for you today?' Will ordered some cuts of meat and cheeses and thought again about the shooting. It was the ultimate paradox of American life: in Evansboro he was surrounded by good, mostly God-fearing, white middle-class families, all trying to live by the same moral code. Into the middle of this community had come extreme brutality, exported from the city and executed not by the villains but by the police. The people of Evansboro would be excited by this in a strange way, strange because they could isolate it from their own existence and rationalise their prurience because the perpetrators were nothing to do with them: they were black, they were not from round here, they were just passing through and their violence would not linger. It was only one step removed from a violent film at the local movie-house, an entertainment that provided thrills but left the viewers untouched and unchanged. How could these extremes of kindness and aggression coexist so easily, Will thought?

He told Rocket the story as they drove back from the deli to his house. He found himself hoping that she would be impressed, that this worldly woman with her hard-boiled exterior would find the news stimulating, and he was secretly pleased that she showed some interest.

'You'll get on Channel 5 for sure,' she said. 'Their news is a non-stop diet of murders. I'll bet the cameras are already on their way.'

'Who'd have imagined that this could happen in sleepy Evansboro?' Will said in self-mockery.

'Oh, I don't know about that. I reckon there's quite a lot of mischief going on behind these colonial façades.'

'You do?' Will asked.

'Take your friend Marla, for instance. I'll tell you two things about her that you don't know. First, she's doing drugs. Nothing heavy, but a little coke and dope here and there. You know, recreational stuff. Second, she's being seriously abused by her husband. Clever guy, incidentally, because you'd never spot it. But he's giving her a very hard time.'

Will didn't want to appear surprised, but couldn't help himself. 'How the hell can you say that?'

'You can see just from looking at her. She's jumpy as hell, and gets too emotional about the smallest thing. She also has a permanently runny nose, after all the crap she's put up there. All the signs are there if you know what to search for.' She lit a cigarette and held it out to Will, but he shook his head. They had reached the house, and he

105

carried the sack of shopping as she followed him into the kitchen. Will retrieved two tins of beer from the fridge and they sat at the table.

'You're serious, aren't you? You really believe that about Marla.' Will felt a little indignant.

'I wouldn't get bent out of shape over it. Wife-beating is like a sport over here, especially if there's nothing good on TV. You ever wondered why so many women wear sunglasses all the time, even in the winter?'

'I think your work has made you incredibly cynical,' Will said cuttingly, but it had no discernible effect.

'Maybe, but that's the world we live in. It isn't all *Homes Beautiful* and the Puritan ethic. There's some bad stuff going on, and it creeps in under the door when you're not looking. We have a society that's built on aggression – it's written into the constitution, condoned by lawmakers. Of course, everyone assumes that the good guys – people like you and Marla – can still differentiate between right and wrong. That's a big assumption to make, and my experience tells me it's crap.'

'Doesn't it sadden you?'

'What's the point in being sad? That won't change the status quo. You just deal with it. As they say, we made our bed, and now we're lying in it. The problem for you folks, the ones that live in these little enclaves of respectability, is that you can't reconcile what you see on the news with what's going on in your own lives. You think there's some enormous canyon between you and them, blacks and whites, managers and workers, or whatever it is that you think divides you. But it isn't a canyon – it's a tiny fissure, and it's closing up all the time. That shooting this morning? You all think that's exciting because it's unreal, because it's transient. It isn't, and it never has been. It's just that the medium of violence is more subtle up here. Poke your nose behind any door and you'll find the same horror and misery as you would in the worst projects. You're just more discreet about it.' Rocket drank some beer and lit another cigarette, brushing her hair away from her face.

'Maybe you're right,' Will said, a little calmer now. 'But I still like to think that there's some inner core of decency within most of us, that our first instincts are benign. If you give up believing that, then we're no better than the animal kingdom.'

'I always think it's kind of cute that the thing that differentiates us from wild beasts is our thumb and forefinger,' Rocket said. 'You know, the ones you use when you're firing a gun? The problem with our society is that we've boiled things down to such an extent that we're closer to the animal kingdom than ever before. Our first instincts aren't benign at all – they're based on survival. If that happens to coincide with something good, then it's just that – coincidence. Perhaps it's different in England, but here we are really living by the laws of the jungle.'

'So do you believe that anyone is decent?'

'The problem with answering that is that you always judge others by yourself. If you're a bastard, you work on that premiss when you deal with anyone else. You and Clare are undoubtedly decent people – even I can see that. But what happens to you in adversity, like you've got now? Do you continue to be decent, or do you gradually let your standards slip? I wish I knew, and I wish I could do something about it. If you're a cop, or someone like me who operates at the margins, you stop looking for solutions eventually. You start out with some pretty altruistic motives, hoping to prevent all the bad things and make the world a safer place. But experience soon proves you wrong, makes you accept the tenet that most people are bad at heart when they're really up against it. You called me cynical, but I think that's just reality. It's wonderful if you can go through life thinking the best of everyone, but you're likely to be pretty scarred by the time they carry you out in a box.'

Will went to the fridge and got some more beer for them. The feeling inside him was like that of a man who watches a repulsive video but cannot take his eyes off it. Rocket was saying things that he abhorred, but he couldn't resist hearing them; he wanted to shake her hard so that the veneer of bitterness would fall away to reveal a gentle, vulnerable woman, someone he could understand more easily and treat in his conventional way. He didn't know whether his unease was because of the message she was sending, or the fact that it was she who was delivering it, but either and both distressed him.

As he sat opposite her she was looking at him intensely. 'So have I shattered some illusions?' she asked.

'About what?'

'Anything and everything. Me, I guess. Here you are, in a pretty weird situation not of your own making, and I come along and you're hoping I'm going to come up with all the answers, and all I do is present you with more problems. Right now you probably hate me like hell for that.'

'I have to admit I'm shaken by what you've said.'

'But why? If Jablonowski had told you these things, you'd take them much better from him. But I'm a different kind of messenger, aren't I? I think you still have a fairly traditional view of women, you know, we're meant to be pretty and genteel and not rock the boat or have big ideas. You probably think that under all this cynicism there's a nice sweet girl just itching to break out.'

'And is there?'

'You know what they say – a woman should be a cook in the kitchen, a maid in the living room and a whore in the bedroom.' She shrugged her shoulders without any sign of embarrassment, but Will could feel himself colouring. He pulled the packet of cigarettes towards him to create a diversion, and fumbled to light one. He would have liked to kick himself for being so unperceptive, for letting his body manifest a feeling that he had not allowed himself to acknowledge.

At that moment, when confusion was rife and the physical took over from the mental, Will wanted to kiss her. For the first time in his life he was consumed by a bestial need for contact, for the closeness of two bodies pressed so hard against each other that their bones scraped and the skin covering them seemed to dissolve. The churning in his gut was a toxic mixture of fear and need and desire, all caution scattered as the chemicals pumped round him and sent thick blood to his groin. He could hear the thrumming of this passion as it sped through his skull, and he made no effort to control it or seek an escape. But in front of him Rocket sat still, apparently untouched by the pheromonal aura around him. He could smell his own scent, could taste it in his saliva, as it seeped from every pore, blurring his sight and transforming him. He saw what he wanted to happen, the way he would take her and have her, and the images only served to heighten the growing excitement.

Rocket moved, a slight inclination of the head and the merest flick of one hand. The signal this sent was enough for Will, and he put his hand on hers. They sat like that for a couple of seconds. Then Rocket got up and, for one beat longer, Will stayed seated, the sickness in his stomach preventing him from instant movement; then he followed her as she climbed the stairs, a painful ascent towards the unknown.

THIRTEEN

The late spring air was thick with the smell of barbecues, of broiling marinaded meat and corn-cobs, as families ventured out on to decks and hosed down the summer furniture. The lighting of charcoal and the searing of steak were like some pagan ritual to announce the end of winter, heralding the arrival of better weather and longer days, with the burnt offerings acting as talismans of thanks. Fathers clutched beers and tongs and stood attentively over their cooking, whilst mothers prepared salads and wondered silently why they didn't simply go to Burger King.

Will and Clare had company: in the kitchen, Clare sliced avocados and tomatoes as she talked to Robyn, whilst on the deck Will and Jack were watching the coals turn white, both preferring to look into the fire than at each other. The visit, they all knew, was not entirely social. Jack and Robyn were friends, supportive and understanding, but Jack was also Will's boss. In the six months since Tom had disappeared Will had been absent more often than he'd been at work; sometimes he'd bring work home and make a dilatory attempt to handle it, and occasionally he'd attend meetings and briefings, but his contribution was limited and half-hearted.

111

The only aspect of this gathering that was uncertain was the timing of the news. Would Jack tell Will before lunch, or would he wait until the girls were washing the dishes and making coffee? This uncertainty put all of them on edge, making them over-polite and reserved, skirting round discussion of any major topic. The imminent arrival of a baby couldn't be mentioned, in spite of Clare's burgeoning stomach; Robyn had warned Jack in the car that this might be altogether too sensitive an issue to broach unless Will and Clare raised it first. But Jack's agitation could not be contained, as if the subject had to be lanced like a boil before it festered and turned septic.

'No more news on Tom, I guess?' he asked, kicking an imagined pebble across the deck.

'Nothing. The trail went cold after they were spotted – if it was them, which I'm beginning to doubt. Anyway, we've heard nothing more.' Will picked up a stray lump of charcoal with the tongs and balanced it on the top of the smouldering pile.

'So when do you give up?'

'Never,' Will replied a little too quickly, knowing the question was loaded. Jack sighed and pushed his hands deep into his pockets.

'Will, this thing'll never go away, I realise that. But you've got another life to worry about now, and you've got to get on with that. If you keep on looking back, nothing's ever going to get achieved.'

'What would you do in my position?'

'Pretty much the same as you, I suppose. But that doesn't make it right. Look, let's be straight about this. I have two concerns here. One is you and Clare and the baby. This is going to tear you apart if you let it, and

Robyn and I don't want to watch that happening. The other, frankly, is professional.'

'Meaning?' Will wanted Jack to spell it out; he wasn't prepared to let him off too easily.

'Meaning that, as long as you're here, you're not focused on work. We've given you a lot of time to deal with this, and I think we've been scrupulously fair. But we can't afford to let things drag on indefinitely – you know that.' Will started to push the coals flat on the grill, little orange sparks flying up as he moved them with the tongs. 'I've spoken to Human Resources, checked out our policy on this kind of situation, and they're in agreement.'

'With what?'

'We're going to offer you a transfer back to London. There's a vacancy in the risk management division – you'd be bumped up a grade, still doing a job well within your capabilities, running a team of analysts. It's a good opportunity.'

'This is serious?'

'Totally. Susan's already doing your job, and we're hiring a replacement for her right now. I know I sound like an A-one bastard, but I'm really thinking of you and the family, Will. You have to believe that.'

Will pursed his lips and drew in a very deep breath. Faced with the inevitability of the circumstances, he prevaricated: he wanted to take some action – shout, or punch Jack, or cry – but the armour he had carefully constructed around his emotions prevented him from doing any of these.

'Jack, you can't do this to us,' he said finally. 'If you're really concerned for us, you'll see how terrible this would be. If we go back to England now we might be separated physically from the problem, but it'll still be with us. We owe it to Tom, and ourselves, to see this through until the end – however long it takes.'

'What precisely have you achieved in the last six months, Will? Eventually you have to face it – being here doesn't do anything for Tom, or you. You're just hanging on right now, and I can see you slipping over the edge. Maybe, just maybe, if you start over in London, you'll get a new perspective on the whole deal.'

'I don't want a new perspective. I don't want to relegate Tom to a position where he's just a fond memory, and that's exactly what will happen if we go now. We have to stay.' Will started putting steaks on to the grill, painting them with sauce.

'What does Clare think?' Jack asked. Will stopped his work and looked up at Jack for the first time in the conversation.

'Is that what Robyn's doing? Is she trying to turn Clare round to your point of view?'

'God, Will, don't be so dramatic. We're trying to help you guys. We all know there's a problem, and it has to be resolved. I can't force you to leave the country, but I want you to understand the practicalities. I don't have any more room for manoeuvre. We have to clear this thing up once and for all, and I'm trying to do it honourably. In your heart you know that. I'm also willing to bet that Clare has already reached the same conclusion. You owe it to her – and the baby – to face up to it.'

'I've faced up to it. Tom has gone, we don't know where, and we have a hole in our lives. Another child won't fill that hole. We'll always be wondering, always thinking about

114

what we might have done, how he would have turned out, and always doubting ourselves and our motives. Everything's already screwed up. We can't undo that. If you really want to know, I think our hopes of finding him are next to zero. There – I've said it. Satisfied?'

'Of course I'm not satisfied. It isn't a question of who's right and wrong in all of this. Everyone's on your side. But if you've got this far, I think it makes sense to try and mitigate some of the suffering by living your future life, not your past. And I'm telling you how we're going to help you to do that. But I'm under pressure here – professional pressure – to get an answer out of you. The bank is hardly a bottomless pit of sympathy. At some stage they're going to ask the question: how long can we go on like this? And it's my job to advise them. We're friends, right, and I'm speaking to you as a friend, not as your boss. I simply cannot stand by and watch you go down.'

'The best I can say,' Will muttered, 'is that I'd rather quit than go back. If that's what you want, you can take my resignation now.'

'Think about it, Will. Call me tomorrow when you've talked to Clare and slept on it.' Jack put his arm round Will's shoulder. 'Now, you still don't know how to cook a good steak, do you?'

Clare was tired, irritable, depressed and very uncomfortable. Whichever way she turned, the baby appeared to move with her and dig a sharp limb into her. They had nicknamed it the octopus because it seemed to have so many appendages available to cause her discomfort, but the name hadn't really stuck: as the months passed their sense of humour and joy had gradually dissipated as they slid towards an event that neither could summon up much enthusiasm for. The stinging pain of loss had turned into a dull, monotonous ache for both of them, a constant bass line in the rhythm of their lives.

Rocket was history. Will told Clare that she was too expensive and offered little hope of discovery, and Clare accepted this decision with a silent nod. It was an acceptance that might have signified knowledge and forgiveness of the original sin, though Will had no reason to believe that Clare knew about him and Rocket. Their affair had been a desultory and disappointing business, conducted through hasty assignations that left Will feeling sicker after the act than before it, but he could not control the primitive urge within his bones and was always drawn back to her in spite of the guilt he felt. Rocket behaved as if she fully recognised his dilemma, as if she were providing a form of rehabilitation or physiotherapy after a long illness, and was calm and understanding when he finally declared it must end.

But the illness was not cured, even if that was what he'd been trying to achieve. He still hurt badly, with internal injuries that had left big scars; he sat in darkened rooms, he walked through Manhattan streets and avenues till dusk and beyond, and he avoided contact with Clare. There was little to pull them together: the cement of Tom's presence had long since crumbled, to the point where they wondered how they had ever existed together before his birth. Clare stayed for long periods in England, relieving the carers who attended to Ralph, an arrangement that no longer merited comment or raised

116

further doubts. Will was pleased to see her go, as it let him fester unchallenged.

They had only argued violently once. Will, returning from a meeting with Rocket, found Clare in Tom's bedroom emptying drawers and packing Tom's clothes into a tote bag. Already fired up with guilt, Will exploded at the sight of this treachery, lunging towards Clare and knocking her backwards against the sharp corner of an open drawer. He shouted at her as she lay on the floor, accusing her of trying to erase Tom's existence, and he kicked her. After the incident she stayed in bed for two days, then appeared one morning as if nothing had happened and they resumed the neutrality of their life.

Now, as they sat on the deck at sunset, they were talking at each other, not fully engaged in conversation but making an effort. Will had told her of his talk with Jack, and how he planned to resist being moved back to London. Clare had reacted predictably enough.

'Surely you're not serious?' she said. 'You can't be.'

'What do you want from me?' Will spat at her. 'What do you want me to say – that I'll give the whole thing up?'

'Will, we can't go on like this. I refuse to go on like this. The whole situation is making me ill, and I can't stand it any longer. You're behaving as if you're the only person in the world who feels any pain, who has any concept of how ghastly everything is. You try to make me feel bad by questioning my devotion to Tom, and it just isn't fair. I want him back just as much as you do, but you seem to think it's some kind of competition. Can't you see what you're doing to us? What kind of life do you think the baby will have if you keep up this attitude? I'll tell you what I want from you – I want some compassion,

117

and some understanding, and some love. You've been utterly selfish, as if you have the premium on grief, and it's time you started thinking about other people.'

'I'm thinking about other people all the time,' Will said. 'I'm thinking about Tom, and the people who took him. That's what I can't understand about you – you appear to have had no difficulty in forgetting all about him.'

Clare didn't want a fight, was too tired for it, and chose not to be provoked. 'This is so stupid,' she said, almost under her breath. 'We still love each other, don't we? Isn't that the most important thing? I know our life is a complete disaster at the moment, but if we stop loving each other then what's left? I don't want to argue with you, Will. I just want us to try and sort something out so that we can get back to some kind of normality. As long as we're brooding over Tom, and living here, I don't see how that can happen. I think Jack is absolutely right – we need a fresh start. That doesn't mean we have to give up on Tom, or that we'll forget about him. God knows, I lie awake every night thinking about him. I still can't get used to the fact that he doesn't wake me up because he's frightened or cold or needs to do a wee. We've got exactly the same feelings for him, but they're just manifesting themselves differently. I don't want us to spend the rest of our lives blaming each other because we can't accept that.'

Clare wiped her eyes and cheeks as the tears came, her face smudged and mottled. 'I can't even think rationally any more,' she continued. 'Last night I lay there thinking about what would happen if we found Tom, if he came back to us and wasn't the same, and I was trying to convince myself that maybe it would be better if he didn't come back. Who knows, maybe he's better off where he is. Maybe I wasn't such a great mother after all, and he's actually enjoying being away from me. That's how far this whole thing is screwing me up, Will – I'm even questioning the really basic stuff that you always take for granted.'

Will exploded again. 'You don't believe all that shit, do you? You don't truly think that Tom isn't thinking about us every minute of the day, wanting to be back with us? You can't believe that, Clare, you just can't. Whatever has happened to him, you're still his mother and I'm still his father and he'll never have anyone who can replace us.'

'Of course that's what I want to think. But these dark thoughts won't go away. Everything's been cast into doubt since Tom went. And then there's the baby: this is going to be hanging over it for as long as things remain unresolved, which is hardly a fair way to bring up a child. I've gone well past the stage where everything's black and white, right and wrong, fair and unfair. All the parameters are blurred, and I just can't make them out.'

Will closed his eyes, squeezing the lids together, and rubbed his hands down his face in a way that suggested he was trying to wipe away his confusion. Then he opened his eyes abruptly. 'I don't think you've ever understood, have you?'

'What? Make me understand, Will. That's why I'm here.'

He waited a long time, rocking slightly in his chair as he battled with himself. Then he sighed and closed his eyes again, nodding as if agreeing that he should say it. 'It's different for you. Of course it's different for you. And you don't even know why.'

'Why?'

'Why? Because I lost him. I let him go. Tom's not here because of me. I'm to blame for all of this. I had a simple thing to do, and I couldn't do it. You have no idea how that makes me feel.'

Clare watched him as he said this, and her perception was that he visibly shrank as he spoke, as if the act of admission physically deflated him. All his features were smudged in the half-light, and he looked more like a boy than a man. In fact, he looked more like Tom than she'd ever noticed before and, in that recognition, she also realised that she was dealing with another lost boy.

FOURTEEN

Tom wasn't Tom any more. Sometimes, in his solitary games, he would give himself the name Tom, but he knew he was just playing. He thought like Ricky and, increasingly, he thought of himself as part of Chuck and Betsy's family and world; his childish pragmatism allowed him to place his mother and father in a separate locker of his memory, no longer called upon every day and no longer integral to his survival. He slipped easily into his new existence, the transition lubricated by the kindness and attention of his new guardians, and rarely cast a backward glance to the life he had been snatched away from.

He was also invigorated by the new freedom he was given: Chuck and Betsy consulted him before making decisions, asking for his opinion and appearing to take it seriously. In his former life he had grown used to doing what he was told – going to bed, going to the playgroup, going to see friends – but now, with them, he managed his own life, reacting to suggestions and proposals with the knowledge that he was likely to get his own way. At first this had given him problems, as he struggled to come to terms with the responsibility, but he soon accepted it as a fact of life and began to deal with things with more confidence. He rarely had to lose his temper to win a fight, as there were no fights: Chuck and Betsy managed each situation as if his wishes were paramount.

Even when he did misbehave – judged by his old set of standards – the ramifications were almost non-existent. If he left his clothes on the floor, or splashed water out of the bath-tub, Betsy might cluck a little, but nothing more. He saw the lines of right and wrong blurring daily, not redrawn but simply fading, and this puzzled him. He still had the childish urge to test the boundaries, and would sometimes try and get into trouble just to get a reaction, but he was always frustrated by the results. Chuck, it seemed to him, was particularly weak in this respect, never wanting conflict when it could be avoided, and Tom soon learnt to treat him with little regard.

His relationship with Betsy was more complex. Every night she would sit on the edge of his bed and talk to him but, more importantly for Tom, she would listen to him. She always had time for him, no matter what she was doing or where they were. He felt he could talk to her, holding no secrets back, and would not be rebuffed with the parental platitudes he'd been accustomed to. If he had a problem, Betsy would try and solve it; if he had a need, she would do her best to fulfil it. He respected her for this, and began to love her a little. He looked forward to that quiet time at the end of the day when they could both reflect on what had occurred and what was planned for tomorrow; she seemed to fill his life, providing the plaster between the tiles of his existence so that he never needed to worry about the past or the future. His world was being managed in a way that made him feel happy and secure.

Betsy too enjoyed their conversations. She liked the

way he recycled her expressions and mannerisms, the way in which he would take a thought or an idea and consider it silently before speaking, the process of working out the concept and conclusion almost etched across his face as he concentrated. She marvelled at his knowledge and intelligence; he seemed to understand many things with a clarity and simplicity that often evaded her, and was not afraid to ask if he needed clarification. Her conversations with Chuck were now exclusively about him – what he had said, what he had done, what he might become in the future. They invested all their energy and emotion in him, leaving nothing for each other but none the sadder for it.

One night he was crying. He lay in his bed and moaned, a sound that cut through Betsy's dreams and woke her with a primal jump. She ran to his room and saw him lying there, eyes still closed as he whimpered, and found herself strangely unsure of what to do next. She wanted to cuddle him, to talk to him through his nightmare and comfort him, but she had no idea why he was sad and, in that moment, she recognised the weakness of their bond, manufactured as it was through a mutual need for affection rather than a stronger maternal cord. What could she say to this little boy who had breezed into her life, whose history was unknown and whose provenance remained uncertain? What were his fears? Was there scar tissue from a previous life? She stood and watched him as he sobbed; then he stopped, turned over and disappeared under his duvet. Betsy went back to bed, but the vision of this little boy caught between peace and tumult stayed with her all night and she couldn't sleep.

★　★　★

It had taken her three days, but the wait was worth it. She had not lied to Will when she had told him that she had friends in Florida who could pick up a scent, and they had done their job quietly and effectively. She had checked into a motel on the outskirts of St Petersburg, returning there only to powder her nose and catch some sleep from time to time. She hated the sunshine: her fair skin burnt and dried and her hair collapsed under the strong ultraviolet, so she wore wide-brimmed hats and covered herself with sunblock.

Now she sat in a sticky sports bar, the huge television monitors rerunning an old football game, and she drank Seven and Seven as if it were water. The agony of knowledge gnawed at her. She could hardly keep still, fiddling with her lighter and shifting her weight ceaselessly on the bar stool. Around her the locals talked of sporting memories and nagging wives, of fishing triumphs and the lack of work, whilst tourists put their heads round the door to check on the ambience, their big city faces and bright shirts and video cameras betraying them as aliens.

Rocket ordered another drink with a nod to the barman and lit a cigarette. It was to have been a simple assignment – find the kid, call the cops, pick up the money and go on a bender – but it hadn't panned out like that. For a start, he looked happy. She hadn't expected that, and it had come like a slap in the face. He was walking with them, not a surly walk but almost with a skip in his step, and she felt he had no right to be so cheerful and carefree. They too looked peaceful and content; they seemed like any other couple, not the tortured monsters she had come to believe they must be. They had no right, she kept on saying. Surely they knew what they had done, and that realisation must weigh heavily on their shoulders. But instead they looked serene.

She had followed them home, and had even got as far as positioning her finger over the doorbell before stopping herself. What would she say? Would little Tom look up at her with those liquid eyes, unable to take in the accusations she would deliver? She retreated. Her courage left her, the desertion of all her convictions denting her strength, and she felt a little afraid. Officially, of course, she was off the case; she had no need to worry about what she had found, but her lingering feelings for Will – and Clare, in a different way – made her uneasy. What to do, what to do?

Other considerations clouded her judgement, darker stains on her memory. She remembered Will's hard edge, when he had told her how much he wanted revenge. At first she had put this down to an entirely understandable sense of frustration and rage, but Will had confirmed his bitterness in the bedroom. He was a violent lover: no blows were thrown, but he treated her roughly and the threat of danger was never far from her when they were together. He could be ruthless with her, abusing her like a child might treat a doll in a fit of rage. It had frightened and aroused her but, reviewing it now, it seemed more chilling. She had seen a side of him that made her think twice about how to proceed. How would he react to this news? Would he seek the revenge he had said he needed?

She caught a cab back to the motel from the bar, showered in cold water and lay naked on the bed. Her conscience argued with her, even through the fumes of alcohol: who is at risk, and whose need is greater? Who is suffering, and who will suffer? She found too many answers to all these questions, all of them conflicting.

Her head swam with the quandaries she faced, and she dragged herself off the bed to try and clear her thoughts.

She wanted to call Will – better yet, to see him and speak to him – so that she could explain how she felt about him and Clare and Tom. Some part of their sadness had rubbed off on her, making her more vulnerable than she wanted to be, and she needed to communicate this to him. She had hated the way he seemed so distant when they parted, as if he felt that their small affair was all there had been between them; much as she'd enjoyed the frenzied way in which they had made love, it was not that which loitered in her memory. She thought of her visits to their house, the stillness and emptiness echoing through every room as they discussed their loss.

Distractedly Rocket picked up a bottle of body lotion and began rubbing the oil on herself as she studied her reflection in the cracked full-length mirror on the door of the wardrobe. Since Will she had been with no other men, not as a conscious decision but more from lethargy; she had not been hurt by him, and was not surprised when he finished it, but she had lost a little of her sparkle, perhaps from the shadow that had fallen across both their lives. Even now, still slightly drunk and naked, she had no real feeling of need, of wanting the warmth of a larger body to envelop her and use her. She felt alone, isolated by the new knowledge she'd acquired and uncertain how to use it, with no one to turn to for guidance. Before Will had come into her life this independence seemed essential – 'I'm Rocket, take it or leave it' – but her brush with such a tragedy, so enormous and ragged, had affected her more than she had bargained for.

The lotion was thick and glistening on her breasts and

126

torso when she finally made a decision. She tossed the bottle on to the bed and hurriedly threw on some clothes, grabbed her bag and left the motel room. The cooling night air helped to invigorate her and propel her forward, and she made her way determinedly along the sidewalk. Within twenty minutes she had reached her destination; she hesitated a little on the steps before ringing the bell briefly, cautious in case he was already sleeping. A man opened the door and flicked a light on, looking at her questioningly; further back she could see the woman hovering in the hallway.

'Hi,' she said as brightly as she could manage. 'I've come to talk to you about the boy.' His expression didn't change, but he looked over his shoulder at the woman and waited for her signal. 'It's OK, I'm not a cop,' she added helpfully.

'Guess you'd better come in,' he said, and pushed the screen door open.

The house was clearly a second home. The furniture was functional, and there were no ornaments or decorations to make it feel warmer; it was all painted a bland magnolia, with brown and cream materials for curtains and covers. There was little to suggest that a boy was living there.

Rocket sat in a large and lumpy leatherette armchair, the two of them opposite her on a big sofa, silent and unwelcoming. If she was surprised that they'd let her in, Rocket was now intimidated by the frozen stares they gave her, almost robotic in their manner. She desperately wanted a cigarette, but couldn't find the courage to ask or to light up.

'Where to begin?' she said. 'I'm Rocket Stubblefield.

I'm a private detective, and I was hired by the parents to find their little boy, the one you've got now.' There was no flicker of encouragement from either of them, no signal that they had any comprehension of what she was saying. 'So here I am. And I'm wondering what we do next, so I figured I should ask you folks about that, see if you can give me a hint.'

There was the merest glance between them before the woman spoke. 'You say you were hired? Does that mean you aren't any longer?'

'That's correct.'

'So what are you doing here? Seems to me you have no authority to be talking to us.' Rocket sensed a small growth of confidence, and it worried her. She'd expected to catch them off guard, but already they were taking control.

'I'm a law-abiding citizen, so I think I have a moral authority, regardless of who's paying me.' Rocket and morality were strange bedfellows, but she calculated that they wouldn't yet know that.

'So what do you think you know?' Betsy asked.

'Not a whole lot, but I'm working on it. I know that that little boy is not yours, and I know that his parents didn't ask you to look after him. Is that enough for you?'

'And what do you propose to do with your knowledge, Miss Stubblefield?'

'That's what I'm struggling with. You see, normally I'd just call the cops and have you pulled in, but things are never quite as simple as that, are they? I've watched you with the boy and he seems to be pretty happy. Let's face it, we all have his best interests at heart, don't we?' She wanted to sound accommodating, reasonable, non-threatening; a fight now would blow the whole thing. 'So

I'm caught between a rock and a hard place. On the one hand, what you've done is wrong, but on the other, he's gone through an awful lot already, and we don't want his little life disrupted any more. Do you see what I'm getting at?'

'Blackmail!' Betsy shouted. 'You little bitch, you're trying to skin us.' Chuck reached across and held her hand to calm her, but she broke free and jumped up. 'I can tell you, you'll get nothing from us.'

Rocket was so shocked by this reaction that she had no reply. She shook her head, more in amazement than denial, and watched nervously as Betsy moved towards her.

'I could use a drink,' Chuck said. 'Will you have one, Miss Stubblefield?'

'I'd love a cold beer if there's one going,' she said, relieved at his intervention.

'Betsy, go fetch some beers for us, would you?' Chuck said. Betsy looked at him for a long time before she left the room. 'Hell, sorry about that, but she's been under a lot of pressure. Now, where were we?'

'Thank you. I quite understand. We're all a little edgy, I guess. Look, I'm not here to blackmail you, any more than I'm here to tell you what's right and wrong, but we have a significant problem. Tom's parents are decent, honest people who've been terribly hurt by what you did. Now I don't know your own position – and in a way I don't want to – but I'm in a no-win situation. Can you see that?'

'Sure can, and I feel sorry for you. But let's take this thing one step at a time. Just suppose we did have their kid – and I'm not saying we do – but supposing that we did, we have to look at it from all the angles. The boy is very happy with us. Betsy and I give him lots of love and attention, and he's really thriving on it. I tell you, he's a livewire. And we're happy too. That counts for a lot, don't you think? So that's three folks who are doing real good. Now, on the other side, you've got some people who are not doing so good. And they reckon that everything would be fine and dandy if they got their boy back – assuming they could. They'd be happy, and the kid would be too – or would he? Isn't that the question you need to be asking yourself?' Chuck spread his hands and shrugged.

Betsy came back with two bottles of beer and a bowl of nuts, setting them on the scratched coffee table before sitting down next to Chuck again. 'I was just explaining how things might be to this young lady,' Chuck said softly.

'I see,' Betsy said. 'And what does she have to say?'

'Well, I think we owe her a little explanation, don't you?' Betsy merely shrugged, and Chuck took this as her consent. He took a long swallow of beer before beginning.

'We had a son, Miss Stubblefield. The best son you could ever hope for, in fact. He was a blessing from God. We'd given up trying for a baby, and then along he came. And he lit up our lives in a way nothing else can. He was kind, bright, very popular, the kind of things you always pray for but never really expect. We had him for seventeen beautiful years.' Rocket felt stapled to her seat as this man spoke so gently, so adoringly, and she didn't want to break the spell. 'But he left us. One day he was there, the next day he was gone. And in all the time since, we've never heard a peep from him. Not a single thing.' He paused and took Betsy's hand again. 'That was five years ago –

five long years of not knowing, of not being able to grieve for his loss properly because we have not the first idea of what happened to him. And for every day of those five years we've never opened a letter or answered the phone without thinking it might be him, writing or calling to say he's OK and coming home. But like this, we don't even know if he's alive or dead.'

Rocket took some beer and wiped her mouth with the back of her hand. 'That is terrible,' she said. 'I am so sorry.'

'Do you have children?' he asked.

'No.'

'Well, I don't expect you to have any idea of how something like that feels,' Chuck said, 'but it's like having a part of you chopped off. You can't think straight, you lose your balance, everything goes. We were way too old to consider starting again, so we just had to live with it. Every minute of every day we're trying to cope with that, with the injustice of it all, and it's tough. We have to fight a major battle every morning just to get out of bed and carry on. We're simple people, Miss Stubblefield. We've never asked for anything much, and haven't expected much either. But we had a little miracle, and it was taken from us. Now how do you recover from that?'

Rocket looked at these two strangers, ordinary people who'd faced the worst and were still struggling to come through it, and tried to reconcile their position with what she knew of Will and Clare. Could she not be sitting in front of them in five years' time, hearing the same miserable account and feeling the same pangs of sympathy and regret?

'We have another chance now, and we don't intend to

131

waste it,' Betsy said suddenly. 'You are not going to screw things up for us.'

'And that's exactly why I'm here,' Rocket replied. 'I have to understand before I can do anything. But the boy has to be the focus. Everything I may or may not do must be driven by what's best for him.'

'I'm not going to beg you,' Chuck said, 'but you have to see our side of it. We will give him everything he will ever want for. He means everything to us, and I can't tell you what it would do to us if we had to give him up now.'

Rocket's options polarised starkly before her. The dilemma had only increased with her visit here, and her stomach churned at the enormity of the power that lay in her hands. She wanted to be far away, to be asleep and at peace, free of the demands of life and its contradictions.

'There isn't an easy answer, and I can't pretend that I've got one,' she said. 'I need to straighten my head out and think things through. I'm sorry for you, of course, and you have all my sympathy. But that doesn't make what you've done any more right. More than that I just can't say at the moment.'

'Do you want to see him?' Betsy asked. Rocket was stunned at the offer.

'Well, yes, that'd be great.' The two of them went upstairs and Betsy pushed open a door. Peering into the room, Rocket could see carefully arranged boxes of toys and shelves filled with books; in one corner there was a huge bed, and she could just make out the top of Tom's head above the blue duvet. She crept in and stood above him, no sound coming from him as he rested in absolute stillness. She lingered for a few moments, then left the room and went back downstairs with Betsy.

'I'll be in touch,' she said to them both as they walked to the front door.

'We're not going anywhere,' Chuck said. 'This is home for us now, and we're staying put. You don't need to worry about that.'

She shook their hands, then Betsy stopped her as she moved out of the house. 'I have a suggestion,' she said.

'Yes?' Rocket replied, eager to listen to anything that might ease the problem.

'Why don't you come round tomorrow afternoon, spend some time with us? You can meet Ricky, and see how we're all getting on.'

'I'm not sure that would be such a great idea,' Rocket replied cautiously.

'Don't worry, we won't try and corrupt you,' Betsy said in a gentle voice. 'Just for your peace of mind, that's all. What harm can it do, after all?'

What harm indeed, Rocket thought. 'OK. Say at three?'

'That'd be fine. We'll be waiting for you.' Betsy smiled for the first time. 'By the way,' she said, 'how ever did you find us?'

'The same way you find anyone,' Rocket replied. 'Luck.'

FIFTEEN

He was late; and she realised, as she sat and swirled the ice around in her glass, that she didn't even know if this were in character, or whether he was truly delayed, or if he'd come at all. Though they had shared a bed on numerous occasions, and performed acts of great intimacy with each other, she really didn't know too much about him: they had never lingered long after making love, never enjoyed that post-sex closeness when the barriers relax and nothing seems too insignificant to mention, when time stands still for just a few moments as the mind rests and the heart rules.

Rocket had been in a state of anguish since she'd met Tom's abductors; the booze had helped to knock the edges off her despair, but eventually she sobered up and asked herself the questions she'd tried so hard to avoid. What she couldn't reconcile in the whole affair was her own reaction to events: she'd tried to understand how she could have blithely allowed them to keep Tom, why she'd called on them without the help or knowledge of the police, and why she'd listened sympathetically to their story without demur or contradiction. In all her life she could not recall a time when she hadn't known the right thing to do, yet now she faced a situation in which, no matter where she turned, there seemed to be a reason for not going in that direction. Her natural inclination should have been to nail the bastards, to turn them over to the law and send Tom home, but that decision wasn't exactly staring her in the face. She'd seen Tom with them, and the vision of him so obviously happy and secure came back time and time again to haunt her; when she'd looked at him in his bed, she had wanted to believe that he was hurting, scared and lonely, but his quiet sleep spoke to her in quite a different way.

The afternoon she had spent with them merely consolidated her doubts. She saw the special bond between Betsy and Tom as he sat curled on her lap clutching a scrap of material and sucking his thumb. Her tenderness towards him, and the affectionate looks he gave her, were no act: this was a family unit, comfortable, secure and happy. She was no psychologist, but Rocket knew that Tom was as committed as they were. When she had left them she could not ignore the wrenching contradictions of their circumstances, nor shake off the warm glow they had bestowed, however temporarily, on her.

Eventually, red-eyed and worn out by the constant battle in her head, Rocket had resolved that it wasn't her decision anyway, that she should simply present the facts to Will and let him be the judge. She was – and here again, she didn't know exactly why – confident that, when they'd said they wouldn't leave, they were being honest. She had returned for a final look, driving to the house and waiting until she saw a sign of them, and this had satisfied her sufficiently to enable her to pack up and fly back to New York. In her apartment she had slumped on to a couch and tried to hide from her responsibilities, finally dragging herself into the shower and dousing her weary flesh with sharpened threads of icy water.

She had a small drink of bourbon when she rang, praying that Clare wouldn't answer whilst subconsciously hoping that Will wouldn't be there and she could put it off. But fate was against her – or with her, she knew not which – and he picked up. Their conversation was stilted: he was cold and matter-of-fact, immediately rejecting her suggestion of a meeting, whilst she struggled to find the right words or phrase that would finally induce him to accept. Eventually she had to let it out – 'I have some new information on Tom' – and even then she had to fight not to tell him over the phone, but he relented and agreed to meet her in Manhattan for a coffee the next day.

Now she sat and waited, preparing her lines like a nervous girl on a first date. She tried not to give the impression that she was waiting for someone who was late, and pulled her diary from her bag and scribbled senseless things in the margins to keep herself occupied. She was just ordering a second drink when Will arrived and, in spite of herself, she felt her cheeks redden and her confidence evaporate. They shook hands lightly as he ordered a coffee from the waitress; then they sat facing each other.

'So what have you got?' he asked briskly.

'Before we start on that, you need to have some background. I think I deserve your indulgence for just a little longer.' He nodded reluctantly. 'We hardly know each other, in spite of what went on. I realise I was just an emotional release for you when your thermostat blew, and I'm not complaining about that. We had some fun, and that's fine by me. But we have some history, however scrappy and unsatisfactory it may be, and what pulled us together hasn't yet been resolved. I don't know how things stand with you and Clare. When you finished it, I wondered if maybe she'd found out about us. Then I figured that it didn't matter anyway, and that I'd get on with my life and let you get on with yours. I swear to God I had no intention of bugging you ever again, but things don't always work out like you planned, do they? Anyway, I wanted you to know that I'm not here to cause a scene or throw any curve-balls at you. This is strictly business.'

Will looked into his coffee cup, then up at her, so that she could see the depth of grief in his face. There was barely a shine to his eyes, as if all the tears had flowed out and there was no liquid left to illuminate them. She could have kicked herself for sounding so selfish in front of him, this man who had lost so much and was still searching for the smallest vestige of comfort.

'Rocket,' he said, his voice cracked and faded like an old recording of him, 'I didn't know what I was doing. I was acting on an impulse that I couldn't control, and you were the unfortunate party on the wrong end of it. I'm sorry for what I've done to you, and that's really all I can say.' He shrugged and looked away again. She leant over to touch his hand, a delicate movement that carried no unspoken threat.

'Hey, I'm Rocket Stubblefield, remember? Indestructible, incorruptible and all that shit. I'm not hurting, and I still like you. Case closed. So let's talk about the real issue.' She knocked back her drink in one and sighed very deeply. 'Don't quite know how to begin this one, though. You may recall that I told you once I had some friends down in Florida who'd keep an eye out for Tom. At the time I thought it was a real long shot, but I said it anyway. As it turns out, they came up trumps – I get a call, and one of them thinks they may have seen Tom. I'd sent them a copy of that photo you gave me, so I figured it was a possibility. But by that time you'd taken me off the case, and I was still boiling a little, so I didn't do anything immediately. I considered calling you, or Jablonowski, but I wasn't thinking straight and I admit that my personal feelings might have got in the way somewhat. But I had an itch, and it needed scratching, so I took a flight down there.'

'And?'

'And – well, to cut a long story short, it was him.'

'You found Tom? Christ, you found Tom and you didn't call us? What the fuck were you thinking of? How is he? Where is he? Jesus, I don't believe this.' She had never seen Will so animated, but she held her nerve in spite of his obviously rising anger.

'Wait up. Just hear me out, OK? Try, if you will, to understand my position. It wasn't nearly as clear-cut as you'd think. I saw him, and he was perfectly happy. He was clearly having a ball, and that really screwed my mind up. Here was this little kid, and we'd all assumed he was being badly treated, and that assumption got blown away. Whatever you may think of me, I promise you I've always had the best motives in trying to find him. But this was seriously weird – here he was, safe and sound, and not in any apparent distress. So I needed to dig a little deeper before jumping in with both feet and simply making things worse.'

'Did you call the police? Did you speak to him?' Will was still very agitated.

'No – but I've spoken to the folks who have him, and that's why I'm talking to you now.'

'Listen, thanks for all your help, but just give me the details and we'll call it quits. I'll pay you for the work you've done, and then you can leave it alone.' Will got up and dug into his back pocket, as if to pull out his wallet.

'I didn't do this for money, Will. I did it because I genuinely thought it would help. Sit down and stop acting like an asshole.'

'You know where my son is, and you haven't told me, and you say I'm acting strangely? Forgive me, Rocket, but I can't quite see it like that. Now, either you give me the address or I make a citizen's arrest and pull you down to Jablonowski's office. What's it to be?'

'I'm going to tell you where he is, of course I am. I only want you to know that going down there with all guns blazing is likely to do more harm than good. He is settled down there – when he sees you and Clare again he's going to be really confused, especially if they've fed him some neat line about why you let him go in the first place. So don't rush it – that's all I wanted to say to you. Think it through, Will – don't react on the basis of your own needs and motivations.'

'Thanks for the psychoanalysis. I think I can take it from here. Where are they?' Rocket handed him a slip of paper, and felt hot tears welling in the corners of her eyes. He studied it and then put it in his pocket. 'Send me a bill, Rocket. And don't ever call us again, do you hear?'

He fled from the café and she watched him hail a cab.

Although stung by his venom, she felt somewhat relieved that it was finally over.

To no one's great surprise, the house was empty. Mobilised by Will's call, the vanguard of officers who burst through the front door could immediately smell the artificial cleanliness, could sense the absence of life: there was nothing to signify even the smallest evidence that anyone was, or planned to be, in residence. The backyard was spotless, with the grass mown and the flowerpots weedless and recently watered.

The dogs were first to find the blood. A large brown pool had stained the rug in the living room and another heavy line tracked away towards the kitchen. As calls were made and notes taken, policemen stood impotent, uncertain how to proceed. The vacuum into which they had plunged seemed to drain them of oxygen, an enervating numbness engulfing them as they came to terms with a failed mission. The blood was the only insistent clue to be studied: there were no other traces of misdemeanour to help them reorientate, and they looked at each other blankly, hoping that one of them might have a shining idea of what to do next. A police psychologist sat in a squad car and smoked, deflated at this loss of opportunity to exercise all his powers; a heavily padded marksman unstrapped the bulletproof vest from his chest and dropped it to the ground outside, the anticipatory adrenalin still pumping despite the lack of a target; a sniffer-dog scratched his ear and looked bored, unable to pick up further scents of blood or fear.

As the caravan of law enforcement trooped in and out of the house, the dog became excited. He barked as his tail swished furiously, straining the lead and pulling his handler towards a pale blue car parked neatly at the kerb. He reached the rear of the car and jumped to put his paws on the bumper beneath the boot, still barking animatedly. Some officers caught the dog's mood and, bereft of other diversions, moved towards the car; the dog was withdrawn, a crowbar was produced, and a burly man snagged it under the lip of the boot lid, pulling up until he heard the lock snap. In unison a group of heads peered into the darkness of the boot as the lid was raised.

The major part of the boot was taken up with a large bundle wrapped in layers of thick cotton sheeting. The smell that escaped left none of the onlookers in any doubt as to the contents, and a space was immediately cleared as the officer in charge moved through the group and took up position in front of the boot. Without bidding, a photographer arrived and started his work; once finished, he stepped aside as two men grabbed either end of the bundle and hauled it out. As they dropped it gently on to the grass verge a screen was erected around them, as if this discovery had finally initiated a routine that everyone knew and could all follow blindly. Large silver scissors cut through the fabric until it was pulled apart; then an officer retched and was quickly pulled back.

The head was covered by a black bin bag, pulled tight at the base by its yellow draw-strings. Gloved hands gingerly removed the bag, which was ferried away for forensic technicians with strong stomachs. The skull had been cleft from behind. Its congealed and blackened contents had spilt and sprayed sideways and downwards, matting the thin surrounding hair. Even from its position, lying on its side, the face displayed the absolute shock of that split second – split in its most literal sense – when the axe, or whatever weapon was used, had rent the bone and tissue in two. Further down, the hands were clamped tight shut, the knees pulled up, in foetal position, into the stomach. A single strike was all that it had taken to fossilise his horror.

A low dispassionate voice murmured into a tape-recorder – 'Male Caucasian, forty-five to fifty-five, single blow to the rear of the skull, time of death to be determined,' – as the photographer snapped incessantly and a man in white overalls knelt beside the corpse. Around this shrivelled shell of a man the crowd rumbled and moved, each spectator suddenly aware of new responsibilities and duties, the house again a focus of their attention as they re-scanned floors and walls and furniture. Radios crackled with fresh information and instructions, and cars arrived and left. The smell of sweat – of anticipation, fear, and excitement – permeated everywhere, swilling biliously with the stench of death.

'Chuck Callahan, age fifty-three, Stone Bridge, New York,' an officer shouted as he held a brown wallet above the body, and the message was rapidly carried, like some unwanted parcel, back from the scene to police headquarters. The John Doe had a name, and now the game could commence.

PART TWO

SIXTEEN

It would have been – and it was, in fact – Tom's sixth birthday. Will sat in his study and stared at a photograph of Tom on the desk. He had been bracing himself for this day, as he had done on every birthday since Tom had gone. He tried to analyse the situation calmly, but found his thoughts constantly interrupted by rising emotion.

The trail had gone cold after Florida. There had been a period of intense activity and one or two false leads, but, faced with the relentless tide of blood that spills daily over their desks, Tom's file was soon consigned to that ever-growing pile of unsolved cases that festers somewhere in the bowels of every American police department. Every so often Will would call them and ask if anything new had turned up, but he was always politely stonewalled with words to the effect that the investigation was continuing and several new lines of inquiry were to be pursued.

Soon after they'd found Chuck Callahan, Will had rented an apartment in St Petersburg and had spent all his waking hours badgering the neighbours and harassing the police for more action. Clare could not be with him; she had flown back to England before his decisive meeting with Rocket in New York, and was too heavily pregnant to return. He had never felt more alone, realising that

147

this crusade was so personal not even his wife could share it with him. Three years on, and the pain had not abated; he wore his grief on his sleeve, visible to all and rarely disguised by any sense of decorum or perspective.

India's birth should have been a major turning point in Will's life, but his feelings were blighted by the constant comparisons he made with Tom, and her development was always, to him, in the shadow of an unmentioned sibling. He and Clare had agonised over if and when she should know about Tom, and had never reached a conclusion: it was one of many issues that they left unresolved in the best interests of all three of them. They had bagged up all Tom's clothes and possessions and put them into storage, a pathetic little package in a huge container warehouse. Clare had a secret locked drawer in her dressing table with some photos, videotapes and drawings in it, but they never looked at them.

Will had no option but to work for himself. Jack had done everything he could to keep him with the bank, even offering long-term disability leave, but Will couldn't face the move back to London with everyone knowing what he'd been through and treating him with kid gloves. He took the easier option and resigned, the red mist of anger and frustration blurring his judgement to such an extent that he didn't even talk through the ramifications with Clare. She was furious but she didn't argue; she merely shrugged and altered her course to stay in line with his. They were lucky: Jack swung things so that Will got a six-month consultancy contract with one of the bank's subsidiaries, and from that he got other assignments and managed to survive.

There was also a fourth mouth to feed. Within days of

moving into the house at St Ives Will had known that it wasn't going to work. He had always viewed Ralph with a certain degree of detached amusement, but at close quarters his behaviour was erratic and intensely irritating. On top of that, the house was cold and very run-down, and Will was too far away from the City to make living there practical. Their own house in Wimbledon was too expensive to move back to: the tenants were paying for the mortgage but they couldn't have managed it, so they rented a mansion flat in Battersea overlooking the park. Ralph's house and all its contents were sold, and they looked after his money for him.

They took care of everything for Ralph. There were some occasional lucid moments when he appeared to be as normal as he'd ever been, but more commonly he inhabited another stratosphere, talking about people who had never existed or incidents that had never occurred. Clare was deeply ambivalent about him: she resented him, never truly forgiving him for the wretched childhood he had given her, but was none the less driven by some powerful force to care for him despite these reservations. To Will it looked like some convoluted form of self-flagellation as she summoned up her strength each day to deal with her father. He made no attempt to acknowledge, let alone reciprocate, any of the tenderness that she showed him; and he barely spoke a dozen words in a day to India. He spent hours locked in his room, watching daytime television. Physically he was as strong as an ox; their new doctor believed he could go on for another ten or fifteen years. Will had come to hate him deeply.

Hate was the new word in Will's vocabulary. He hadn't ever hated anyone before, but now his anger, prompted by very little, spewed out in vitriolic waves. He had a long and growing list of those at whom this hatred was directed – Rocket, Ralph and Betsy Callahan being the most frequent targets – and it took up a lot of his energy. He would be sitting on the train, trying to concentrate on the newspaper or the project he was working on, and the bile would bubble up inside him, engulfing all other emotion and rational thought until he could feel nothing else but the white heat of hatred as it burned at his very core. His eyes would literally water at the fierceness of this fire, his cheeks flushing and his palms sweating until he was bursting with a rage that wanted to explode. Only very rarely did this actually occur – spectacular arguments with Clare, mainly about Ralph or money – but, to Will, the feeling was oddly similar to orgasm. There was a perverse, toe-curling excitement when the uncontrollable torrent erupted from within him, followed by a longer period of depression and remorse.

There was no joy in their lives. There was little to look forward to, and even less that Will wanted to cherish from their past. Their lives were existential, secure in their cloistered environment but lacking sufficient stimulus. The last time Will had been really stimulated was with Rocket. Both he and Clare had enjoyed a healthy, if conventional, sex life until Tom's disappearance; but from that moment on, he found it difficult to hold Clare in a sexual way, always regarding their physical interactions as comforting rather than sensual. Rocket had allowed him to focus all his emotions – anger, frustration, misery, hate – on the act of making love, a contradiction in terms that he couldn't reconcile. She drew the toxins from him so that each session with her became a purgation. He would leave her feeling exorcised of all his demons, numb and calm and free from the turmoil that normally welled inside him. It was a stupid, reckless affair, with no purpose or commitment, and it still made him bite his lip when he thought of it.

To Will, now, Rocket was a traitor. She had used Tom as a hostage in her game of revenge. She had behaved appallingly and was probably responsible for Chuck's death and Tom's continuing absence. When he recalled that there was a time when he couldn't bear to be apart from her, it chilled his blood. Time and again he would revisit the events of that period – the meeting with Rocket, the flight to St Petersburg, the interviews with the police – and he would try to make sense of it all. When he had called the police and alerted them to Tom's whereabouts, he had had no idea how it would all turn out. He'd needed to be nimble, to think on his feet: the police had asked many questions and he hadn't wanted to give them all the answers. He recalled the clumsy way in which he'd tried to implicate Rocket in Chuck's death, and how they had seemed curiously uninterested in this. They were much more concerned with him, and how he knew where Tom was. That still perplexed him, that they could treat him almost as a suspect.

On leaving Florida he had the deepest sense of a mission unaccomplished, a failure that he could never accept. There were too many strands left untied; now, as he looked at the photo of Tom and tried to imagine a suitable way to commemorate his birthday, he began to formulate his own private programme for a final resolution.

SEVENTEEN

It was Christmas Eve, and Will was late. He had stayed too long in the comforting warmth of a wine bar in the City, relaxing with some old friends who plied him with port as they celebrated their temporary reprieve from work. Will had always viewed the Christmas break with mixed emotions: it was too expensive, and lasted too long, and he had never quite understood the excitement of these people who spent the rest of the year complaining about their domestic lives, yet became quite animated at the thought of a prolonged spell of exile with their families.

Will now faced Christmas with growing dread; experience had taught him that the day itself would be marked by a brief period of familial unity which might last until the pudding had been served, followed by a gentle decline into depression and possibly acrimony as the afternoon wore on. India would be the centre of attention as she scaled the mountains of presents that were laid before her, whilst Ralph would open his with a puzzled look and would barely consider the contents before returning to his usual dazed condition, helped by a glass of the single malt that Will always bought him for the occasion. But India and Ralph had merely bit-parts in the year-end drama: Will and Clare seemed almost destined to fight on this day, fired up by the artificial goodwill and the steady flow of alcohol, and they each followed an invisible yet preordained script that led them remorselessly towards conflict.

As he staggered somewhat uncertainly along Prince of Wales Drive, Will felt disappointed. He had drunk enough to be feeling festive, but the pain he carried continued to nag at him, and his apprehension about the next twenty-four hours hadn't lessened with the intake of port. Foolish as he knew it to be, he still couldn't help remembering Christmas with Tom: the last one, in the States, had been particularly good, with snow deep on the ground and every house in the neighbourhood dressed for the occasion with lights and decorations. By comparison, Battersea was dreary and uninspiring, and Will let himself unkindly use the comparison to draw some muddled conclusions about the differences between Tom and India.

This train of thought was interrupted, however, as he neared home. He was on the opposite side of the road to the flats, walking by the perimeter railing of the park, with his head tucked into the upturned collar of his coat. The sky was very clear and a frost was already forming on car windows; Will only looked up when he stopped to cross the road and, as he waited for a van to pass, he glanced up at the front windows of his flat. At first he saw nothing unusual: the large sitting-room window was curtained, although he could see that lights were still on in there, and his gaze drifted across to the next window, which was floor-length with double doors and a very small terrace and protective rail. The room behind this was Ralph's, and Will's assumption – that Ralph would be in the sitting room with Clare – momentarily overpowered what he actually saw, so that it took several seconds for the image to penetrate.

The double doors were open, and Ralph was standing on the terrace. He was stark naked, and he held his erect penis in one hand as he clutched the guard-rail with the other. From where Will was standing it was impossible to see the expression on Ralph's face, but his fixed stance suggested that he was concentrating very hard on the job in hand. Will's immediate impulse was to shout out, but he caught himself. Perhaps Ralph was sleepwalking, he thought, and a sudden shock would be enough to send him hurtling head first over the rail. Instead, he ran across the road, unable to take his eyes off the spectacle above him, and pounded up the stairs to his front door, fumbling with the keys before finally bursting in. The flat was quiet, and the sitting room was empty. Clare had obviously gone to bed, although he knew she wouldn't be asleep yet. He had to choose between facing her now, or rescuing Ralph, and he decided that Ralph's plight was more urgent. He gingerly opened the door and crept into the darkened room; Ralph's silhouette was framed by the window, and Will reached him and swiftly wrapped both arms around him, pulling Ralph back until they were well inside the room.

They stood facing each other, Ralph still carrying his throbbing erection yet entirely oblivious to the absurdity of the situation. Will looked around for a dressing-gown or a blanket in a desire to cover his own embarrassment, not Ralph's. He went to the window and pulled the doors closed, then drew the curtains and walked back past Ralph.

'I know about you,' Ralph said, catching Will totally unawares.

155

'What's that supposed to mean?'

'Tom told me everything. I know all about you. You stay away from me, do you hear?'

Will snorted in disdain and walked out of the room. Clare was standing down the hall, and her head was cocked in a look of surprise.

'What was all that about?' she asked.

'Come with me and I'll tell you,' Will said, grinning broadly. They went down the hall together and into the kitchen. 'Do you want a drink?' he asked as he got a beer out of the fridge.

'No, and do you need one?'

'As a matter of fact, yes. It's Christmas, and I'm relaxing. Is that all right?' She shrugged, unwilling to start the fight early, and let it pass.

'So what was going on just now?'

'I've just caught your father exercising his manhood on the balcony,' Will said, trying to keep a straight face.

'What do you mean?'

'What I mean is, he was beating the meat, banging the bishop, pulling his hood, flipping his lid – he was having a wank. Right out there, on the balcony, in full view of all and sundry. I've just pulled him in and closed the window.'

'You saw this? You saw him doing this?'

'What do you mean? Of course I did – do you think I'm making it up?'

Clare thought for a moment, then chewed her bottom lip. 'I just . . . it's so difficult to believe, that Dad could still be . . .'

'Well he is, and I can vouch for the fact that everything appears to be in full working order. I've got nothing against that – God, I hope I'm still functioning like that when

I'm his age – but I'd prefer it if he confined his activities to the inside of his bedroom. Do you think that's being unreasonable?'

She laughed a little, which was encouraging, then frowned. 'No, that's fine, but who's going to speak to him about it?'

'Well, obviously you are. He's your father, and you have to sort him out.'

'I realise that, but it might be better coming from you – you know, man to man, all that kind of thing.'

Will put up both hands to stop her line of attack immediately. 'Absolutely not – this is nothing to do with me, and I don't want to be involved,' he said.

'But look at it another way, Will,' she said evenly. 'What if it were your son? Then . . .' She knew instantly how badly she had erred, what a terrible thing she had said, and his look merely confirmed it. He got up and took his beer from the table, silently moving away and out of the kitchen.

'Shit!' she said vehemently, but not all the anger was directed at herself.

Predictably enough, the row came in the evening. Having taken a walk in the park after lunch – an idea, it seemed, that was shared by every other family in south London – they settled down in the late afternoon with the television on and India happily playing with her new toys. Ralph slumbered, Will drank, and Clare read.

Clare was already seething, but experience had taught her to hold it in. Will had been lethargic and taciturn for the whole day, showing no interest in lunch and making no effort to smile or convey any notion of the Christmas spirit. She regretted her remark of the previous night, and had told him how sorry she was, but he had merely shrugged and walked away from her. His biggest crime, in her eyes, was that he paid scant attention to India; she craved the strength of her father's embrace and the reassurance of his smile, but he seemed completely unaware of this. 'Why is Daddy cross?' she had asked Clare, and the answer was so hard to find.

When Clare went out to the kitchen to start clearing up, Will followed her. At first she thought it was a conciliatory move, that he was coming to be with her and to talk things through. But he merely reached into the fridge and pulled out a can of beer without even speaking to her. She sighed, gathered her strength, and spoke.

'What is it, Will? What's the matter?' She started in a low, understanding voice, trying to sound helpful and gentle. He turned round quickly, and she could see immediately the flash in his eyes that suggested an imminent explosion.

'Christ, you can be so insensitive sometimes. Don't you know what the matter is? Isn't it obvious, even to you?'

'I've already told you I'm sorry about what I said last night. But you can't still be brooding over that. For one thing, it's not fair on India. You've gone round all day looking like thunder, and the poor little girl doesn't have the faintest idea why.'

'Incredible. You do it every time – bring India into it, make it look as if I'm being a bastard and you're absolutely perfect. You really are unbelievable.'

The conversation was quickly sinking to its inevitable depths, but not even Clare had the will-power to stop it.

158

'Come on, Will, that just isn't fair and you know it. We're all on tenterhooks, not knowing when you'll blow into a rage or storm out because of something we've inadvertently said. When you're India's age that doesn't seem very reasonable – all she wants is a normal daddy who gives her some love and attention, not someone who's likely to explode at any moment.'

'And I don't give her love and attention? I don't believe this. I'm bloody depressed, and all I get from you is a barrage of criticism about my shortcomings as a father. Well thanks a lot – I really appreciate it.' She could see his facial muscles starting to tense, a sure sign that trouble was on the way, and she tried to avert it.

'You know what I'm saying, and you're just twisting my words around. India loves you – adores you – and she's confused. So am I, to be perfectly frank. You have a family that loves you, and yet you can't take any happiness from it. I'm very worried about you, that's all.'

'You don't understand, do you? You think we're one big happy family, and everything's rosy in the garden. Jesus, you really have no idea of how I feel, do you? I get absolutely no support from you at all – even now, all you want to do is have a go at me, and tell me what I'm doing wrong. Do I ever criticise you? Have I ever told you how to behave with India? But you don't get that, do you? You just wade right in, and point out all my deficiencies, as if you're so bloody perfect. Well that's it – I resign as a father. From now on you can take full responsibility, seeing as you think you're so wonderful.'

'Oh, don't be so bloody melodramatic,' Clare said, her face now flushed with anger. 'Stop behaving like a child. I'm trying to find out what your problem is, and all you

159

can do is throw everything back at me. That's always your defence, and it's pathetic. Why don't you just admit it – that you're bored with us and you'd like to leave?'

Will almost jumped from where he stood to land right in front of Clare, and he grabbed her jaw with his hand, squeezing hard. 'That's enough, you little fucking bitch. Shut up, shut up, shut up!' He pulled his hand away and pushed her chest hard so that she stumbled back against the wall.

'You bastard,' she shouted, the tears welling. 'You're determined to ruin everything for us, aren't you? Why don't you just fuck off out of here and be done with it?' She raised her arm to hit out at him but he was too quick and he grabbed it, twisting it back so that she was bent double. As she struggled to free herself she saw India standing in the doorway, her bottom lip trembling as she watched the violence in front of her. Will saw her too and immediately released his grip, moving quickly away from Clare and brushing roughly past India as he made for the front door.

EIGHTEEN

Betsy lay on the bed and waited. In the dark stillness her eyes were wide open, her hands flattened across her abdomen. She listened, but there was no sound close by. Nothing else mattered: the silence was all she sought, the signal that life might be returning to the strange condition she now considered normal.

The fight had been a bad one. There were punches and kicks, and harsh things were said. Both had cried, both had screamed, and both now lay on opposite sides of the wall. Betsy tried to set things straight in her mind as she lay there, but echoes returned to cloud her thinking – the call from the school, the words he had said, the blows he had struck – and she found no solace in prayer or thought. She couldn't sleep whilst these fresh memories churned inside her, and she couldn't find a way to purge herself of them.

She realised, as she fought against it, that she needed Chuck tonight. Had he been there, he would have known what to do and say, and the realisation only deepened her unease. Betsy had never needed anyone: her life was driven by a certain knowledge of what was right, a divine guidance that couldn't be questioned, and she hadn't the capacity to accept that another person could supersede that power.

But Chuck, by his absence, exerted a force that she couldn't deny, a gravitational pull that kept her feet on the ground.

Betsy hadn't missed him for the obvious things. She had never asked for his help, and had always assumed that his need for her was greater than hers for him. She had often fretted that she would die first, leaving him stranded in a world where he lacked the craft to survive. She watched him sometimes, as he pulled his big frame from a chair or rummaged through the icebox, and wondered how he'd get along without her – a child in a man's body, she'd thought, and yet his presence was part of the deal she'd struck with God.

Alone now, and faced with this latest crisis, Betsy reassessed that deal. Perhaps he meant more than she'd noticed; perhaps his aura had been more magnetic than seemed possible; perhaps a little of Chuck had seeped into her body and soul and would never disappear. As if to reinforce this a shiver ran through her, and she moved her arms and folded them across her chest, hoping to warm and protect herself. The day's events came back into sharp focus.

She'd been on her way out to the store when the phone rang. It was the school secretary: Ricky had been caught in the washrooms, stuffing tissue paper into all the lavatory bowls and flushing frantically until the floor was flooded. He was standing calmly in the water, his feet soaked, when the teacher found him, and he had given no explanation and no apology for his actions. Was he sick? Did he have some problems at home? Had anything like this happened before? The secretary sounded concerned, but Betsy couldn't determine whether it was concern for Ricky or

162

concern for the school. She jumped into a cab and went straight there, braced for the inevitable contrition she would need to show on his behalf.

Their journey home was silent: his behaviour was so irrational and so alien to her experience that she didn't know how to tackle it. He sat and sucked his thumb with his scrap of blanket, now no more than a few threads of grubby yellow material, and made no effort to explain or justify; once home, he slumped on a couch and waited, as if he knew he would have to face some retribution, however slight. For a while Betsy simply ignored him; finally she summoned the courage to face him and discuss it.

'Ricky, what you did was a bad thing. Do you understand that?'

He looked at her over his curled fist and continued to suck. She waited for him to nod, or show some sign of agreement, but nothing came. She pressed on.

'Ricky, everyone's kind of mad at you right now. It's very important that you understand why. You cannot do what you did at school today, otherwise they're going to get even madder. And so am I.' She didn't want to say this, but hoped it might spur him into some demonstration of remorse. His big eyes stared at her, unblinking. This test of wills was uneven, and she knew it.

She sat down next to him on the couch and touched the top of his head. This had an effect: he pulled his thumb out of his mouth and shifted himself away from her until he was cramped against the arm. Then he laughed, a dry and nervous sound that she misinterpreted.

'You think it's funny, do you?' she said, her voice raised. This only encouraged him to laugh some more, almost manic now. Betsy raised a hand, not intending to strike him but merely as a reaction to his laughter, and he swiftly vaulted over the arm of the couch and on to the floor. She followed him round the couch as he began to run, but he was too quick for her and he escaped as she tried to grab him, all the time laughing. He raced into the kitchen and spread himself on the floor, face up, with his legs in the air as she approached. She bent down to try and lift him but he kicked out wildly, one foot catching her on the side of the face. The blow stunned her, not from the force of it but from the obvious abandon with which it was delivered, as if he didn't care whether he hurt her or not. She stood still above him, and he pushed himself between her legs whilst she paused, nimbly getting to his feet and running off again, this time to his bedroom. He slammed the door and leant hard against it, still laughing uncontrollably.

Betsy was panting from the effort of this; she didn't want to struggle with him at the door. She waited for even breath to return, then started to talk calmly.

'Ricky, we have to talk. We have to sort this out, little man. Come on out, and I promise I won't be mad.' The laughter stopped on the other side of the door, and she felt she was getting through to him. 'Come on, come and have a hug and we'll make up.' She waited until she sensed that he had moved back, then pushed at the door; it gave without effort, and she found him lying on his bed, curled up with his face to the wall. He looked so small, so vulnerable, that all her anger ebbed away and she moved to sit on the edge of the bed, careful not to impose too much on his space.

'What's up? You can tell me. What's your problem?' He

continued to stare at the wall, and then a huge sob shook him from head to toe.

'Nobody likes me,' he said in the smallest voice she'd ever heard.

'What do you mean, nobody likes you? We all love you, Ricky, you know that.'

'The teacher hates me, the other kids hate me, and you do too.' It was the kind of definitive statement that only a child could make, and yet Betsy felt compelled to rebut it.

'Sometimes you say the weirdest things. You know how fond everybody is of you. They're always telling me at school what a popular guy you are. What's really eating you, huh?'

He rolled over on to his back and stared up, not quite looking her in the eye. 'That's bullshit,' he said.

'Ricky!' she cried, shocked beyond belief at the word. 'Where did you learn that? You need to wash your mouth out, young man.'

'Bullshit, bullshit, bullshit,' he said with increasing vigour, and he started kicking his feet down on the bed. This violent outbreak frightened her and she flinched as he continued to thrash on the bed, not knowing whether to shake him or leave him to work it out of his system. Eventually he stopped and looked at her defiantly. 'I want to go home,' he said, his voice even now, betraying none of the emotion he had just displayed. This proclamation was like another foot in her face, so powerful and unexpected that she almost saw stars. How to answer, what to say – her head swam with panic and incomprehension. He sensed it with his childish instinct, and said the words again. 'I want to go home.'

'I . . . I don't understand,' she said falteringly. 'You are home. This is your home. What do you mean?'

'You're not my mummy. I know that. I want my mummy, and I want to be at her home.' His tone was still level but firm.

'Who has said these things to you, poppet? Who has said these terrible things? You mustn't listen to them. I'm your mom, and I always will be.'

'Chris says you aren't. He says you're just someone who's looking after me, and I don't have a real mummy and daddy. He says they just left me because they didn't like me, and you've got to have me now because no one else will.'

'And you think Chris knows better than me, do you? Chris is being a very silly little boy. You mustn't pay any attention to him, do you hear?' Betsy tried to stay calm in the heat of all this, but she felt her cheeks burning and her eyes stinging from the force of it. Ricky seemed to think for a while.

'Are you my real mummy? I mean, did I come out of your tummy?' Truth or dare – Betsy weighed the options, and decided on a compromise.

'Listen. If I tell you the truth, will you promise me you'll never talk about it again?'

'OK.'

'When you were a little kid, you had to come and stay with Chuck and me. Your parents couldn't look after you any more – they wanted to, I promise, but they just couldn't. So we helped them out, and that's what I'm doing right now. I've made a promise that I'll be your mom, just like I was your real one, and I'll take care of you. This is your home now, and it always will be, for as long as you want.'

'What about Chuck?'

'Chuck has gone, sweetie. He's happy now, up with the angels, and he's looking down at you and me and thinking of us all the time.'

'Does his head still hurt?'

'No, baby, there's no pain any more for Chuck. He's doing just fine.'

Ricky lapsed into silence, but she still wasn't sure whether he'd accepted her version of events. She ran her hand gingerly through his hair and watched him as he blinked his way towards sleep, sitting there silently as he subsided into stillness. She sat there for an hour, not daring to move, and tiptoed away only when she was certain he was deeply gone.

Now she lay on the bed and ran through the conversation again, a victim of total recall. Initially she worried most about his interpretation of circumstances: how had he managed to carry the memory of his former life for so long in that little mind? But now, having accepted that this was possible, another more pressing concern attacked her. What else would he remember? There were fresher memories, much darker and more dangerous, that he could retrieve at any time. How could she protect herself and him from these? The questions swirled endlessly around her as she lay in the dark, unfettered by other stimuli, and she found no respite as she shivered and shook.

Clare awoke with a shock. The room was still lit; she must have dozed off in the armchair. She had been dreaming about Tom, and there was a sharp pain in her ribcage. He had been crying, and the noise had woken her from a mother's light sleep. She could hear a noise back in the real world, similar to a child's mewling, but she knew immediately that it was not India. She dragged herself up, her limbs less ready to act than her senses, and walked towards the source of the whimpering. In the kitchen she found Ralph, dressed in his suit and sitting at the table with a bottle of Scotch in front of him. His chin was resting on one hand whilst he clutched a glass in the other; his face was streaked with moisture so that he looked smudged and abstract.

'Daddy, what is it?' His eyes moved up a fraction, but nothing else. He showed neither surprise nor recognition. Clare wondered whether he was in one of his less coherent periods, and she approached him carefully, mindful of the need not to alarm him.

'Hallo, Clare. What are you doing here?'

'What are you doing here, more like? It's the middle of the night. What's wrong?'

'I couldn't sleep. I'm ready, so I thought I'd just wait.' Ralph drank from the glass and looked into it as if it might hold some secret that he'd been searching for.

'What are you waiting for?'

'Death,' he said flatly.

'Death?' she almost shouted. 'Whose death?'

'Why, mine of course. There's no point hanging around here any more. Everything's done, and Peggy's not coming back to get me, that's for sure. You and Will don't want me hanging round your necks, so I'm better off out of it for good.'

The shock Clare felt was on many levels: Ralph had been completely out of it for many days, unable to grasp

168

even the simplest things and, when he did speak, he rambled on about imaginary events or behaved as if Peggy were still alive. Now he sounded with it, in spite of the booze, and the pity she felt for him was compounded by the fact that he was so lucid and clear-minded. But she was determined not to let him get away with it.

'Dad, you're crazy. For one thing, you're as fit as a fiddle. Dr Cassidy said you'll probably outlive us all, God help us. And secondly, we love having you around. So don't be such a noodle. Come on – drink up and then we can go to bed.' She tried to be cheerful and light, battling against his mood.

'You go on, my dear. I've got to sit up a while yet.'

'You look tired, Dad. You should get some sleep.' But she sat down with him anyway.

'I am tired. I'm tired of the whole thing, and I wish it was all over. I've served my time, and I deserve a break. Christ, I can't even paint any more. What's the point?'

Clare had never seen or heard him like this. When she was a girl she was hardly conscious of his periods of depression, hidden as they were by her mother and the way he would lock himself in his studio. Even when she had seen him down, he never gave the impression of being out; he was always ready to fight against himself, and move the family so that he could break free of the lethargy and blockages he routinely suffered.

'Is life really so bad?' she asked. 'I think you're doing pretty well, all things considered. No one expects anything from you. You've earned a little time to yourself, and you should enjoy it. Don't wallow like this – it doesn't become you.'

Clare found herself feeling sorry for him; the years of

pain that he had inflicted on her and Peggy became distant and faded, and, whilst she tried to resist this shift of emotion, the genetic bond was somehow too strong.

'You're young,' he said. 'It's your prerogative to know everything, but eventually you'll see that nothing's really quite as simple as it seems. I appreciate your concern, but I'd be much obliged if you'd just bugger off and leave me to it.'

'Fine,' Clare said, snapping out of kindness. 'You just go right ahead and stew. What difference does it make to me? You know, sometimes you can be a royal pain in the arse.'

'Spoken like your mother,' he said, a little energy returning to his voice. 'Good night.'

Clare sighed, the accumulation of exhaustion and despair finally catching up with her. She left him alone with his thoughts and his whisky, resolving not to lose sleep over his private torture.

NINETEEN

'Life's a bitch and then you die,' Jack said as he smiled broadly. Will poured some wine into his glass, despite Jack holding up his hand to signal that he needed no more. They sat opposite each other in the wine bar, wedged into a corner well away from the mass of drinkers and revellers.

'Early death doesn't seem to be an option,' Will said. 'What do they say: "Only the good die young"?'

Jack was in London on a business trip, and his conscience dictated that he see Will and catch up on the news. He genuinely liked him, and Clare, but he knew that the evening would be tough going, and so it was proving. Will had changed in an unpromising way: gone was the laid-back, relaxed character who took victory and defeat with equal grace, to be replaced by someone harder and angrier. He was physically changed, too: his edges seemed sharper, his face leaner, and his clothes were hanging off him.

Will drank with a purpose, and Jack noticed that as well. In New York Will had hardly drunk at all, but now he was chugging back the wine without giving himself the time to savour it. They were already on the second bottle, and Will's pace was increasing whilst Jack sipped slowly and thoughtfully.

'Well, how's that family of yours?' Jack asked.

'Ah, the joys of the nuclear family,' Will said bitterly. 'The problem with nuclear families, my friend, is that they have a tendency to explode, as their name suggests. And ours is pretty near to boiling point.' Jack had the feeling that Will was without a friend in the world, and that he was expected to listen whilst all the bile was vented. It was a role he didn't want, or invent for himself, but he played it anyway; he saw it as his contribution to Will's continued well-being.

'What's the problem?'

'Me. It's as simple as that. I'm no longer satisfied with the way things are. Good old Will, the happy-go-lucky guy you once knew, is history. I'm boxed into a corner, and the only way out is to fight – just like a rat, you might think. But it's nothing to do with Clare or the others. It's my problem, and I'm dealing with it.'

'How?'

'How – by getting pissed as often as possible and avoiding the family. The work comes in sporadically, and most of it I can do with my eyes closed. So money isn't much of a problem – but life is. I just can't accept that this is it, that there's nothing more out there for me, or us. I'm still young, and I'm meant to be having fun. Adding everything up, I think I missed out somewhere.' Will waved anxiously at a waiter and pointed at the empty bottle, signalling that he needed two more.

'Hey, we all have to pay a price. That's the deal, and there's no point looking back and thinking how things might have been.' Jack watched as Will fiddled with his empty glass and bit his lips, restless movements that distressed him. He could still see the headlines in the

172

papers, the stories about Chuck's murder and how close they'd come to finding Tom; he and Robyn had talked of little else, stunned by their proximity to such a tragedy and powerless to help. He could not imagine how Will and Clare had coped with all of that and somehow managed to keep on going.

'Right,' Will replied, looking round to see if the waiter was coming back with the wine. 'Unfortunately, that gem of wisdom, with which I have much sympathy, hasn't helped me. I know I should be content with my lot, but I'm not. So what do I do?'

Jack was afraid to ask the next question, but knew it would soon come up anyway. 'Do you still think about Tom?'

'Only all the time. He's like the monkey on my back – wherever I am, whatever I'm doing, he's there with me, chastising me and digging his claws in. The pain doesn't go away, you know, it just takes on a different form. Sometimes I can't sleep, sometimes I can't stay awake. But all the time, twenty-four hours a day, it's there.'

'How has Clare coped?'

'About me, or about Tom?'

'Both, I guess.'

'About me, she doesn't know how to deal with it. She tries to understand, but she'll never feel the guilt I do. God knows I've tried to explain. But she doesn't begin to see how the whole thing's eaten away at my guts, and what it's made me become.' The waiter arrived at their table and Will snatched a bottle and filled his glass. He drank a large part of it before speaking again. 'What she thinks about Tom she keeps to herself. We've got a sort of truce about that one. I think she hopes that it'll just go

173

away if we never talk about it. So India is meant to be the palliative – you know, if we expend enough of our energy and love on her, the pain of Tom will eventually recede.'

'It sounds as if you're being hard on both of you. Surely there's a middle ground here?'

'You always were the compromise merchant, weren't you? I used to respect that about you, I really did. But I now see that compromise is really just a polite way of saying cowardice. Don't face up to the issues, just negotiate your way around them. I've come to the conclusion that confrontation is by far the best method of dealing with everything. Be a man, not a mouse, all that macho crap. You see? Will Easterbrook is finally getting angry, so you'd better watch out, world.' He finished his wine and poured some more; Jack put a hand over his glass as Will moved to fill it up. Will shrugged, then smiled.

'Jack, you'll have to forgive me. I've not been myself recently – or perhaps I should say, I haven't been myself until recently. All those years I was bottling it up inside, and now it's coming out. And the funny thing is, I feel much better for it. You may well look at me like that, but it's true. Keeping all those bad thoughts hidden away was doing me no good at all. Better out than in, that's my motto now.'

Jack closed his eyes briefly, then stared at Will and leant towards him. 'Listen, buddy, it sounds to me like you need a break. If you're feeling claustrophobic, it's probably affecting Clare and India as well, you know? Why don't you take yourself off for a while, get yourself fit and healthy and sort out some of your anxieties? I could give you the name of a real good place to stay – the bank uses it for stressed-out executives all the time. What do you say?'

From the fevered pitch of his last remarks, Will now dropped his tone and became much quieter and calmer. 'Jack, my old mate, you don't get it, do you? I've left that world behind. I don't need help from the men in white coats – I need a permanent refuge. A diet of uppers and downers isn't going to fix it. Whatever state of mind I'm in, Tom's going to be there. He's become part of my life, and he's not going to let go so easily. Callous as it may sound, I really believe that it doesn't matter too much whether he's alive or dead. He's always close by. That's the saddest part: how do you grieve for someone, and get over that grief, when they're still with you?' Now Will looked as if he might burst into tears, and Jack was seriously worried, so he decided not to say anything in case it sparked off more emotional activity.

All around them were groups of people talking and drinking together; some laughed, others listened, but they all seemed to Jack to be inhabiting a different world to Will. He had nothing left in common with these people, and he looked out of place in the mainstream of life. Jack suffered the agony of one who knows he can do nothing to help a friend.

Will must have caught his mood, for he brightened and smiled instantly when he looked at Jack. 'Anyway, enough of this maudlin crap, we're here to have some fun, right? So let's get on with it.'

'Are we going to eat soon?' Jack asked, following Will's diversion.

'Sure, as soon as we've made an impact on this wine. Look, just forget about everything I said. It'll all work itself out in the end. It's probably nothing more than my mid-life crisis. A couple of bimbos and I'll be as right as rain.' Will winked crudely, and Jack tried to smile.

Much later, when he had poured Will into a taxi and given the driver enough money for the fare and a very big tip, Jack sat in his darkened hotel room and suffered for his friend. The only man who could rescue Will was Will himself, and the potential for that looked bleak.

'I dare you. Go on, just do it.'

Ricky stood with the book of matches in his hand; Chris was right in his face, leaning against him.

'Mom'll get real mad if she ever finds out.'

'But she won't. Who's going to tell her? You calling me a snitch? Go on, get going before someone comes.'

Ricky considered this for a brief moment, then bent over towards the pile of scrumpled newspaper that they had made against the building. He carefully pulled off a match and held it over the striking strip. He made one final protest. 'Why don't you do it?'

'Because you're the one who thought of it, dummy.'

'No I didn't.'

'You did too. It's your idea. Go ahead; it'll be neat. And I'll always be your friend.'

'Promise?'

'Promise.' Chris made a cross over his heart with his fingers, and this seemed to be enough for Ricky. He struck the match, waited for the flame to grow, then lit the paper. They stood back, watching as the fire got under way, then they ran as fast as they could, Ricky stuffing the match-book into his pocket. They were well away from the scene before the flames and smoke began to billow into the sky.

TWENTY

Clare walked; she would take India to Battersea Park and they would wander down the broad alleys and across the lawns, past the zoo and through small gardens. They could spend hours at a time when Clare had nothing to do but think; India, unlike Tom, was quite self-contained and silently happy, leaving Clare to try and bring order to all that raced through her mind.

Clare watched other women as they pushed buggies, or held little hands, and wondered if they too carried some great disappointment. For that was truly the state at which Clare had arrived: she was no longer angry, just disappointed. She had passed through the phases of grief with textbook efficiency – denial, anger, depression, despair – and had reached that stage where life, and all it contained and promised, was deeply lacking. She'd always thought that she expected nothing from life, that Will's sense of fatalism had rubbed off on her to such an extent that she would follow the path that led where it may, but now she realised that there was something subliminal, implicit, that lay within her and which had quietly driven her on. If asked, she couldn't have said what it was she wanted, but she knew it wasn't what she had got.

There had never been a time when she and Will had

mutually discovered some fundamental turning point, when it was time to make some radical changes to their lives and set off in a different direction. They had always accepted the twists and turns with equal grace, simply shifting like sand dunes in a storm until they found their new shape. Now she was nearly ready to search for something new, actively pursuing an altered course of her own making.

But the legacy of her life restrained her. Every time she dared to ask herself what it was that she wanted, she recoiled from finding an answer because of all that had gone before and all that still surrounded her. Clare's loyalty to circumstance made her wary of change: she looked at what had accumulated, and the experience of what she had suffered, and instinctively knew that to break with this would be too hard to manage. Will, Ralph, India, even Tom – they were all factors that caused such inertia, as if she were chained to an engine that carried her unwillingly to stations she'd rather not visit. She suspected that this was the junction where she should jump off, but that in itself was not enough to impel her to do it.

Will had regressed to the point where Clare saw him as a child. She still loved him, but the love had changed so that now it was more protective than anything else. He no longer owned her respect; what she felt for him was partly residual for what he had been, and partly sympathetic for what he had become. She recognised the way in which her feelings for him had changed, but refused to accept that this would corrode the relationship; instead she believed there was still a bond that held them together, constitutionally different but none the weaker for that. Love was absolute in Clare's mind; the reasons for it, the means by which it was demonstrated, and the manner in which it grew, were not her concern. Will was her charge, and in some incomprehensible way she had reinvented her love for him to accommodate this.

He could frighten her now, which was new; and his thoughts and actions worried her. He was often distant, rarely close. At another time, under different conditions, she might have perceived that this was the start of a crisis brought on by boredom or frustration on his part – perhaps an illicit affair was the key to it all? – but she barely considered this option. The need for sex, for physical love and affection, was something she felt much more than he; often she found herself yearning for the heat of a body beside her or on her, surprising herself with the power of the emotion. In spite of her feelings, Clare still harboured some innocent doubt over the propriety of raw sex, almost as if the pleasure it gave her could not be entirely healthy. When she lay next to Will in bed, watching him struggle to reach peaceful sleep, she chastised herself for the throbbing she felt within her and the ache of her unfulfilled passion, a passion which seemed absent from his limp body.

What frightened her most about Will was his volatility. His moods swung from one side of reason to the other, and there was never an easy way to forecast how he might react to any given situation. Sometimes he would merely sulk and brood in response to perceived slights; at other times he would rant and rave, physical anger never far from the surface as he shouted at her or at India. He could come home from a meeting in the City and be in a perfect mood, seemingly anxious to please and pacify, or he could storm through the door and curse at them all.

179

She never even knew if he would carry his rage through the night, or would sleep it off like alcohol and awake with his balance intact.

And yet still she managed to hold things together. The family functioned, though hardly as a unit, with Will on the outer limits and Ralph floating in and out of reality. Clare stood firm at the centre, nurturing India and fighting to insulate her from the storms that swept around them, aware that she at least must retain her childish hopes and dreams whilst the rest of them strove to deal with their demons. This one cause was all that Clare needed to stop her from calling a halt and breaking the cycle: she felt some duty, much more profound than simple maternal instinct, to save India from further harm, and she saw her role as an anchor, holding the ship as it lurched against choppy waters.

But that night, as she lay fully clothed on the bed and listened for the sounds of his return, she knew she was losing him. Through some medium of accrued intuition, she felt that this was the night when it might well finish, when the darkness finally engulfed him and he could no longer see a way out. He hadn't phoned, which was strange in itself: even in his blackest moods he would call to say where he was and when he might find his way home, but she'd heard nothing from him and the absence of that vital call, the single cord that still held them together, worried her. Of course he might have got drunk and simply forgotten or been too lazy to phone, but it seemed to Clare that this was a deliberate omission, carefully designed to send her a message of exclusion and doubt. As the clock frantically ticked on the bedside table, the persistent sound amplified in the dark, she held her hands to her face and sobbed tearlessly.

At four in the morning the burst of the phone bell rattled her awake and she fumbled to pick up the receiver. She did not expect to hear Will's voice, and was surprised to find it was him. He wasted no time on explanations.

'Could you come and get me?' His voice was thick, his tongue too big for his mouth and saliva deserting him.

'Of course, where are you?' Her natural response – to help him – overcame her premonitions of doom.

'At the police station in Bishopsgate. There's been some trouble, but don't worry about that now. Just come as soon as you can.'

'What trouble?' Involuntary images flashed through her mind.

'Please, Clare, just hurry up and get me out of here. And could you bring a clean shirt?'

'I'm on my way.' She swung her legs off the bed and rubbed her eyes vigorously. She stumbled around the room and found a fresh shirt, then crashed towards India's room. The girl lay peacefully under her duvet, and Clare made the instant decision to leave her there, a maternal judgement that this would be better than to subject her to whatever horrors might lie ahead with Will. Grabbing her bag and giving herself a cursory glance in the mirror, she rushed out of the front door and into the emptiness of the fading night.

He was hollow-eyed and pale, with blotches on one cheek and the first signs of stubble on his chin. Leaning against the wall of the police station, he held his arms around his midriff as if he were hurting or cold; he hardly moved as

181

the car drew up beside him and Clare wound down her window and shouted at him to get in. On the journey across town she had become angry, feeling it was her right to treat him harshly. When he pulled himself up straight she could see that he had no shirt on under his jacket and, as he lurched into the passenger seat, she thrust the new shirt into his lap. He said nothing, made no noise at all, but she waited before driving off.

'Well?' She made no effort to disguise her annoyance, and stared pitilessly at him.

'Can we discuss this when we get home and I've had a shower?' he asked, ignoring the shirt on his knees.

'No. We'll discuss it right now. What the bloody hell's going on, Will? What have you done?'

He let out a big sigh and leant his head back. 'I got a little pissed and there was some trouble, that's all. It's all over now, and it doesn't require any further debate. I was an arsehole, OK?'

'What kind of trouble? Have you been charged with anything?' She was insistent; Will had perfected a way of turning everything round so that she was to blame, and she was determined that he would not be allowed to get away with this.

'I've been let off with a caution. They put me in a cell to sober me up and I'm being sent home with a flea in my ear. Now can we please go home?'

Clare gripped the steering wheel hard, now looking straight ahead into the lights of the oncoming traffic, then drove off. They were silent for some time and she thought he might have dropped off; she glanced at him and saw that he was leaning his head against the window, his eyes wide open.

'Right,' she said. 'This is it, Will. We can't go on like this any more. It's not fair on me or India. I'm warning you now, things have got to change. Do you understand?' She heard him sigh, a long slow exhalation carrying so many emotions that she had no idea what it meant. She wanted to maintain her fury, but something within her prevented it and she could not control a rising tide of pity. Above all she was tired, and Will's continuum of trauma and anguish exhausted her beyond reason.

'I know,' he said thinly. 'I just can't explain what's going on with me, Clare. It's as if there's some superior force driving me and I just can't handle it. Believe me, if there was a way to change everything, I'd be doing it. But I'm just ground down by whatever it is, and fighting against it is pointless.'

Clare didn't want to have this conversation, and she certainly didn't want it to be going in this direction. But she felt compelled to continue, hoping that it might purge them of the cancer that was growing inside them.

'Do you want to be with us? You're so far away from us, and you're so unhappy, I wonder if you even know what it's doing to all of us – especially to you.'

'No, Clare, that isn't the question. The real question is this: do you want me to be with you? You've every right to kick me out, God knows. My head's so screwed up, I can't make any decisions about our future. You've got to sort out what you want, and then I'll go along with that.'

They were driving along the Embankment, and Clare pulled the car over to the side and parked. The river swept silently along next to them, and Clare suddenly remembered the happiness of swimming in open water, the freedom of standing against large waves as they broke around her. It was a childhood memory, and she wanted to be very small again and feel the salt water against her skin and the pebbles under her feet. She longed to be engulfed by the biggest waves and enjoy the thrill of being swept along by the undertow as the shingle rattled against her ribs.

She turned to look at Will; shrivelled like some plant that has had too little light and water, he presented himself almost as a challenge to Clare. She wanted to squeeze him tight until he was free of all the misery, but he shrank from being touched, both physically and emotionally, and she knew better than to treat him in the same way she would a child, even though she could not envisage any better way of dealing with the problem.

'I can't answer that,' she said. 'We want you with us – of course we do – but we want the man we knew, the man we've always loved. We want you to come back to us and be part of us, not be some dark cloud hovering menacingly in the distance.'

'Should I go away, just for a while? Do you think it would help?'

'I don't know, I really don't. You have to sort yourself out, and we'll do whatever we can to support you. But you've got to work all this out for yourself. Only you can do that.'

There was silence, and she wasn't sure if he were thinking this over or merely playing for time. They sat motionless for a long time; then he shifted his weight so that he was directly facing her.

'Do you think about Tom?' he asked.

'Of course I do.'

'And what do you think?'

'I try to think about the good things, about the joy he brought us and how happy he made us.'

'And that's it?'

'No. Sometimes I wonder if we'll ever see him again.'

'And?'

'And I tell myself that nobody knows, and that there's no point speculating. Will, we did everything we could. You have to accept that. Until you face up to the fact that we've moved on, and Tom isn't here, we're never going to get this whole mess sorted out. It hurts like hell, and I don't think you realise how much it's affected me as well. But I cannot allow us to carry that grief in everything we do and say, because it's not fair to India or ourselves. Can't you see that?'

'Yes, I can see that, but it doesn't make it any easier to let go. And . . .' His voice faltered, signalling some confession. 'I'm not sure I want to.'

'What do you mean?'

'I've turned it over a million times, believe me. I can see everything that you're saying, but it never changes for me. Tom's always there, you know, like some voodoo sign. It's as if . . . well, I don't know, but it's as if even the thought of giving up on him would mark the end of life for me.'

Clare raised her hand and put it gently against his cheek, and he leant into the caress and closed his eyes.

'I know,' she said. 'I know.' And, though her disguise was better formed, she felt the same pain in her heart.

TWENTY-ONE

Rocket was still shaking from the experience when she got back to her hotel room. He was one of the biggest men she had ever seen, so tracking him through the backstreets had been no problem, but she had not figured that he would stop her. He had disappeared briefly around a blind corner and, as she turned it, he sprang out from a doorway and confronted her. In that split second she had to decide whether to run or stand her ground, but the jelly in her legs told her that she wasn't going to get very far. She was aware that he held a gun in his hand, a fact that became more obvious when he pulled her towards him and thrust it up under her chin.

'What the fuck you doing, lady?' he had whispered in her ear, his breath rancid in her face.

'My job,' she said. 'Just my job.'

'And what is that?'

'To find you, that's all. Now I've done that, so let's call it quits.' He was hurting her a lot, and she believed he was quite capable of hurting her a lot more.

'Who wants me?' He shook her as he asked this, and the gun butt jabbed into her throat. She struggled now to remember the name of the company who had hired her.

'First National Finance of Princeton, I think,' she said.

'They made you an auto loan?'

'Shit,' he said, lengthening the word so that it practically became a sigh. 'Is that the deal? You working for them? Kiss my ass, lady.' He threw her backwards and started to laugh.

'I told you, I'm just doing my job,' she said, marginally relieved that the gun was no longer pointing directly at her.

'Well, you just go ahead and do it someplace else. I'll be watching out for you, you hear?' He emphasised the point by waving the gun at her again, and she nodded rapidly.

'I hear,' she said, but she stood still. She expected him to run off quickly, but he turned and ambled away with all the arrogance that fire-power invested in him, never looking back until he disappeared from her view.

Rocket drank one glass of bourbon straight off and her hands were still shaking when she refilled it. Having traced him to Chicago, she was loath to let him go: a fat commission rested on her success in giving the client all his details but, weighing it all up in the light of her recent experience, she was rapidly reaching the conclusion that the money wasn't quite as important as her continued health.

She sat on the bed, propped up with two thin and stinking pillows, and surfed through the channels on the television, her mind still turning over the events of the day. She was tired and hungry; she was also, unusually, very lonely. On the cold streets in Chicago, as the wind whipped in from the lake, she had felt alone in a way she hadn't experienced before. She wanted company – a girlfriend, or a strong man – to lift her out of her rut and stimulate her. She ascribed the feeling to a temporary frustration with business, even though she suspected it might be deeper than that. Rocket had worked only sporadically over the last three months, and money was tighter than ever; with little to keep her busy, she bothered herself with what she believed were trivial matters, like the meaning of life and her place in it. With a fresh glass of Seven and Seven in her hand, she turned her attention to the screen in an effort to chase away her doubts.

She watched the news presenters – strong white male, strong black female – as they catalogued the latest manifestations of violence in the city. For once, the news seemed immediate to her, all the more powerful since she had looked down the barrel of a gun herself that very day, and she listened attentively as the reports of killings and brutality were read out. Then an item came on that pinioned her to the bed, forcing the breath from her as she watched.

'In Palatine today, an extraordinary story unfolded at the Douglas A. Harriman elementary school. A second-grade pupil, Ricky Callahan, was arrested by local police officers after setting fire to the school gymnasium. Ricky, aged just seven, was seen by teachers as he ran from the building and was apprehended with a book of matches still in his pocket. But, in a late-breaking development, it appears that Ricky Callahan's mother is wanted by the Florida police authorities in connection with the murder of her husband, Chuck Callahan, in St Petersburg two years ago. From Palatine, Judy Noriego now reports.'

Behind the newsreader was a picture of Ricky, confirming what Rocket already knew. Riveted by this recognition, she watched unblinking as the reporter reiterated the facts of the story and added some suppositions of her own. There were interviews with teachers, and neighbours of the Callahans in Palatine, but the information they provided was lost to Rocket as her thoughts reeled from what she had seen. Tired as she was, she felt a latent propulsion to act, and she scrambled off the bed, spilling her drink as she rushed for her diary to find the phone number of Lieutenant Jablonowski in New York.

He was not there; and no, she could not have his home number. They would leave him a message, and he'd get back to her as soon as he could. Stunned, Rocket stood alone and the memories she had long since consigned to experience came rushing back in a huge torrent. She thought first of Will, the tortured, angry soul she had last seen running from the bar when she'd given him the details of Tom's whereabouts. Briefly she dwelt on the physical intimacy they had shared, the way in which he drained himself of everything when he climaxed, so that he was almost transparent after their sessions. It surprised her that she could still feel aroused by the thought of him inside her, groaning and swearing obscenely as he moved erratically on top of her, the sweat gathering in the gutter of his spine as he pushed them both hard against the headboard. She remembered the rough way in which he pulled himself away from her when he had finished; how he would lie with his back to her as her skin still prickled with the heat and intensity of their closeness; and how he always behaved as if that were the last time, and she had always assumed that it was.

She thought of Clare then, a painful but obvious juxtaposition, and she wondered how she was coping.

How had things turned out with the baby? Were they still together? Had he regained some perspective on life? It all seemed so long ago, and yet the pain of it returned with full freshness. Suddenly Rocket wanted answers to her questions, and she knew that the only way to get them lay in her being able to mediate in this new business. She ached for the phone to ring and, as she waited hopefully, the vision of little Tom asleep in his bed returned to haunt her.

Two uniformed police officers had been entrusted with the task of controlling the scrum that had formed outside the Callahans' apartment building. There was the usual assortment of video journalists, many of whom appeared to be taking footage of each other, along with interested onlookers and outraged mothers. Every time some innocent resident tried to get into or out of the building they would be assaulted by a barrage of lights and lenses and microphones as desperate news teams tried in vain to find some new angle on the story.

To one side of this mêlée stood Rocket with a detective; he was holding a mobile phone in one hand, a pad and a cigarette in the other, and he seemed to be the calmest person on the scene. He listened to Rocket as she told her story, occasionally nodding or glancing to one side to watch the proceedings. Whenever she paused – to take a drag on her cigarette or a slurp of coffee – he would look at her, waiting patiently for her to begin again. He said nothing until she'd finished.

'That's a very interesting story, Miss Stubblefield, and I'm sure my colleagues in Florida will want to hear it all over again. I guess you realise you're in deep shit here?'

'Tell me something new,' she said. He grinned at her; he liked her, and felt she might be good company for the evening and – who knows? – even the night.

'This guy Easterbrook,' he said, looking at his pad for confirmation of the name. 'You say he's back in England?'

'I don't know that for sure, but that's what Lieutenant Jablonowski told me last night.' Rocket had had a difficult conversation with Jablonowski; he had struggled to remember the case and was uninterested even when he remembered. It seemed to her that he resented the fact that he would have to reopen the file, and he took out his frustration on her. He'd also told her exactly the same thing as this guy, that she was in trouble and would be spending much time explaining herself to various law-enforcement agencies.

'Well, look,' the detective said, 'we don't have a whole hell of a lot to go on up to now. She's furiously denying everything, kind of like you might expect in her situation, and you're about the only lead we've got. That makes you pretty important to the case, so I guess we're going to cut some sort of deal. You planning to go anyplace soon?'

'I think not,' Rocket said.

'Why don't you come downtown with me and we'll see what we can sort out?'

'Fine. Can you tell me what's happened to the boy?'

'He's with the social-work people having his head stroked. You know, he's the victim in all this, so they reckon, so he'll be pretty well cared for.'

'And if it turns out that he is Tom Easterbrook?'

'After negotiating a pile of paper the size of the Rockies, he'll probably be allowed to go home.'

'Probably? You mean there's some doubt?' Rocket

192

ground her cigarette-end under her foot and opened her eyes wide.

'I'm not an expert in this kind of crap, but there's any number of reasons why a court could decide that he shouldn't go back to them. Who knows?'

Rocket chose to keep quiet; inside she was bursting with fury and indignation at the thought that this boy, a victim in more ways than the police would ever understand, could be dragged through a series of hoops that might ultimately lead to him being treated as little more than a foundling. How would he ever recover from what lay in store for him?

They walked over to an unmarked car and got in. All the way to the station she tried to justify her actions to herself, and all the way she failed.

TWENTY-TWO

It had been a snap decision, and Will was too tired, or too lazy, to fight it. Clare had arranged that Bea would look after Ralph, and India was going to stay with her best friend from playschool. They were lucky to get the place – a small Victorian terraced house on the outskirts of Southwold – at such short notice, and she had packed the bare minimum for the trip. A week by the sea, alone together, seemed to her to be the best tonic for whatever ailed them. Will was amenable, but nothing more. Since his run-in with the police he had changed tack, working long hours and never initiating a conversation. With India he was formally kind, treating her almost as a visitor from another family with whom he wanted to create a good impression; and generally he behaved like someone convalescing from a debilitating illness that had left him weakened and unable to function normally. Clare took this as a good sign, hoping that his silences portended the end of his manic phase, and she took care to keep the habitat neutral and calm.

Ralph, however, remained consistent in his inconsistency. Whole days would go by without a hint of his problem, and then it would strike without warning. He had started telling anyone who would listen that he

195

was planning to emigrate: this plan never fixed on a definitive destination, although many had been mentioned. He had brought home numerous travel books from the library and spent hours flicking through them, occasionally taking notes and stuffing them down the sides of the sofa or taping them to his walls; he called in at a travel agent and picked up brochures which he scattered on the floor; and he would lock himself in the bathroom with all his material and make strange noises as he lay in the waterless tub, fully clothed, and scanned the pages.

The abnormality of their lives had become normal for Clare. Whilst others might be startled by all this erratic behaviour, she had learnt to accept it and manage it. Ralph's fantasies she greeted with the same equanimity as Will's unstable behaviour, never cracking until she reached the safety of the dark bedroom. The idea of a break, where she and Will might start to rebuild their relationship as equals, was both enticing and terrifying. She realised the dangers involved, that nothing might change, or, even if it did, it might be for the worse. It was almost a blind date, where she was going away with a man she hardly knew but for whom she held secret hopes.

They reached Southwold by midday, and had lunch in the Swan Hotel. Afterwards they walked on the beach – strangers on the shore, she couldn't help thinking – and she tried to hold his hand. But she knew that he needed the conscious silence and distance, and she left him to himself on that first day. She suspected that he might be grieving, that he was finally acceding to the inevitability of circumstances and was entering the first phases of a new episode in his life, a life that she hoped they could share, and she steeled herself to wait for it to arrive.

There was no phone in the house, and Clare had reluctantly agreed that she would only call home once during the week. To herself she had promised that she would try not to think of India and Ralph; this was her time, and Will's, and she should focus on them to the exclusion of all other background distractions. It was tough going: when Will rested in the afternoon, or walked down to the shops for bread and newspapers, she would struggle to contain her anxieties for what she had left behind. She knew that everything else must fall into place if only they could return refreshed and revitalised, but that knowledge could not restrain her sufficiently to stop her from thinking of the lives of those that depended on them for support.

On the third day he was much brighter. He woke up before her, got dressed and made her tea and toast which he delivered to her bedside. He smiled and kissed her on the mouth, and said he was going to the baker's. Clare lazily went through the motions of getting up, showering slowly and wandering naked around the house as if unable to bring herself back to full consciousness. It was unplanned, but, when he returned, she was still undressed as he came into the kitchen. He looked at her in a dispassionate way, evaluating what this meant before deciding on what to do or say. Without thought she slid up to him and rubbed herself against him, wrapping her arms around his back.

'Remember this?' she said, taking his hand and placing it between her legs. He held it there, still saying nothing but making no active motion of interest. 'It's been too long, Will. Please?' She placed gentle kisses across his face, encouraged by his inaction, and then felt his fingers begin to stretch and test her warm flesh. As he began to explore, she pulled at his belt buckle and fiddled with zippers and buttons until she could reach inside and grasp him. She felt a certain hardness and worked her hand underneath it, using her nails to scratch lightly at its stem as it grew. Pushing down with her wrist, she freed him from the restraining material and began to caress him more forcefully; his fingers had stopped moving, resting inside her, and he shifted his other hand to hold on to her buttocks.

Suddenly he pulled away, kicking off his shoes and letting his trousers and pants drop to his ankles. He pushed her to the edge of the sink; compliant, she spread her legs and he fell against her, both hands now clasping her rear as he entered her. She gasped loudly, the mixture of pain and ecstasy forcing the breath from her chest, and he held himself still for several moments. Then he started to move with a long, powerful rhythm, the strength of his grip on her tightening as he drew himself up and down. Clare steadied herself by splaying her arms and grabbing the work surface behind her; her head was bent backwards by the force of his strokes until she threw herself forward, hitching her body around his with her feet round his thighs and her arms at his neck. He took her weight on his hands and began to pump more erratically; then, as she bit into his shoulder, he stiffened, his legs locking straight and his fingers digging deep between her spread buttocks. For an eternal second they stood like that as he emptied himself within her; tightly wound together, she wanted to be like this for ever, and she squeezed every muscle she could to extend the moment.

He dropped her gently back on to her feet and pulled himself away before hugging her. She was wet everywhere, but his embrace kept her warm.

'We needed that,' she said huskily.

'I think you're right. I'd forgotten.' He was smiling in a way she hadn't seen for years, and the feeling was almost as good as the physical pleasure; she was winning him back.

Jablonowski was cleaning his ear with a paper knife, prodding carefully and inspecting the tip when he withdrew it. The Easterbrook file lay open in front of him, and Rocket sat on the other side of his desk. As she waited for him to say something, she wondered if this had been the chair in which Will sat when he came to report Tom's disappearance.

'Problem is, Rocky, we're caught in a truckload of shit here.' In this brief summary of the situation he managed to offend her twice: she hated being called Rocky, and she already knew only too well about the consequences of Ricky Callahan's actions, for her more than anyone else, and didn't need him to confirm them.

'I think we're all agreed that there are a few problems. But shouldn't we be concentrating on what happens to the kid?'

'Oh yeah, sure, that's paramount,' he said unconvincingly. 'But with this murder business, that puts a whole new spin on things. Look at it this way: what if the kid saw something or, worse still, what if he was an accessory? Kind of spooky, huh?'

'Can I ask you something really stupid? What if she

didn't do it? The way I'm hearing it, your friends down in St Pete's have got absolutely nothing to go on. Isn't there a chance that it wasn't her?'

'It was her, believe me. She's a fruitcake, Rocky, I'm telling you. She's got the religious thing in a major way, and says she doesn't need no lawyers because God's going to see her right. You ask me, they'll nail her sooner or later. And anyway, that's none of our business right now. Florida's taking care of that. We just need to worry about his abduction. And that's a royal pain. I've got paperwork coming out of my ears, and social-worker do-gooders drifting in and out of this office like it was some kind of mission house.'

'Have you spoken to the Easterbrooks yet?' She watched as he pulled a large piece of wax from his ear, examined it between his fingers, and then let it drop on to the file.

'That's a tough one, and you know it. You see, if I call and tell them we've got the kid, they're naturally going to ask when they can come and pick him up. And I don't have an answer for that. In fact, I can't even advise them to come over here, because I doubt that anyone would let them see him until all the bureaucracy bullshit has run its course.' He shrugged and applied himself to an exploratory search of his other ear.

'This cannot be right. He could be in limbo for months, years, before he gets back to his rightful parents. What's that going to do to him? Is anyone worrying about him, and his feelings?'

He seemed to ignore this totally, but he stopped digging for a moment and looked up at the ceiling. 'I tell you what,' he said, still facing upwards. 'This is out of left field, but it might work. What if you were to have a little chat with them, sort of soften them up? Do you think that would help?'

Rocket grimaced and shook her head. 'I'm really not the most popular person to choose, in light of all that's happened.'

'Yeah, yeah, I know all that, but you got on with the wife OK, didn't you? Couldn't you wheedle your way back in there, use all your feminine charms? It's got to be an option, hasn't it?'

'A very poor one, in my judgement.'

He thought again, leaning right back in his chair until Rocket felt he might topple over. 'Think it over, Rocky. We'll work on the problem with the kid, and you can make yourself damned useful by working on them – you know, managing expectations and all that crap.'

The proposal was outrageous, but she couldn't dismiss it out of hand. She wanted to see the whole business reconciled and everyone back in place, and she yearned to be a part of it and make some redress for her mistakes. Her guts churned at the thought of speaking to Will again, even in the unlikely event that he would listen to her. Her life was going nowhere right now, and she felt that resolving this situation at least might help her regain some semblance of order.

'I'll think about it. That's all I'm saying.'

'Think about it real hard. You've done yourself no favours at all so far. Florida even suggested that you might be a suspect, and I had to vouch for you. So it's time for you to repay the debt, OK? Meanwhile, I suggest you get yourself a good lawyer. You're going to be spending a lot of time in court. But who knows? If you do some good work for us, maybe we can forget about all this. What do you say?'

'Thanks. I think I get your drift.'

'I always said you were a smart lady.' Jablonowski resumed his aural inspection, and Rocket got up and left.

He was growing tired of the attention. Since torching the gym, Ricky had been poked and prodded by doctors and nurses with rubber gloves and stethoscopes, interviewed by a dozen people, and hardly allowed to go the bathroom on his own. At first it had been an adventure; everyone was very kind to him, and spoke in soft tones, but now he wanted to be back home. He even missed Chris.

He was, above all else, confused. He'd figured that there would be major trouble about the fire, and he had prepared himself for the worst, dreading his mother's reaction and what the school might do to him. Instead, they all wanted to ask him questions about his home life, his friends and, time and again, his parents. What did he know about his father? Could he remember when he had last seen him? How did his mother treat him? It just didn't seem to make any sense. Every time someone came to see him, he got ready to talk about the fire and how it had all been Chris's idea, but they never asked him. It was weird.

For the first time in four days he was on his own, sitting on his bed and reading a comic. The house was big and very shabby, and there were lots of other children there – maybe as many as twenty, Ricky estimated – all of whom appeared to have serious problems too. But he was kept pretty separate from them, eating his meals in his room and spending a lot of time with a large black woman who kept on giving him hugs, made less enjoyable because Ricky didn't like the smell of her armpits. He longed for his mother without recognising the contradiction in this: he had convinced himself that she was to blame for all his troubles, but he still needed her to come and take him home.

The door opened and another woman walked in. He knew her vaguely from a previous meeting, and he gave her a hesitant smile which she returned enthusiastically.

'Hi, Ricky, remember me? I'm Ellen.' He nodded. 'Can I sit with you?'

'Sure.' She sat down next to him and stretched her legs out in front of her.

'So how are you doing?'

'When can I go home?'

'Well, that's what I've come to talk to you about. You see, we have to get everything sorted out here first before we can decide on what to do next.' He didn't quite follow this, but stayed quiet in the hope that she might elaborate. 'I wanted to ask you a few questions. You don't have to answer them, but it would help a lot if you did.'

'Can I go home if I do?'

'Maybe. Shall we try and see what happens?'

'OK.' He was getting used to questions.

'I want to talk with you about a long time ago. You'll need to think real hard. Can you remember the very first thing in your life?'

'What, like being born and stuff?'

'No, later than that. What's the first thing you can remember after that?'

Ricky fiddled with his fingers and tried to concentrate. He didn't know exactly what this woman wanted, and he was anxious to please her so that he could get out of this place. 'I remember my birthday last year,' he started, studying her face to see if this was well received. 'And I remember going to Disney in Florida. That was neat.'

'Do you remember who went with you to Disney?'

'Yeah, my mom and dad. Before he died, you know.'

'Excellent. That's very good. Can you think of anything else – even further back than that?'

He struggled, desperately wanting to find a memory that would really please her. 'Well, I don't remember it too good,' he said, 'but something happened when I was a real baby.'

'And what was that? Was it something good, or not so good?'

'I don't know. Kind of good and bad, I guess. I went somewhere busy, like a big city, with some guy and I think I was having a good time and he was nice, and then it wasn't so good and I was frightened and then it turned out to be good and I was OK. But I don't know who that man was, or what happened to him.'

'You've done very well, Ricky. I'm really proud of you. Would you like some candy?' She dipped into her bag and pulled out a chocolate bar.

'Thanks,' he said as he started ripping the paper off. 'So can I go home now?'

TWENTY-THREE

'This is going to sound very deep and meaningful,' Will said.

They were walking along the beach, seen by others as two careless lovers with their hands and hearts together. At this early hour a thin haze hovered above the sea, unmoved by the breeze and the weak white sun.

'Go on,' Clare replied. 'I can take it.'

'I know I'm not very good on emotional things. I tend to think that if we don't say anything about how we're feeling then there can't be much wrong between us, and I know that's rubbish but it's just the way I am. Anyway, I was thinking about everything last night, and it occurred to me that you need to ask yourself a single question when it comes to evaluating a relationship.' He was clearly uneasy about talking in this way, and he wouldn't look at her, preferring to stare out at the waves or watch his feet as they crunched the shingle. She felt the best way to encourage him was to say nothing and look elsewhere, squeezing his hand as the sign that she was interested and attentive. 'It's this: if there was a nuclear holocaust, and the end of the world was imminent, with whom would you want to spend the final hours?'

'That's a pretty bleak way of looking at things, isn't it?'

'Maybe, but it concentrates the mind wonderfully. We all have forces pulling us in so many different directions, so many calls on our time and attention, that we never really get a chance to work out what's important to us and who needs us most. But if you were sitting in a concrete bunker waiting for Armageddon, you'd have nothing better to do. So I thought it was quite a good scenario.'

'Have you been facing Armageddon? Is that what it feels like to you?' They stopped walking and Clare looked at him closely. He still seemed uncertain and refused to return her stare.

'In a sense. I know that sounds a bit dramatic, but it's the best analogy I can come up with. Everything stopped; nothing had any relevance any more; there were no reference points or signposts and no clear view ahead. I imagine that's how it would feel, and that's how it felt to me.'

'Felt? Is it in the past tense?'

'Who knows? This week has been a real catharsis. I know you planned it that way, and I'm eternally grateful for it. I've never had the time – or given myself the time – to look at where we're going and clear out the debris in my head. But this week has really helped. And the funny thing is, I'm itching to get home. I want to get started again, and I want to do it now.'

'It wasn't just for your benefit, you clot. I needed it just as much as you did. I know you think that everything's your fault and your problem, but it doesn't work like that. We've shared it all, even if it hasn't always seemed like that.'

'That's the point, isn't it? What I was trying to say is

that you're the person I want to spend the rest of my life with, whether that's two minutes or fifty years. But it's taken all this time for me to understand that. I don't want to be on my own. I can't survive without you. That's all I know.'

She had never heard him speak like this; Will's emotional changes were signalled by action, not by an articulation of feelings. In their earliest days as a couple he had told her he loved her, and had appeared to believe that these protestations would suffice for the rest of their time together; he had shown no subsequent need to reaffirm his love in any other way than to stay with her and continue to provide for her. It was an old-fashioned method, but it had worked well enough for him. Now, as they stood right at the edge of the bubbling sea, he was taking them back to the start, as if the accretion of all their experience were no longer enough to keep them together and he needed to say these things to keep her. Touched by this, and sensing the intense vulnerability that he felt in delivering such a message, she didn't know what to say or do.

They stood there a long time, silenced by his confession. Clare wanted to laugh or cry, to show some reaction to it, but the overwhelming effect had been to make her stop dead in her tracks and wait. If she were to begin the same process, and repeat to him what he had said to her, she feared that it might overload his system.

'I'm sorry,' he said at last. 'I'm talking crap. It must be the sea air.'

'No you're not. And I love you for it.' She moved close and hugged him protectively; looking over his shoulder towards the sea, she could see that the mist was starting to lift, burnt off by the growing heat of the sun.

Ralph was not there when they returned to the flat. Bea had left a note to say they had gone shopping, and that everything was fine. They sat together and enjoyed the stillness, sifting through the mail and acclimatising themselves. Clare went over to the answering machine and replayed the messages, scribbling notes until one froze her fingers.

'Hi. It's Rocket Stubblefield from New York. Lieutenant Jablonowski asked me to give you a call to update you on developments here, and I'd really appreciate it if you'd call me back. Just in case you've lost my card, the number is two-one-two seven-seven-three four-five-four-five. Thanks.'

Had someone sprayed her with mace, the effect on Clare could not have been greater. Just as she was beginning to see daylight ahead of her, the old doubts returned. Her immediate reaction, once she had recovered from the shock of the message, was to ignore it. There had been plenty of useless conversations between New York and London, heavily laced with platitudes and empty promises, and Clare had no desire to engage in yet more of the same. But she was intrigued that Rocket should call: why her? Why didn't the police ring if there was something more to tell them?

Lacking trust in her own judgement, Clare's first thought was to speak to Will. Then she recalled his new confidence, and its fragility, and decided that she should wait. Will was already in his study working on the computer. He smiled and shrugged as she stood in the doorway. 'Got to pay for the holiday now,' he said, and she nodded and turned away. It was time to fetch India; she wanted real life to intervene and interrupt her troubled thoughts.

Having watched Will thrash from side to side, and being satisfied that he had finally won his nightly battle to get to sleep, Clare lay on her back and held her hand over her eyes. Will breathed evenly beside her, but she was not yet confident enough to get out of bed and go to the kitchen. Rocket's number was burned on to her memory like a monitor that has had the same characters on the screen for too long; she rehearsed the conversation again, whispering the words as she tried to infuse herself with the strength to make the call.

Finally she pulled herself up and padded out of the bedroom. Ralph's door was closed and no sound came from behind it; he would be comatose after the amount of wine she'd let him have. She looked in at India, safe and graceful under her duvet, possibly dreaming of the new clothes they had brought back from Suffolk for her. That in itself had been a major event: Will had insisted they drive into Ipswich to find something for India, and had been heavily involved in the choice of dresses, surprising Clare with his enthusiasm and the pleasure he derived from giving them to her. He had even taken photos of India as she modelled them.

Clare walked into the unlit kitchen and sat at the table. With no sounds to distract her, she could concentrate on her indecision; again and again she weighed up the reasons and excuses for not calling Rocket and not telling Will, but her justifications became no more acceptable and she knew that she had to take some action. A part of her felt uneasy about the relationship between Rocket and Will, knowing that there had been an unreported event that had soured Will's perception but unable to discover what might have caused it. The darkness helped her to see nothing, and she went to switch the light on. She made herself some strong coffee and hovered over the phone before finally dialling the number.

Rocket answered almost immediately, briskly announcing herself.

'Oh, hallo, Rocket, it's Clare – Clare Easterbrook from London. I'm returning your call.' Clare had often heard people talk of having their hearts in their mouths but, until now, she had not experienced it for herself. She sounded clumsy and nervous but could do nothing to control it.

'Hi. Yes, thanks for calling back.' They were embarked upon the elaborate opening ritual of a long dance in which neither appeared keen to take the lead. The pauses were anxious and heavy.

'You said you wanted to bring us up to date?'

'That's right. That's right.'

'And?'

'Just let me get the file, will you? I won't be a second.' Clare listened for background noise as Rocket put down the phone; her hand was already wet and her cheeks glowed with anguish. 'Right. Sorry about that. OK – here we are. Look, before I begin, has anyone else called you in the last couple of days?'

'We've been away, so I don't know, but yours is the only message we've got.'

'Fine.' Clare could hear the click of Rocket's lighter and imagined her inhaling deeply. 'There've been some developments, and I wanted to let you know about them.'

'I appreciate that.' Glacially they were moving towards the moment of truth, but neither cared to rush it.

'You'll remember that after Florida the trail went pretty cold,' Rocket said, her voice thick and uncertain. 'The police never got anywhere with the murder investigation. Well, they may have made a major breakthrough. Seems like they have a suspect.'

'That's good,' Clare replied, gently encouraging Rocket to continue.

'Isn't it? Anyways, the woman they've got is now in custody and that's led them to something more significant, from your point of view. She was taking care of a boy.'

The admission hung in the ether, softly echoing between them as both tried to assess its significance. Clare's eyes watered whilst her mouth dried. Her metabolism was in complete control, overriding any commands and wishes from her brain.

'A boy? Is it hers?' The questions needed to be graded in their severity.

'They don't think so – they're working on the basis that he isn't, and the social workers are looking into all of that. I just thought you ought to know.'

'What does that mean?'

'This is all off the record, Clare. That's why I'm calling you rather than Jablonowski. Until they have something firmer to go on, they don't want to say anything much. But they realise there's a possibility – a probability, I guess – that the boy might be . . .' Rocket tailed off, preferring to let Clare finish the thought.

'Might be Tom,' Clare said. 'What do you think?'

'I haven't seen him in the flesh, so to be perfectly

211

honest, I can't give you an informed opinion. For what it's worth, though, I don't think they would have asked me to call unless they were pretty sure. They're just scared as hell that they go down that route and it turns out to be a dead end. They want you to know, but they don't, if you see what I mean.'

'So what happens now?'

'I don't know. Clearly it's important enough that you should be aware of it, but they're not suggesting you come over right now. If they put a foot wrong, some judge or lawyer will pick up on it and blow everything – for you and them. But I have to tell you, they seem to have the boy's best interests at heart. They're moving heaven and earth to make sure he's protected from all the crap that's flying around.'

'What do we do, Rocket? What can we do?'

'All I've ever told you to do is wait, and now here I am doing it again. I know that's a tough one, but I can't see that anything else is appropriate.'

'So what's the timing on all of this? How long do we have to wait?'

'I wish I had an answer to that. But I just don't know, and I suspect they don't either.'

'Can I ask you something else? What's your role?'

'I don't know that either exactly. I suppose I'm sort of a go-between until they've got their act together and can do something official. I hate it as much as you do, but that's all there is at present.'

Clare found herself gripping the receiver so hard that her hand was getting pins and needles, and she tried to relax. In her deep breaths she could hear her own fears. 'Well, I really appreciate the call, Rocket. You've been very kind to us. Will you keep in touch?'

'Of course. First news I get, I'll be on the phone. If it is Tom – and that's a big if – I just want you to know that we're all pulling for him. I truly believe that.'

'Thanks. I'll talk to you soon.' There was nothing more to say, even though there were so many unanswered questions. Clare put the phone down and steadied herself on the work surface. She wanted to vomit, to purge herself of all the agony, but her throat was tight and unyielding. Her eyes still swimming, she turned unsteadily away from the phone. As she looked up, she saw Will standing in the doorway.

'I think we both need a drink,' he said flatly.

TWENTY-FOUR

Betsy was indignant. She had tried to remain calm and composed, but the questions they asked her, and the manner in which they were posed, had eroded her thin film of serenity and she was fighting back. Through the power of incessant prayer she had hoped for some divine intervention that might take her away from all the misery she now experienced, but nothing had changed. She had decided that these fools would not listen to reason, so she attacked them vehemently when they made their absurd suggestions and innuendos.

They had charged her – abduction of a minor – but had not appeared to take much interest in this. Instead they pursued a single line of questioning about Chuck. When had she last seen him? Why had she not informed the police of his disappearance? What was she trying to hide? They had gone deeper, asking personal questions about their relationship which she refused to answer, and had exposed her to various different techniques to try and get under her skin. Through all this Betsy had represented herself, denying her right to a lawyer for reasons she wouldn't disclose, and had blocked, stalled and parried all lines of inquiry. Finally, though, her patience had snapped and she demanded to know

215

where they were trying to lead her.

'Mrs Callahan, you have got to face up to reality,' an officer had said to her. 'You're in serious trouble. Your husband was murdered and you were the last person seen with him. It's in your best interests to cooperate with us. We need to get all the facts straight if we're to eliminate you from our investigations.'

She was shocked into a response. 'You aren't honestly suggesting that I had something to do with Chuck's death? It's unbelievable that you can even think such a thing. Do I strike you as the kind of person who would do that? What sort of people are you?'

The police were perplexed by her intransigence. She had readily agreed that Ricky was not her son, and had maintained that she had never sought to hide this fact. Although she did not accept that what she had done was wrong, she raised no objections to the charge, claiming that God would see that natural justice prevailed. The religious angle was a mystery to all involved in the case; Betsy repeatedly called on them to seek His guidance in their pursuit of the truth, but the concept proved alien to the hard-boiled officers she encountered.

They were left in no doubt over the strength of her feelings towards the boy. 'When can I see Ricky?' was the first and last question she asked at every interview; she punctuated every response with fresh claims that everything she had done was in his best interests, and that all she wanted was to go home with him and put all this behind them. Whenever they probed her about Chuck she shook her head slowly and drew breath to berate them for their ignorance. In case conferences they would argue about her, no one certain that she was simply a brilliant felon whose will was so robust that they were ill-equipped to crack it. In the backs of their minds they all dreaded the option that she was telling the truth, and they fought hard to dispel their doubts.

One night they felt they might have a break: she insisted on seeing her priest, and he dutifully arrived just before midnight. They briefed him, though he already knew many of the details from media coverage, and he went to her. She was an intimidating presence, even in her dull blue prison clothes, and he flinched at her cold and penetrative stare. He was tempted to believe that her faith was stronger than his.

'I'm searching, Father, and I need a little light.' She sounded just as full of conviction as he had known before.

'What are you searching for, Betsy?'

'Forgiveness.'

'For what?'

'For those who doubt me. God knows I'm innocent, and that's enough for me. Now I must find it in my heart to forgive those who cannot yet see the truth. I know that in the end it must all be resolved, just as He planned, but these are troubled times for me and I need your help.'

He sighed, disappointed that her plea would not be as easy to fulfil as he'd hoped. Her view of life was so monochromatic that he found it difficult to present her with the compromises that satisfied most of his customers. He could see no way forward, no soothing words that might soften her resolve; she had illuminated the limitations of his power in a way that was both frustrating and irksome.

'They have a job to do, Betsy, you must realise that. There are . . . incidents that need to be explained, and they are looking to you to help them in their investigations. I know how strong your faith is, and I share it. But we must give them all the assistance we can.' He knew how weak this sounded; he even felt himself tending to side with the authorities, try as he might to suppress it. Here was a woman whose beliefs transcended the need for rational explanation and the due process of law; her moral code would not permit the intrusion of more temporal considerations, however desperate the need was, and he could fully understand their exasperation.

'Yes, yes,' she replied impatiently. 'But that's all irrelevant, surely you see that. We answer to a higher authority, and I am not prepared to let these people try and supersede that. If I could just have some affirmation, some signal that my feelings are true and pure, then I know I could find it in my heart to forgive them their transgressions.'

He was defeated; there was nothing he could say or do that would give her the imprimatur she sought, and he resented her for it.

'Sometimes we must follow our paths without His light,' he said after some reflection. 'Even in the darkness, we must believe that He is there, watching over us. And, in the very blackest times, He will protect us.'

Betsy moved her stare away from him for the first time since he had come in, and he welcomed this relief. She seemed to look at nothing in particular, as if examining her own soul, completely still save for the slow rise and fall of her shoulders as she breathed. When she spoke again she was much quieter.

'You're right. I've been a fool, thinking that I needed a sign. He's always here, even if I can't see Him. I will travel more peacefully knowing that.' He relaxed now, hearing her talk like this. He felt that he had done all he could, and he wanted to escape from her frightening intensity. But she hadn't finished with him. 'Can we pray together?' she asked, but he took it as an order. They knelt together in silence for several minutes; then she shook herself back to reality, and thanked him for his time and guidance. When he was outside two officers approached him, eyebrows raised expectantly.

'I tell you boys,' he said, 'I don't envy you your job. May God go with you.' He cursed at himself for his own weakness, and hoped he would not be called upon to repeat this latest experience.

Ralph was coughing blood. When he wasn't coughing he was vomiting, and sweat poured down his pallid cheeks. The doctor was on his way, Clare's role confined to dabbing a cold flannel across Ralph's forehead and holding him as he shuddered through his hacking fits.

'This is it, this is it,' he kept on saying whenever he had the strength and the opportunity. She knew what he meant, but couldn't bring herself to agree with him. He was too fit to die, even if he wanted to, and she was sure that this was just a chest infection that could be controlled and beaten. Nevertheless, she didn't like what she was seeing.

Having unwrapped him from around the lavatory bowl she steered him back to his bed and he lay there shivering, occasionally bursting into another bout of coughing. When the doctor came Ralph drifted into a state of acquiescence, letting the stethoscope move over him without complaint or comment and choosing to ignore any questions.

'How is he otherwise?' the doctor asked Clare.

'Mentally or physically?'

'Both.'

'Mentally he's much the same as before. Sometimes he's with us, sometimes not. There's really no pattern to it. Physically, he's been very well recently. He eats regularly, never complains of any aches and pains. The way things are at the moment. I'd say he's got a strong chance of surviving us all.'

The doctor ignored this allusion to Clare's other problems, and scribbled a prescription. 'This is an antibiotic, and should clear it up in a week or so. Make sure he finishes the course, and let me know if he doesn't appear to be getting any better.' She took the prescription and the doctor left. If only, she thought, all our ills could be cured as painlessly as this. Ralph had presented them with a temporary diversion, but she knew they would soon have to return to the critical issues in hand.

Together, Will and Clare had been as indecisive as she had been alone. The initial fires of rage that burned in his eyes were soon dimmed as they talked through the situation; she was relieved to hear him discuss it calmly, listening to her opinion and appearing to value it, thoughtfully putting his own point of view across without recourse to anger or, worse still, violence. They had agreed that no good could come from a premature visit to the States, much as they both wanted to go. But they could not exorcise the spectre of Tom, and they struggled to find some definition of what their next actions might be. Unable to sleep, they had drunk coffee and sat dazed by Rocket's revelations, both incapable of suppressing internal hopes and fears but with an implicit pact that prevented them from speaking of them.

At seven Will was showered, shaved and dressed in his suit. He claimed to have a meeting in the City, but Clare's unkind belief was that he merely wanted to be out of the house. When she guiltily checked his diary, there was no note of any meeting that day. Now Ralph demanded attention, and she held small gratitude for it. For a short while she stood by his bed and listened to him. Then he suddenly opened his eyes and stared at her.

'If Tom calls you will let me know, won't you?' he said very clearly. 'I wouldn't want to miss him.'

'I'll do that, I promise.' She shook her head in puzzlement at the way in which his tortured mind now functioned. She decided to go to the chemist and pick up the medicine straight away. She buckled India into the buggy and set off, leaving Ralph to meander in and out of consciousness.

Will was determined not to get drunk. He had eaten two sandwiches before starting on the bottle of wine, and he drank slowly, trying to savour every mouthful. The bar was empty this early in the day, and the staff were still rearranging bottles and cleaning ashtrays. He liked this time, before the market masses intruded and spilled over into his private world, subsuming all in their endless rattle and hum. He no longer felt any kinship with them; they had left him far behind to battle on with his solitary crusade, and he studied them with detachment but little remorse. He disliked their superficial companionship and their deeper rivalries; he resented their blind acceptance of the status quo; and he questioned their motives in the endless round of drinks, laughter and tears that they perpetuated with every visit to the bar. They were avoiding reality, whilst he was facing up to it.

He felt no shame or guilt in sitting here alone. He justified his actions with the thought that he needed the time and space to set everything in order, and this was as good a place to do it as any other. Though he hardly cared, he knew that Clare would approve of this dispensation, and might even have encouraged it had he asked. But he was not yet sure enough of his own equilibrium to go to her; the news from Rocket had slammed against his temple like a well-delivered left hook, and he needed to test his reflexes to see how he would recover from the blow.

He had managed to distil the rights and wrongs of his existence into neater packages, and was pleased by the progress he had made. He had surprised himself with the manner in which he had gone about this, vaguely recognising Clare's contribution to it. All the time, he thought, I've had this inner reserve of courage but have never used it; I've just been cruising, but now I'm in control. He liked the feeling that he had a new element of power over his destiny, that he could actually work to change the course of events if he would only put his mind to it. He could see that his instinctive reactions were no longer good enough, and that he would have to plan more carefully if he were to achieve his private ambitions. As part of this he would have to manage Clare and her desires, but the prospect wasn't daunting: in baring his soul to her he had actually won a measure of supremacy that he could use whenever it suited him.

He was stiffened by events; rather than bend to them, and let them lead him where they might, he was now empowered to challenge them. What had happened could not be changed, he knew, but the consequences of this history could be turned to his advantage. He sneered at the weakness he had formerly displayed and swore to himself that he would not allow such frailty to manifest itself again. He had the chance to set everything straight, and he had no intention of letting it slip. There was no point in brooding on past failures and crimes; all that mattered now was how he manoeuvred to ensure that the future went in his direction.

He felt strong; he felt no need for others' support, and no desire to ask for help. He was certain that Tom was still in his life, ready to break out of the brackets of the last few years and reclaim his place at the centre. It only remained for Will to develop his strategy and sharpen his tactics; Clare was pliable and would be easily outflanked, and he had already begun to soften her up with his openness and apparent change of heart. Nobody could stop him and, he felt, nobody would want to. His was a righteous crusade, and that in itself would bring him victory. He drained his glass and refilled it, his eyes sparkling with vigour and confidence. He was ready, and he knew what he had to do.

TWENTY-FIVE

It came in such a rush, and was so unexpected, that she hardly had time to take in the information. Ricky needed a haircut – and had insisted on one – and Ellen had volunteered to escort him into town to the local barber's. He sat completely still in the chair, watching her reflection in the mirror as the barber snipped and combed. From the moment they had got into her car, she had sensed that Ricky's mood was changing, as if a great weight were being lifted from him as he moved away from the house. Although he was quiet during the short journey, she saw him sitting up and taking an interest in the passing scenery, his face brighter and more expressive.

She let him savour this short burst of freedom, and echoed his silence. When the haircut was finished he came across and sat next to her, showing no signs of wanting to leave in a hurry. Ellen had an idea and put it to him.

'What say we go get something to eat?' He nodded enthusiastically, and they wandered off to find a coffee shop. Once inside she ordered milk and a double chocolate-chip muffin for him and a coffee for herself. As he sat opposite her she noticed for the first time just how small he was: his chin barely cleared the table top, and she remembered the medical report that suggested he

225

was in the bottom percentile in terms of height and weight. His size merely emphasised his vulnerability, an insecurity that was heightened by his attachment to the small scrap of fabric he carried everywhere.

'Can I ask a question?' he said.

'Shoot.'

He pulled himself further into the table, signalling that the subject he wished to discuss was confidential. 'Does everyone have a special friend?'

'Yes, most folks do,' she answered, not knowing where this was leading.

'Do you have someone at the table, right now, who's your special friend?'

'Well, you're a very special friend of mine,' she said, still not understanding.

'No, not like that. I mean someone you can see but no one else can.' Suddenly many little lights came on in Ellen's head. Ricky had insisted on sitting in the back seat of the car, but had opened the front passenger door first; he had made sure that he sat next to an empty chair at the barber's; he had wanted to sit at a table for four in the coffee shop; and he always left or made a space on his bed when she came to see him in his room.

Now he began to swing his legs frantically under the table, and she realised that this was a difficult moment for him. 'Do you want to tell me about your special friend?' she asked.

He plunged a hand into his pocket, pulled out the worn square of yellow material and rubbed it against his mouth and nose. The action seemed to calm him a little as he considered her question. 'Yeah, I've got a friend,' Ricky said. 'He's here now, but he's shy.'

'That's OK,' Ellen said. 'Tell me about him.'

Ricky looked at one of the empty chairs by the table. 'He's sitting right there. He doesn't want a drink or anything to eat, and he didn't want a haircut. But he did want a ride, so he came along with us.'

The waitress came over with their order and Ricky drank some milk, waiting until she was gone before looking at Ellen to judge her reaction. 'It's neat to have a special friend like him, isn't it?' she said.

'Well, sometimes he gets me into a lot of trouble,' Ricky said. 'Like that fire. You know, he did it. It was Chris's idea, but he did it.' His tone suggested that it was important for Ellen to know and believe this, so she nodded in acceptance of the fact. 'Most of the time he's good, though.'

'Does your mom know about him?'

'No. Well, I mean, she told me never to talk about him to anyone. It was like she didn't like him much, so he just sort of hung out in my room. He doesn't mind.'

'And does he want to go home now?'

'Kind of. But he came from someone else's home, and sometimes he gets real homesick and cries. Then I have to tell him what my mom said, that he's not going back there and he's going to stay with us now.'

Ellen was fascinated and frightened; they had reached the point where Ricky was finally opening a door on his life and the confusion he faced. Such a transfer of emotions was not uncommon but, in his case, it was especially important.

'Tell me some more about him. He sounds really cool.'

'He's seven, and he's a bit bigger than me. He doesn't

227

go to school with me. He doesn't like it there. But he's always there when I get home, and he sleeps in my bed with me. And he has a friend too.'

'Does he? That's nice. Who is this friend?'

'He's called Grandpa. He lives a long way away, so he doesn't get to see him much. But I know they used to talk on the phone some.'

The pieces started to come together in Ellen's mind. 'Ricky, what's your friend called? Does he have a special name?'

'You're not going to tell anyone, are you? 'Cause Mom would be real mad if she knew.'

'No, Ricky, I promise I won't tell anyone.'

'He's called Tom.'

'It's time to bring them in. At the very least you should give them the chance to ID him.'

Rocket had called in on Jablonowski unannounced, and he was clearly irritated by her presence. 'I thank you for your concern and interest but, as of now, your involvement in the case is over. The guys in Chicago are sorting it all out, and they don't need you to help. Push your luck any further on this one and they're going to blow you away. And I'll back them up. Comprende?'

'I've done your dirty work, and I think I have a right to some input at least,' Rocket said, not in the least perturbed by his threat. 'Now they won't even let me near him, and I could probably identify him. Don't forget, I found the kid when you'd all failed.'

'Oh, we haven't forgotten that. How could we? One guy had an axe through his skull, thanks to you. If you'd just left it to us, and given us all your information, we could probably have avoided all this aggravation and the kid would be home by now.'

'We've been over this a thousand times, and it never gets us anywhere. The point is, the Easterbrooks are worrying themselves shitless whilst all you boneheads shuffle paper and pass the buck. What do the social workers have to say about all this?'

'It's none of your business. This discussion is terminated. It was nice knowing you, and now I want you to get the hell out of my office.'

'Just tell me one thing. If he were your boy, and you knew they had him, what would you do?'

'That's a question I can't answer, and there's no value in trying to. But you're looking through the wrong end of the telescope. What you should be asking is what will happen if we screw this up and it turns out that the Easterbrooks can't get him back. That's what worries me. You're in panic mode because you're trying to atone for everything you did wrong before, and you've lost your sense of perspective. Loosen up, Rocky. You're heading for major grief if you don't let go of this.'

'Thanks for the advice. You know, you really are as dumb as everyone says.'

'Get out!' he shouted, and Rocket slowly rose and walked out of his office. She needed a drink to soften the sting of his accusations and clear the red haze of anger from her eyes.

It was a strange feeling and Clare was still getting used to it. Far from collapsing when he'd heard about Tom, Will had drawn additional strength from the news and was now in command of their thoughts and deeds; he had retained the sense of balance he'd discovered in Suffolk, and was almost too calm for Clare's liking. She had never known a time in their marriage when he had dominated her so totally, but she wasn't complaining: having held the family together for so long, she was glad of a break and was grateful for his intervention.

In this exact reversal of roles, Will was now the instigator of suggestions and proposals with Clare relegated to passive concurrence. He no longer waited for her to come up with ideas as to how they should behave or react; and he played his new part with such assurance that she wondered if he had always had this side to him but had suppressed it all these years. In any case, she let him take the lead because she so totally lacked any sense of what was right and wrong and how they should proceed. Having carefully constructed a force field around her feelings for the past, she had seen it breached by Rocket's call, and now it was she, not Will, who found their history hard to manage and imposing painfully on the present.

She had been a good nurse to Ralph, even though he scarcely noticed it. His chest still rattled but the antibiotics had taken hold and he was recovering well. He was very weak and the exhaustion meant that it was hard to tell when he was lucid: he spent much of his time in a half-sleep, huddled in front of the television or prostrate on his bed, occasionally mumbling broken phrases to no one in particular or coughing sporadically. Clare found respite in his illness, as it took him away from the real world and placed him in a semi-conscious state from which he rarely ventured, allowing her to worry about the more important challenge.

And to Clare it was a challenge. Finding her judgement

clouded and her reactions fuzzy, she needed to separate the emotional and intellectual strands of her life so that she could decide what was necessary and what was superfluous. Emotionally she needed Tom to return or, more accurately, she needed resolution of Tom's plight either way. She knew that their biggest problem – especially for Will – had been the absence of a clean break; whilst Tom's fortunes were still indeterminate, they couldn't properly grieve for his loss and pass through the stations of that grief with any real conviction. In Suffolk Will had tried to come to terms with that and meet the problem head-on. She had encouraged this because she felt that she had already achieved it, but now she knew that this was just an act, and that her emotional disturbance was just as great as his. The only difference was that she had been better at hiding it from herself and him.

Intellectually, Clare wanted to evaluate the options and judge them on their merits. Were Tom to return, what effect would it have on their family unit? How would India cope? How would they all cope? Was reunion the only – the best – course of action, regardless of the consequences? Will, it seemed to her, was wrestling with none of these dilemmas, his mind's eye clear and his principles unshakeable, but she was struggling to see everything from every angle, with kaleidoscopic results. Confused and frustrated by her inability to focus, she deferred to Will.

She wanted to talk to Rocket, not in her professional capacity but as a woman. Rocket had seen inside her, attuned herself immediately to Clare's rhythms, and that insight was what she needed now. Much as she hated the medium of the telephone for communication, devoid of nuance and subtlety, she ached for someone with whom she could share her confusion and who might present her with a new set of alternatives. Rocket seemed to offer this chance to her.

Before she had made the decision to call, the phone rang.

'Yes, hallo, is that Mrs Easterbrook?'

'It is.'

'Please hold. I have a call from Captain Feehan, Chicago Police Department.' The nasal tones of the operator jarred on Clare's ear. She closed her eyes as she waited for contact to be re-established.

'Hi, Mrs Easterbrook? Brendan Feehan here, from Chicago Police Department. Is this a good time to talk?'

'As good as any.'

'Great. Look, we have some encouraging news for you, I think. Seems like we may have found your boy, Tom. I should immediately qualify that with a heavy caveat, because we can't be sure until we've run some more checks, but I wanted to put you on stand-by. We'll be needing you to come over real soon, I'd imagine.'

Clare lacked any sense of what to say next: she didn't know whether to be pleased or anxious, elated or calm, and she had no immediate questions for this man. Wanting to fill the silent gap, she could only say: 'I see.'

He picked up on this. 'Yeah, well, it must be a bit of a shock for you, I know, and it'll take some time for it all to sink in. Best news is, the kid is in great shape and fighting fit. He's being well looked after here, and you can rest assured that we're doing all we can to get him back to you ASAP.'

He had given her time to collect her thoughts. 'What

happens now? I mean, when we come over, what's the procedure?'

'We'll ask you to identify him and, assuming he is Tom, then there'll probably be a few legal processes to go through, but that shouldn't take too long. But I advise you to line up an attorney here so that he can guide you through the whole thing.'

'Fine. Is there anything else I need to know?'

'That about covers it. I'd estimate that we have three or four more days of paperwork ahead of us, then we'll call you again and get everything arranged, OK?'

She needed more, but was uncertain of how to ask for it. 'I know you probably can't say, but can you tell me how you found him?'

'I'm sorry, Mrs Easterbrook, but I really can't give you those details over the phone. All I can tell you is that we've charged someone in connection with his abduction.'

'I understand.'

He gave her his phone number and asked her if she needed anything else, but Clare was too shaken to think any further. She wished that Will had taken the call; he would have known how to handle it much better than she. She let her hand rest on the phone after the call was over, and tears fell erratically on to her fingers, but she couldn't tell whether they were from joy or fear.

TWENTY-SIX

Faced with a torrent of evidence, there was little to stall the decision. Ellen had persuaded, cajoled, argued and sulked by turns through the entire process; Ricky, now increasingly referred to as Tom, could not provide them with the final proof of his identity, but his frequent talks with Ellen and others had convinced them that he was Thomas Easterbrook. The police in Chicago and New York quickly lined up behind Ellen to support her; they wanted the file closed and responsibility shifted elsewhere.

The Easterbrooks were due to arrive in Chicago that afternoon; at the morning case conference a schedule had been mapped out which would include tests, interviews, checks and counter-checks. They had fixed the next morning as the time for a formal identification and, assuming it would be positive, they had set aside the rest of the day for group and individual counselling. Ellen was assigned the task of explaining all this to Tom.

'I need to talk to both of you,' she said to him. He looked confused. 'You and Tom.'

'Are we going home?'

'I can't tell you that just now,' she said. 'But we're going to be doing some things tomorrow that will start to sort everything out, and I want to tell you about all that.' He

235

looked disappointed. 'We need to do these things before we can send you home, Ricky. You'll just have to trust me on that.'

'What things?'

He had confessed that he knew Betsy was not his real mother. He knew no other, but was aware that there had been a life before, even though he could remember nothing of it. He was unwilling to talk about Chuck, and would pull his knees into his chest whenever his name came up. They had tried to get to the bottom of this, but without success: Chuck remained a memory he had locked away or discarded for undisclosed reasons, and nothing they could do would entice him to talk about it.

'You remember that you told me a little about your mom, and how you knew she was looking after you even though you didn't come out of her tummy?'

'Yeah.'

'Well, how would you feel if I told you that we may have found your real mom and dad, and that they were coming to see you?'

'Have you?' He seemed neither overly interested nor dismayed by this news.

'That's what we're going to find out tomorrow. They're coming here, and they're going to meet with you and talk with you.'

'How will I know if it's them?'

'That's a good question, Ricky. You see, it all happened such a long time ago that you may not remember them, but they'll remember you. They've never forgotten you, and they still love you so much.'

'Then why did they leave me?'

She was ready for this. 'Honey, they didn't leave you.

That's what you have to get straight. They lost you, and Chuck and Betsy took care of you while they were looking for you.'

'But I didn't feel lost.'

'No, and that's because Chuck and Betsy did a real good job of looking after you. But now we've found you, we think you should go back to your real parents – if you want to. How does that sound?'

'I don't know,' he said after thinking about this. 'What if I don't like them? What if I don't want to go back with them?'

'I think you'll like them, Ricky. I think Tom will, too. But you can take your time – as much time as you need to decide. Is that fair?'

'I guess.' He took his comforter out of his pocket and clasped it. After some more thought he spoke again. 'What if they don't like me, or Tom?'

'They will, I know they will. They can't wait to see you again. They're so excited.'

'Do they have a dog?'

'I don't know. You'll have to ask them.'

'I'd really like a dog, but Mom wouldn't let me have one.'

'Well, you'll have to talk to them about that.'

'A dog would be neat.' This set his train of thought in an entirely different direction, and Ellen knew he had lost his concentration.

'So, tomorrow morning you're going to meet them. You'll need to have a good scrub tonight so that you look your best, and you'll have to decide what clothes you want to wear. OK?'

'OK,' he said, with a small shrug of his shoulders.

* * *

Clare was amazed by his performance. Faced with a thousand questions, many of which sought the same information, Will remained calm and amenable. He answered them all with polite detachment, never betraying any frustration or annoyance. He was courteous, patient and consistent, taking the strain from her and setting his face against the cold wind of bureaucracy. By the time Ellen arrived in the interview room, they had seen eight different policemen, doctors, counsellors and social workers.

'You guys must be shattered,' Ellen said as she set her coffee cup down on the table.

'We're bearing up,' Will said, still bright and alert. Clare's limbs ached with exhaustion, and she tried to draw on his stamina to see her through this ordeal.

'Well, I'm the last, you'll be pleased to hear. My name is Ellen, and I've probably had more contact with Tom than anyone else involved in the case.' Clare's senses were stirred on hearing this; at last they were going to talk about him. 'Everyone else will already have warned you that it might not be him and that, even if it is, you face an enormous challenge. Assimilating him back into the family unit will be no joke. He's obviously built some new attachments, and he doesn't seem to remember his life with you at all.'

'We're ready for that,' Will said.

'Good, because you'll need to be. My role now is to tell you a little more about him. You don't need me to tell you that he's changed a lot; but maybe I can help you with understanding what kind of a child he is, and what's important to him.'

238

'That'd be very helpful,' Will said.

'Physically, he's pretty obviously recognisable as Tom. I've seen the photos you brought in, and I don't think there's any doubt it's him. Was he always small for his age?'

'Yes. We'd been taking him to see a consultant, and his bone age was way behind,' Clare replied.

'Well, he's still on the small side, but I can't see that it's given him many problems. He never talks about it, and he doesn't use his size as an excuse, which is good. I guess you can always consider hormone treatment if he doesn't have a growth spurt later on.'

Clare and Will briefly glanced at each other; they had never been able to agree about this treatment and had deferred a decision. Memories of old arguments came to the surface, reuniting the present and the past uncomfortably.

Ellen continued. 'The most interesting thing about him is that he's retained something in his subconscious, even though he doesn't know it. He's invented a friend called Tom. It seems that he transfers a lot of his anxieties to Tom, and it's obviously no coincidence about the name. He told me that Tom had different parents and wanted to go back home. In fact, that's how we cracked the case.'

'How do you suggest we deal with that?' Will asked.

'Trial and error, I'm afraid. He may want to keep Tom; I'd say it's highly likely, because Tom offers him some security. For now, though, I wouldn't mention it. Tom is a well-kept secret, and he wants it to stay that way. If he chooses to talk about it, just be encouraging and open. That's all you can do.'

239

'What about these attachments you mentioned?' Clare said.

'Clearly he loves Betsy, and that isn't going to go away in a hurry. You can't expect him to make a clean break; it would be unhealthy if he did. You'll have to earn his love all over again, I'm afraid. But you mustn't try and compete for it. We don't want to confront him with a choice between you and her. And I would suggest that you only discuss her, and his feelings for her, if he raises it.'

'Does he know we're coming?' Will asked.

'Oh yes. I've talked with him about that.'

'And how did he react?'

'Much as you'd expect. He's apprehensive, and worried that you won't like him, or vice versa. He asked how he'd know you, and whether he'd have to go with you.'

'And what did you tell him?'

'I told him not to spend too much time worrying about that. We need to make him feel as if it's under his control, and he has some say in the process. Otherwise he'll store up resentment and it'll manifest itself at some later stage.'

'Do you think he understands what's going on?'

'He's grasped the concept, but he's having trouble turning that into reality. Once he's met you, and can see and touch the whole thing, I think he'll feel much more comfortable.'

'What else should we know?'

'I'd have to say that his little adventure with the fire was a complete aberration,' Ellen said. 'It could have been a cry for help and attention. Perhaps he was facing a crisis and didn't know how to deal with it. But we don't think he's dysfunctional in any way, and we're leaning towards the view that the fire can be dismissed as a one-off. Other than that, he has a pretty healthy mind and normal interests for a kid his age.' As they were taking this in, Ellen checked her notes and put a finger up. 'There was something else – probably not important, but I thought I'd better mention it. He told me that his friend Tom had a special friend too – called Grandpa. He said he lived a long way away but he might have spoken to him on the phone. Does that ring any bells?'

'Oh my God,' Clare said, immediately seeing the connection. She looked across at Will but he merely raised his eyebrows. 'My father. When Tom was little, he learnt my parents' phone number. You know, we used to teach him all the numbers he should ring if he were ever in trouble – our number, 911 and his grandparents. But it's too fantastic to believe that he might have remembered them all, surely?'

'You never know what a little kid is capable of,' Ellen said. 'But is there any evidence that he actually did call?'

It all came flooding back to Clare, those times when Ralph had said that Tom had called and she'd ignored him. 'He might have, he just might have,' she whispered, haunted by her failure to take Ralph seriously.

'Well, it doesn't matter much in any event,' Ellen said. 'I just thought you'd like to know that he still remembers Grandpa, for what it's worth. It could help the readjustment process.'

Clare tried to put this to the back of her mind as she wanted to know something that she believed to be very important. 'Do you like him?'

Ellen grinned broadly, a beautiful smile that changed her whole face and the way she held herself. 'I've worked with kids all my life,' she replied. 'All different shapes, colours and sizes. I was one of nine children, so I got plenty of experience early on. And I've never met one I didn't love. They all have their charms. But I'll tell you this for nothing. Tom is a dazzler. He's been through the wringer and out the other side, but he's still hanging in there and he hasn't lost any of his sparkle. He's a great kid.'

Clare returned the smile and reached out to put her hand on Will's. A tricky piece of the jigsaw had just been fixed in place for her, and the feeling was liberating and uplifting. Everything will be all right now, she thought secretly.

It had been a *tour de force*, but now Will was drained. He lay on the bed in their hotel room and held one hand over his face. Clare sat next to him and picked at the huge sandwiches they had bought, although her appetite was dulled by anticipation and jet lag. The night ahead would be a long one, she knew, with little sleep as the prospect of meeting Tom haunted them; they hardly dared to think about it, let alone mention it, although she knew they should discuss their roles and behaviour.

'So how do you think it went?' she asked him.

Will pulled his hand away from his face wearily. 'Pretty much as I expected. They're just doing their job, I suppose, although I can't see much point in it all. He's ours, and we've proved it a dozen times over. What else needs to be said?'

'You really believe it's him?'

'They wouldn't have let us get this far if they didn't think that. They know all right, and they're simply covering their arses. Once we've got tomorrow out of the way we're home and dry.'

She was awed by his certainty, and the manner in which he took everything in his stride. For her this whole process was no less traumatic than Tom's disappearance, but Will seemed to have arrived at a point of such confidence and security that nothing could knock him off his chosen course. Whilst envying him, she also fretted that this confidence was fragile, and any set-backs or delays might easily damage it. She wanted to avoid another decline, and she needed to manage his myopic expectations.

'I'll bet you there's a snarl-up tomorrow,' she said testingly.

He sat up. 'How could there be?'

'Oh, I don't know,' she sighed, 'but something's bound to go wrong. It always does. I think we need to be prepared for that.'

'I think you're being unduly pessimistic. He's our son, and they know we're reasonable human beings. They'll be glad to see the back of him. They won't want him hanging around any longer than is absolutely necessary.'

'I hope you're right, Will. We've come so far, and I don't want to be disappointed now.'

'Tom is coming back,' Will said firmly. 'There's no debate about that. Very soon he'll be back with us, and we can put all this in the past.' He watched her reaction. 'You're not having doubts, are you?'

She was startled by the change of tone in his voice. 'About what?'

'I don't know. You just sound . . . ambivalent, I think. You do want him back, don't you?'

'How can you ask me that? Of course I do, just as much as you. Whatever can have given you that idea?'

243

Will lay back on the bed again, the flash of anger subsiding. 'Forget it.'

She tried to; she told herself that Will was just as tired as she was, and that he had every right to expect loyalty and encouragement from her. She decided to let it go.

'Shall I book a wake-up call?' she asked.

He let out a small laugh. 'I don't think we'll need that. I'm dog-tired, but I know I'm not going to get much sleep.'

'No.' Clare got up and walked over to the window. She looked down at the flow of traffic on the streets and the gleaming buildings downtown. She had never seen Chicago before, and yet now it was the most important place in the world for her. It was here that she would reach a critical moment of truth, when the course of the rest of her life would be determined. Tom was at home here; this was now his natural habitat, giving him a measure of power that struck her as unnatural. He would be driving their relationship; ultimately, he would be the one who could make or break it. To him, they could be visitors from another planet, such was the distance between them. She was desperate to talk about these feelings to Will, but had no idea where to start.

'Do you think he'll recognise us?' she asked, still gazing at the river of lights.

'I'd think not – not in any tangible way, that is. But I do think it's significant that he's invented this *alter ego*. That must show he still carries something with him, however subliminal it might be.'

'What did you think about the story with Ralph?' Clare asked as it returned to disturb her. 'That's incredible, isn't it? How could he have remembered Ralph, let alone his number?'

'Who knows how a child's mind works?' Will said, sounding a little distracted.

'But Ralph told me. Christ, it makes me shudder to think. I clearly remember him saying once, maybe more, that he'd had a call from Tom. I just dismissed it as another of his fantasies, but it wasn't. Did he ever say anything to you?'

'Never,' Will said firmly. 'I'd have done something about it if he had.'

'The whole thing seems so bizarre. Tom was inside me for nine months, and yet he's going to be a complete stranger. It's almost like being a surrogate mother.'

'No it isn't, Clare. Surrogates never get emotionally attached. They're doing a job for money and that's it. You – and I – have got very strong bonds with him, and time hasn't loosened them. I guarantee you, as soon as you see him, all your maternal feelings will flood back.'

'They already have,' she said, and she meant it.

Cold; very cold; shivering; a wet kind of cold. Dark, too; he was not sure where the door was. He turned on the light to see if it would help. Better, but he was still frightened. It must be the middle of the night; I shouldn't wake anyone, Tom thought, they'll get real mad with me. Might stop me coming out of my room. He didn't want that; he wanted to be with his mom. Where was his friend Tom? He'd gone, couldn't find him, probably scared of the dark too. He wished he could be in his own bed, have his own things.

He wished he didn't have to see those guys tomorrow. Who are they, anyway? Ellen says . . . what did Ellen say? They'll like me, sure they will. But what if they don't?

What if they're real mean? And I don't know them, never seen them before. What do I say? Tom says it'll be OK, but he doesn't know. He never liked my mom. Says she's crazy. I don't know. Sometimes she is, but I just don't know. Wish I could see her. Wish I could have a hug. So cold.

He took off his pyjamas; they were all wet. So were the sheets. Am I in trouble; they don't like that. Shall I get dressed? I'm real cold. What's the time? Is it time to get up? They said they'd come, but no one's here. Ellen said she'd be here. My legs are hurting inside, like I've got a headache in my bones. He lay down on the floor, but it was too cold, too hard. He got dressed and sat on his chair. I'll just wait, see what happens. Must be time soon. Should he brush his teeth? He was a bit warmer now. He wished Tom were here. Where's he gone? I want my mom.

TWENTY-SEVEN

Clare shivered, not from the cold, but from terror. They were sitting in a large room with a jumble of odd pieces of furniture – two sofas, an armchair, a battered and scratched table with four wooden chairs, and a huge cupboard from which one door was missing, stuffed with toys, books and magazines. The carpet tiles were brown and worn, dotted with several black patches of discarded gum; the unlined curtains, fraying at the hems, had been hung irregularly; and the walls were covered with posters, pock-marks and traces of old Sellotape. It was exceptionally hot, but still she shivered.

Will got up and walked around with his hands in his pockets. He seemed oblivious to the surroundings and looked at nothing in particular. There were no words to share, no final thoughts to articulate; both knew that this was their destiny, their destination, and nothing they felt or said now would make any difference. There was no turning back.

There was a knock on the door and they both looked round, Clare springing up to move towards Will. They watched as Ellen entered the room, a little hand in hers. As Ellen came in they could see another woman further back. Then they saw him. He was partially hidden behind

Ellen's legs, and made no move to come out. Ellen was smiling, and she gently pulled on his hand. Reluctantly he stepped to one side of her, still holding her hand, close to her. He looked at the floor.

Clare's throat tightened immensely as she saw what he held in his free hand. The scrap of blanket was just visible within his fist, and the sight of it was enough to validate all her hopes. She bit so hard on her lip that it broke open; the taste of blood awoke new consciousness within her, and she could feel adrenalin coursing to every part of her. Will crushed her hand in his, but made no other movement.

'Will, Clare, I'd like you to meet someone very special,' Ellen said. Clare crouched down in front of him, still several feet away, and offered him the palm of her hand.

'Hallo,' she said quietly. He ignored her hand, still keeping his face down and his eyes on the floor.

'I'd guess this little man didn't get much sleep last night,' Ellen said brightly. 'Am I right?' There was no response. 'Shall we all sit down?' Ellen and Tom sat together on one sofa, Tom careful to leave a space next to him, whilst Will and Clare sat on the other. The woman went to the table and placed a big file of papers on it before sitting down. 'Coffees and cookies on their way,' Ellen said.

The silence was as sharp as a knife. Clare had not expected to be so bereft of speech and thought; she had anticipated that, in her nervousness, she would have to control the flood of words, but nothing came.

'So, I'm Will. And what's your name?'

Tom looked up at Ellen for confirmation before answering. 'I'm Ricky.'

'Hallo, Ricky. That's a good name. I like it.' Will sounded calm.

'Ricky, would you like to see some photos?' Ellen asked. 'Of you?'

He nodded, and briefly looked up to see where they would come from. Clare dug into her handbag and pulled out a big folder.

'Do you want to come over here and look?' she asked him. Again he looked at Ellen, who smiled and nodded. He let go of her hand and inched his way towards Clare, who shifted across the sofa to make room for him next to her. But he stopped short of her and turned himself so that he could look at the photos in her hand without sitting down.

Will and Clare had spent hours selecting these photos – Tom's birthday parties, Tom at the beach, Tom on the deck, Tom with them – and had whittled the pile down to just twenty, all chosen to show him as part of a happy, caring family. In several he was in their arms or on their laps, always smiling and always secure. He looked at the first one: it had been taken shortly before he went missing, and showed him with Clare outside their house in Westchester, the sun bright and several rhododendrons in full bloom.

'Is that me?' he asked, incredulity in his voice.

'What do you think?' Clare replied. He looked at it closely, then looked over to Ellen.

'It might be, I guess. And that's you, right?'

'That's me. We used to have a house in New York; that's where we all lived. And I think that looks like you, doesn't it? Here, look, here's another.'

Clare was relieved to have found him interested in

these; he studied each one carefully, like a tribesman from the jungle who has just discovered the miracle of photography and fears it might take his spirit away. Several times he stopped her from moving on, fascinated by what he saw. When they reached the last one, he looked at Clare for the first time, suspicion in his face as if he were unwilling to be tricked so easily. Then he went back and sat down next to Ellen.

Throughout the whole exercise, Will kept his stare fixed on Tom. He ached to pick him up and squeeze him tight, hoping that the touch would awaken memories and finish this alienation. Above all, he wanted to say he was sorry.

A black man with thin grey hair came in with a trolley; he took off a tray and put it down on the table where the woman was sitting. Ellen thanked him and he left. The woman took a glass of milk and a plate of biscuits to Tom, then delivered coffee to everyone else. Tom drank some milk and wiped his mouth on the scrap of blanket that he still clutched tightly.

'Ricky, I have something to tell you about that,' Clare said, pointing at the material. He looked at it in his hand, and then at her. He was curious. 'You know, that's a corner of a blanket that you used to have in your cot, when you were really tiny. And you know what? I still have the rest of the blanket at home.'

His eyes opened wide in disbelief. Now he stared at her, no longer sure of his own position. Ellen put her arm around him. 'I wish you'd brought it with you,' she said, 'because that piece is pretty well worn out.'

'Well, it's waiting safely in the airing cupboard,' Clare said.

'Can I see the photos again?' Tom asked Ellen.

250

'Sure, go right ahead.'

More confidently this time, he walked over to Clare. She gave the photos to him and he shuffled through them until he came to one of him on the grass outside the house: he was squatting beside an old dog that lay on its side as he stroked its belly. He looked at it for ages.

'Is that your dog?' he said at last.

'No,' Clare answered. 'He belonged to the neighbours. He was called Sam. He loved you, and you loved him. He'd follow you everywhere, and you used to give him chocolate drops.'

'Is he still there? Can I go and see him?'

'Well, we don't live there any more. But I suppose he might still be there.'

'Do you have a dog now?'

'No we don't. But I really want one. It sounds like you do, too.'

'Yeah.'

'What kind do you like best?'

'They're kind of yellow, and they've got lots of hair. My friend at school, Chris, he has one and it's real neat.'

'What's it called?'

'Jake. I like Jake, but he never comes to my house. Mom doesn't like dogs.'

'That's a shame.' Clare tried to pretend that the reference to his mother didn't affect her.

Tom had nothing else to say on the matter, so he took the photo and went back to his sofa.

'Ricky likes all animals,' Ellen said. 'I think he's going to be a zoo keeper when he grows up.' She stroked his hair and he looked bashful. To hide his embarrassment he nuzzled into his square of blanket.

'Have you ever been to the zoo?' Clare asked.

'Once,' he replied, pleased to be involved again. 'I saw tigers, and lions, and elephants, even a shark. And lots of snakes.'

'I don't like snakes,' Clare said.

'They're OK. You think they're going to be real slimy, but they're not. I touched one at school.'

'You're much braver than I am.' He liked this idea, and produced a little smile.

'Well, listen,' Ellen said, 'perhaps Will and Clare can take you to the zoo one day. How would you like that?'

'That'd be great. But will you come?'

'If I have time,' she said. It was a breakthrough, as they all knew, and no one wanted to rush it. 'Look, I've got to run now, Ricky, how about you stay here and talk some more? Would you like that?' Immediately his face changed, now anxious and uncertain.

'Do I have to?'

'Only if you want to.'

'Can I come with you?'

Ellen looked at Will and Clare; Clare shrugged and opened her hands to show she wouldn't mind if he wanted to leave. Will remained impassive.

'OK. You come with me, and we'll see Will and Clare later. Agreed?'

'Can I take this photo?'

'You'll have to ask Clare.'

'Of course you can,' Clare said. 'Would you like to take any others?'

'No,' Tom said, 'this is fine. Thanks.'

They all got up together. 'It was really nice meeting you,' Clare said. 'I hope we'll see you again soon.'

'Bye,' Tom said. He slipped his hand into Ellen's and they walked out of the room. The woman at the table spoke for the first time.

'A little heartbreaker, isn't he?'

'You can say that again,' Clare replied. She turned to look at Will, and he quickly enfolded her in his arms as the sobs began to shake him.

'So sad, so sad,' he repeated over and over again. And, though he made little sense, Clare understood him completely.

TWENTY-EIGHT

'Let's try this one more time.'

Betsy's resistance had been nothing short of heroic; in the face of continued questioning, she had remained steadfast in her refusal to alter her story or elaborate on any of the details she had given in her very first interview. The investigation of Chuck's murder had gone precisely nowhere; the DA's office was frustrated beyond endurance as she gave them no evidence to pursue any other line of inquiry, and nothing with which she might incriminate herself. She now sat in front of Brendan Feehan as he flicked through previous interview notes in her file, trying to find some different way to the truth.

'We can do whatever you like, Mr Feehan,' Betsy said, 'but it won't alter a thing. I've told you all I know and cannot tell you what I don't.'

'I appreciate that,' Feehan said, 'but indulge me for a moment.' She put her head to one side in a gesture that suggested she might accede to his request. Her hands lay still in her lap, and she sat upright and steady. 'Let's go back to the morning of your husband's death. You went out to the store at what time?'

'After breakfast, so that would have been about nine o'clock.'

'And Ricky went with you?'

'As I've said.'

'And what time did you return?'

'Around midday. Ricky and I went to a coffee shop after the shopping, then we walked home.'

'How did you enter the house?'

'I don't understand the question.'

'Well, did you go in the front or the back? Were you together or separate?'

'Ricky ran ahead, and he went in the kitchen door at the back. It was open because Chuck was in the house. I followed him in and then I closed the door.'

'And where was Ricky?'

'Waiting for me in the kitchen. Why do you ask?'

'No particular reason. Just trying to establish everyone's movements, I guess. Were you aware of anything unusual in the house?'

'Nothing whatsoever.'

'And when did you realise that something was wrong? I mean, did you know immediately, or did it take something specific to alert you?'

'As soon as I knew Chuck wasn't at home I thought something was wrong. The car was parked out front and he wouldn't have gone out without leaving a note. Obviously, once I had seen all the blood, I feared the worst.'

'So what did you do?'

'I have to be honest, Mr Feehan, and tell you that I panicked. I didn't know what to do. You'll understand that my position was somewhat complicated, and I wasn't thinking straight. So I gathered up Ricky and fled. I needed to be away from that house and to get my thoughts in order. That was my instinct.'

'And where did you go?'

'As you already know, I checked us into a motel. It's all in your file there.'

What rankled most with Feehan was the flat, calm manner in which she spoke of these events. Even the mention of her husband seemed to elicit no noticeable change in her demeanour. It was as if she were talking of some happening that she had seen on television and about which she were totally uninterested.

'Did you look at or in the car at any time?'

'No. Why should I?'

'You see, one of the major problems we have is that no one can verify your story. There's no one at the coffee shop who remembers you, and the store can't say whether you were there or not. So what we have is your word and nothing more.'

'As you say, that's your problem. I know what I did and when I did it. That's what I've told you.'

'If we could just get some verification of this, we'd all be in a much better position, you know.' Feehan tried to sound encouraging, but it didn't work.

'How can I be in a better position? I am innocent, and that knowledge is all I need. These interviews are entirely for your benefit, aren't they?'

'Not exactly. You're looking down the barrel of a gun, Betsy. All roads of the investigation lead to you as the prime suspect. Surely you can see that?'

'God knows what happened, and His justice will prevail.'

It had taken a few minutes, but they had come back to God, as in every other interview. Feehan sighed. He

257

decided to play his trump card.

'I guess we'll have to lean more heavily on Ricky then,' he said apologetically. This got a reaction.

'No!' she said, leaning forward in her seat. 'That's not part of our deal. You said he'd be left out of this.'

'But that agreement was on the basis that you'd cooperate, Betsy, and frankly I'm not seeing a lot of cooperation. All I'm seeing is obstruction.'

Betsy moved back into her former position. To Feehan it looked as if she might be regretting the temporary flash of emotion and was trying to expunge it. She looked him straight in the eye, a penetrative stare that made him feel as if he were the culprit, the suspect, the one under interrogation. Feehan had little stomach for the idea of interviewing Ricky, a sentiment shared by most of his colleagues, but they needed a result and would have to follow this course if they couldn't crack Betsy.

To break the spell he referred to the file again, but the words swam before his eyes; he could feel her look upon the crown of his head, and he struggled to find something new to say.

'Are you finished?' she asked, calmer now.

'For now.' He flipped the file closed and picked it up as he rose from his chair. 'Betsy, let me tell you something for free. You could save yourself from a lot more trouble if you'd come up with something new. I advise you to rack your brains and go over the facts again. See if you can't think of something that will get you off the hook. There must be some information that'll clear you of suspicion once and for all. Otherwise . . .' He shrugged to show that the alternative was grim.

'I can't give you what I don't have.' Feehan turned

away from her and went to the door. But then she surprised him. 'I have a request.'

'Yeah?'

'Could I see that private detective – you know, Miss Stubblefield?'

He was intrigued by the question, and tried to think quickly. 'I'll see what I can do. Any particular reason?'

'Just taking your advice, Mr Feehan.'

He left the interview room as a uniformed officer went in to escort Betsy back to her cell. He couldn't identify any good reason to deny her request, but it made him uneasy.

Rocket's pride, always a volatile commodity, had almost died. She slopped around her apartment in grey sweats and drank beer from the bottle. She watched television when she should have been working on the few remaining cases she had on the go. Her enervation was total; she ate sporadically, went out rarely and let the dust and dirt build up around her. The days were long and painful, unpunctuated by constructive activity or thought. A dozen times she had picked up the phone to call Jablonowski and put it down before dialling; she could see no way to intermediate, and had no strength to try.

Dizzy from lassitude and too much beer, she would lie on the couch and breathe in small gasps; the ash dropped from her cigarette on to her chest and the floor, and a thin layer of smoke hung constantly above her. Visions of Tom in his bed revisited her frequently, but they had taken on a life of their own, like an interactive video in which both she and Tom could alter its plot. Sometimes he would wake up and stare at her with big, tear-laden eyes; at others, he would turn and grin before returning to sleep. Once she had heard him speak: 'Help me,' he had said weakly, but she was too far away and couldn't move any closer.

She had also constructed an unseen scenario, where Betsy stood over Chuck's limp body, an axe in her hand and Tom some distance behind her. Her conscious mind had never allowed her to exercise this option; she had never believed that Betsy could truly be capable of such an act, notwithstanding all evidence to the contrary. But, as she meandered between fact and fantasy, this powerful image would come back to her, and Tom was always part of it. In it, she could almost smell the blood and fear, and her body would snap uncomfortably at the sensation. Her heart raced as if trying to escape from her ribcage and she would clench her hands on her thighs, hoping for release from the terrors she had seen.

In the brief periods when she was fully functional, Rocket would avoid any effort to reconcile past and present. She tried to make herself busy with menial tasks, keeping her thoughts away from Tom and his troubles. But whatever she did or did not do, there was always a backdrop of anguish accompanying it, and she couldn't determine whether this was caused by self-pity or her feelings for Will, Clare and Tom. She let herself ignore the reasons and concentrate on the symptoms: dosed up with alcohol and nicotine, she wandered along a bleary path between mute coherence and frightened dreams.

When the call came from Chicago she was slouched in a corner, her head and back resting against the wall with her knees pulled up to her chest. She fumbled with the receiver and slurred her name.

'Hi. It's Brendan Feehan here – from Chicago PD.'

'I remember.'

'Are you OK? You sound pretty beat up.'

'Just tired. What can I do for you?'

'I've got a strange one here. Betsy Callahan wants to see you.'

There was a long pause before she answered. 'Did she say why?'

'I was hoping you might know. Seems it's important, though. Any ideas?'

'Beats me.' Another silence.

'Will you come, then?'

'Sure. When do you need me?'

'As soon as you can make it. And we'd like to see you first, give you a briefing. OK?'

'No problem. One question, though. Who's paying?'

Feehan laughed with relief. 'Oh, we'll pick up the tab. What's one more air fare? Our budget's shot to shit as it is.'

'OK. I'll be on the first available flight. I'll call you.'

The conversation over, Rocket pulled herself up and called the airline; she had to juggle with her credit cards before one was finally accepted and the ticket was booked. One further hassle out of the way, she made her way to the bathroom and showered. Betsy was no fan of hers, that was for sure, so what possible reason could there be for such a request? As she stood under the prickling jets of water Rocket searched unsuccessfully for an answer.

Feehan was almost as nervous as she was.

'I'll be frank. She's the toughest lady I've ever encountered. The only thing that gets to her is any mention of the kid, and how we might involve him in our investigations. Other than that, she's damn near inscrutable. Nothing fazes her, nothing changes her story.'

'I met her just the once, and that was enough,' Rocket said. 'But she's given no indication of why she wants to see me?'

'Zip. But she's insistent, and we're willing to try anything.'

'Tell me something. Do you think she did it?'

'Bottom line, yes. But I have serious doubts as to whether we'd ever be able to prove it. She is cold, colder than any bitch I've ever dealt with. We could put her on the stand and she'd mesmerise the jury. She is awesome, and I can't see any way to break her.'

'So what do you hope to get from this interview? What do you want me to ask her?'

'I don't think it's going to be like that. I think you're going in there to listen. She's got something on her mind and, for whatever reason, she figures you're the one she's going to tell it to. It might be nothing – but it might be everything. Just bite your lip and listen good.'

'Oh, I'm a good listener,' Rocket said. 'I've heard every story under the sun – and then some.'

'I'll be waiting for you.' Feehan smiled at her, and suddenly she realised that this was not a professional look of encouragement but something more personal. To herself she described the feeling as a twinkling, and she liked it.

'Wish me luck.' She got up and was led to the interview room by a burly woman in a tight uniform. She opened the door for Rocket, then remained outside as she closed and locked it.

Betsy was sitting at the table, her hands resting on it. She wore no make-up, and her hair was tied back severely. Her eyes were dry and clear and registered nothing at Rocket's entrance. Rocket sat down opposite her. The room was well insulated from external noise, the silence oppressive.

Betsy spoke without moving. 'I guess you're wondering why I asked to see you.'

'Correct. We didn't exactly hit it off at our last meeting.'

'That's neither here nor there. Personal feelings shouldn't be allowed to get in the way of what is going on at the moment. But I need to talk to you.'

'That's why I'm here.' Rocket tried to sound friendly, but it made no impact on Betsy.

'You know, of course, that they think I did it. Maybe you think the same. Either way, it doesn't matter. I didn't.'

'Is that what you wanted to tell me?'

'No. We'll get to that in a minute. First, though, I need to ask you some things.' Betsy sought no approval for this, but Rocket nodded in agreement anyway. 'Tell me, apart from you, who knew about us? Who did you tell?'

The questions unlocked a floodgate in Rocket's memory: she thought of Will and the way he had reacted to her news all those years ago in Manhattan. But she was uncertain about sharing this information, even though she had given it to the police. If Betsy didn't know, was she entitled to tell her? Rocket hesitated.

'You told the parents, didn't you?' Betsy said, still emotionless. 'I guessed as much. I knew when you came down to see us in Florida that you'd do it eventually. I told Chuck, but he never listened. I guess I can't blame you. But now you have to do something for me.'

263

'I'll try.'

'Before that, let's get one thing completely straight. I don't care who believes me. I don't care what they believe. I did not harm Chuck in any way. That's the truth. But there's more to it than that. I am facing a dilemma and I need to talk it through. You faced one too, remember?'

'I'll never forget it.'

'Good. Then you'll understand what I'm going through. That's why I asked to see you. When you came to us you could see that Ricky was happy and safe and well cared for. You knew that anything you did to undermine that would have an adverse effect on him, and I believe that you faced some agonies over that. Am I right?'

'Totally.'

'Well, maybe you made the wrong decision, maybe not. Anyway, we all have to live with the consequences of your actions, however you arrived at them. There's no point looking back. It won't change a thing. But tell me – how do you feel now? Are you still as sure as you were then that you made the right choice?'

'Betsy, I wasn't sure then, and time hasn't helped. If you only knew the sleep I've lost and the pain I've suffered, you'd realise that.'

'I can see that in your face. But what you've gone through is nothing compared to what I've endured. So hear me out. I'm not looking for absolution or approval. I just want you to know what I'm going through.'

'I'm listening.'

Betsy exhaled deeply. 'I haven't told the police the truth. And my reason for that is simple: Ricky must be protected from everything. He must not be allowed to suffer with the rest of us from those decisions you made. I love Ricky

264

more than anything else on God's planet, and I won't see him harmed if I can avoid it.'

'Even at the expense of your own liberty?'

'What liberty? They've got me locked up now, and they'll keep me locked up for his abduction. The sickness inside me will finish me off before I'm released, and anyway, what does my liberty matter if I can't be with Chuck and Ricky? What's the value of my life without them? There is no price that is not worth paying to keep Ricky away from all this.'

'So what haven't you told the police?'

'There are things I know and things I've done – bad things. I am wrestling with my conscience about them, and I've tried to find justification for my actions. I've been searching for understanding from God as much as His forgiveness. Your presence, and your continuing interest in the matter, may just be the salvation I'm looking for.'

'You didn't answer my question.'

'No I didn't. And I'm not ready to yet. For now, it's enough that you know – that you hear from me – that the truth is very different from what is being presented. I think you should be able to work out the rest from that. I'm certainly hoping that you can – not for my sake, but for Ricky's.'

They looked at each other for a long time then, as the effects of Betsy's admission seeped into them. Rocket was not sure that she could speak.

'Do you understand what I'm telling you?' Betsy asked eventually.

'I guess,' Rocket replied huskily. She understood everything and nothing; dazed by this revelation, she was totally clueless as to how to react. But she couldn't let this go now. 'This is unfair,' she said. 'You're simply transferring your problem on to me, and I don't need it. In fact, I refuse to accept it.'

'Too late, Miss Stubblefield. This is your second chance. You faced this once before and you failed the test. Now's your chance to put that right.'

'How? By listening to some half-boiled confession from you that adds up to nothing? What good will come of that?'

For the first time in their conversation Betsy's face changed. She smiled, not kindly and not with her eyes, but with her mouth turning up at the corners. Rocket recognised this as a vague and unusual effort.

'This is God's test for you. You've held the power before to shape the destiny of others' lives, and you were found wanting. Now you can try again, and see if you do any better.' Betsy folded her hands in front of her and waited for a response.

'Betsy, I don't play by the same rules as you. I think you have seriously misjudged me. I cannot – will not – subscribe to your beliefs. I'm not that strong. We seem to have diametrically opposed agendas in all this. I'm sorry, but if I'm being asked to take some test, I'll flunk it.'

'No you won't. And you're quite wrong about our motivations. We share much more than you allow. You want to see Ricky safe and sound, and so do I. Where's the difference? Now you know what I'm going through as a result of what you did. And you know what Ricky will go through if you make the same mistakes. So think of it this way: if you can grasp the importance of what I've told you, you'll be on the path of righteousness. But if

266

you can't, I don't need to remind you of the consequences for Ricky.'

'Why bother to tell me this? I don't get it. If you want me to suffer, I can promise you I already have and will continue to do so until my dying day. What's the point?'

'You harmed us. You tore us apart. But I'm not mad, and I don't want to get even. I just want you to be involved. It's better that way.'

'I didn't harm you!' Rocket shouted. 'You did it to yourself by taking him in the first place. You were bound to get caught sooner or later. I was merely an agent in that process, not a principal. Sure, I'm sorry about the grief you've had to go through, but I'm much sorrier for Ricky's real parents and Ricky himself. There's a limit to my sympathy, and you've overstepped it.'

Betsy was unmoved. 'Sleep on it, Miss Stubblefield. You might even try a bit of prayer. You'll feel differently in the morning, I promise you.'

Rocket steadied herself before speaking again. 'Betsy, I'd like to help you. Really I would. But this is one favour that's not in my power to bestow. I have a moral obligation to divulge what I know, and I intend to fulfil that.'

'No. Your moral obligation is to Ricky. Focus on that, and everything else will fall into place. Put your faith in the Lord and you'll be repaid.'

'Sorry, but you'll have to do better than that. Faith was never one of my strong points.'

'Then work on it, young lady. Nothing else matters.'

'And in the meantime?'

'You'll work it out. I don't think you'll make the same mistake twice. Now, if you'll excuse me, I need to get going.' It sounded so incongruous but, in the manner in which she said it, Betsy showed no sign that she saw this.

Rocket got up and knocked on the locked door. She looked at Betsy as she waited for the door to be opened; to Rocket, she seemed to be in a different world, driven by different motives from all those around her. Her certainty and serenity was, just as Brendan had said, awesome. Rocket was relieved when she was rescued.

Brendan was waiting for her when she reached the hall at the end of the corridor. 'Well?' he asked, palms open to show he was desperate for information.

'Where's the nearest bar?' she said. 'I need to get wrecked.'

TWENTY-NINE

That first night, when they had returned to their hotel after meeting Tom, was a time of postponement and evasion. Will lay on the bed whilst Clare showered; the few words they spoke to each other were brief and meaningless, and the thoughts they had were strangled by unexplained but recognised forces. Neither had the desire to illuminate the other's hopes and fears, and both took care to hide their faltering inner light. They faced a continuum of darkness without the courage to break it. Their weary agony had overcome a brief explosion of ecstasy, and they tried to guide their thoughts to safer territory.

Will was in a trance. He had proceeded through the rest of the day's interviews with increasing vacancy, his thoughts locked deep inside himself, and had answered questions with all the vigour of an android. Clare was hardly better, but dug her nails into her palms to make the blood flow and deliver stimulation to her brain. They had listened to long explanations of the process that would follow, and had nodded automatically at suitable points. Details of their domestic life, their financial situation and their family backgrounds were sought and given, inked on to five-part forms that were date-stamped, signed, subdivided and sent to unknown destinations. Some conversations were taped and labelled, others were merely noted on yellow legal pads. Interviewers were white, black, young, old, male and female; all were consistent in maintaining that Tom's best interests were at the heart of everything they did and would do in future.

The undertone, unspoken but plain, was clear to them: Tom would be theirs sooner or later, once they had battled through the maze of papers, processes, hearings and interviews. But to them it felt as if they were the offenders: the constant checking and rechecking of details, the validation of information already given and proven, seemed designed to put them on the defensive. One wrong answer, they thought, and all this would slip away from them as they were caught out by artful questioning techniques. By the end of the day they felt no nearer to Tom, and their threadbare confidence had long since ebbed away.

They tried to defy that night: they left the lights on and stayed dressed, unwilling to yield to the unknown images that would materialise as they tossed and turned. Clare turned one hundred pages of a book without reading a single word, whilst Will flicked from channel to channel on the muted television. Just before dawn Clare threw down her book and wept. It was a quiet, private moment of despair, and Will watched her without the means to share it or offer any consolation. There was nothing he could do or say; in her solitary grief he saw his own vulnerability but was unable to conform with it or provide mitigation. She sat for a long time with her head bowed, tears softly dropping on to her lap. Outside a drizzle of rain reflected her feelings.

Later, with a grey light breaking through the window, Clare called Marla. They had kept up a sporadic correspondence, and had always spoken at Thanksgiving and Christmas. Marla's letters were laced with an implicit, resigned sadness; Clare responded with breeziness and an optimistic tone, never lingering on the past but preferring to catalogue current affairs.

Marla's immediate reaction to Clare's news was an offer to come to Chicago; and Clare knew that she needed another friend who could supply a different perspective, however flawed and uninformed it might be. Will's closeness to her own feelings was unintentionally suffocating, preventing her from expelling the vast reservoir of emotion that seeing Tom had created. Marla might give her the chance to breathe again, and Clare wanted to take it. They had nothing much to say to each other on the phone: their tacit agreement was to save themselves for when they met, and Marla promised to jump on a plane and get there as soon as she could.

'Was that a good idea?' Will asked when she'd hung up.

'I think so. What I want is someone to talk to. I know I've got you, but it's different. We're too wound up in everything that's going on, and we know too much about each other. Can you understand that?'

'Not really. I certainly don't feel the need to go and pour my heart out to anyone else. You're the only person whose opinion matters to me. I'm surprised you don't feel the same.' Will was not angry as he said this; exhaustion had drawn all venom from him. But Clare was anxious to keep him calm.

'Will, of course I feel like you do. And of course I value

271

your opinion more than anyone else's. But I just want to see Marla. I think it would lighten the load. There's nothing sinister in that, is there?'

'It's your call. Just don't expect me to be wild about the idea, that's all. We need to stay completely focused on events, and I don't want her diverting your attention.'

'She won't, I promise.' Will's anguish, she felt, was verging on the selfish; it was as if he took some pride from carrying this burden unassisted, and resented the idea that anyone else could offer help, or that he might need it. The intensity of his vision, and the way in which he was trying to enclose the family in an impenetrable force field of his own making, was having a perverse effect on Clare: she needed someone else to shine a beam on to their lives and break through the barriers he was creating.

'Do you want to talk to me?' she asked him.

'Not especially. I know exactly what you're thinking, and vice versa. Spelling it out won't change a thing.'

'I'm not sure I know what you're thinking. In fact, I'm a little frightened to ask, just in case I don't like what I hear. But it might help.'

'Well, if you must know, the overwhelming thought is frustration. Here we are, minutes away from him, and we can't do a thing about it. Seeing him has just magnified that a thousand times. And I don't like being made to feel as if we're on trial. All that stuff about Ralph and India really made my blood boil. It's none of their business how much I earn or where India goes to school. Tom is ours and I want him back.'

'They're doing their job, Will. I'm as frustrated as you, but I do believe them when they say they've got his best interests at heart. And this is all very temporary. It seems

272

like an age, but it'll be gone before we know it.'

Although he had no answer to this, Clare knew that he didn't really agree with her. Will's world was now black and white, right and wrong, have and have not. The grey areas in between were unseen through his eyes; but this served to give her strength. If he had been the old Will, willing to be pushed in any direction by the current of events, she doubted that she'd have had the stomach for what lay ahead. By defining the parameters of their life so acutely, Will was helping her through her own considerable doubts. Sometimes she missed his relaxed approach; but now, faced with such a daunting challenge, she was glad he was so committed.

'I love you, Will,' she said quietly.

'That's good, because I love you too.' It was a simple, time-honoured exchange, but it swept away a layer of despair.

Tom sat on his bed. His hands were unoccupied, resting limply on his thighs, and he gazed at nothing in particular. Ellen sat with him, a space between them in recognition of his little friend.

'You don't need to feel bad, you know,' she said. 'No one said it was going to be easy.' He said and did nothing. 'Listen, soldier, do you want a hug?' He shrugged, so she got up and went to crouch in front of him. She placed her hands on his knees. 'Come on, let's have a little cuddle. No one's looking.' He moved forward timidly, then threw his arms around her neck. She knew he would cry, and she knew she had to stop herself. At first he sniffed; then he sobbed and pushed his face deeper into her flesh. She could feel the hot moisture of his fresh tears on her skin.

'I want to go home.'

'I know, and we're working on it, we truly are. Just a little longer, that's all.'

'Are they going to take me away?'

'What do you think? Would you like that?'

'I don't know. I guess . . . I guess it'd be OK, wouldn't it?'

'It'd be fine, if that's what you want to do. They love you so much, and they'd look after you so well, I promise.'

He pulled back and looked at her through puffy eyes, his face smeared. 'Can I see my mom? I mean, ever?'

'Who knows, Ricky? Right now, your mom has a lot of problems that she's dealing with. But she's thinking of you all the time, I bet. And I know she wants you to be happy. If we asked her, she'd probably say that you should go with them, because she can't look after you now the way she wants to.'

'Can we ask her?'

Ellen was stumped. She had no idea of how to proceed: letting him see Betsy might work as a final release, but it might complicate everything. No manual, no training, could advise her now.

'We'll see.'

'You always say that, and nothing ever happens. Why can't I see my mom, just for a little while?'

'Tell you what I'll do. I have to go and talk to some other folks, see what they think. I promise I'll do that today, then I'll come back and tell you. Is that a deal?'

He nodded; then relapsed into stillness. She had painted herself into a corner and she knew it. Nothing would appease him until this was resolved, and she would be the facilitator. Another difficult day lay ahead, and Ellen sighed deeply at the prospect.

Brendan was good in bed: not the best, but more than adequate for her purposes. Rocket sat on the edge of the bath, the door locked and the light off, and slowly smoked a cigarette. He was sleeping soundly, and his peace disturbed her. This was aggravated by the dryness in her mouth and the first signs of a hangover. They had drunk too much, eaten too little, and rampaged across the bed in various positions until he finally collapsed. She couldn't remember exactly what she had told him about her meeting with Betsy, but she was pretty sure she'd been discreet; she had certainly decided that he need not know the main reason for Betsy asking to see her, and had fluffed her way through some poor lies that she hoped had put him off the trail.

She was nowhere near to reaching a conclusion about what to do next. She didn't even know what the options were. Through the beginnings of a pounding headache she made a feeble attempt to justify various alternatives, all of them seeming to place her in an impossible situation. As she dropped her cigarette into the lavatory bowl and listened to the short hiss as it expired, she felt envious of Betsy. The woman had manufactured an impregnable security out of impossible circumstances, driven by a faith that rose above all rational consideration. Rocket wanted some of that, too, but couldn't find it – and didn't know where to start looking.

It was masterful of Betsy to have dropped this conundrum so squarely into Rocket's lap. Like a well-aimed, laser-guided bomb it was destined to explode in her hands unless she could find a way to defuse it. The

275

simplest action, to tell Brendan and hang the consequences, was totally unappealing. Rocket couldn't initiate a fresh line of inquiry that would undoubtedly involve Tom and might also draw in Will and Clare. Having sparked off the chain of events that had led to Chuck Callahan's death and, ultimately, Tom's discovery, Rocket was in no mood to kick off another round of misery and destruction.

But the other choices were even starker. If she were to say nothing of Betsy's confession, she faced the prospect of a life haunted by the knowledge that loose ends, important strands, had been left to dangle. She continued in her belief that Betsy was innocent; but if that were so, someone else killed Chuck. She pushed the thoughts away before they had enough time to crystallise and torment her. So what? She wanted to use this as her credo: did it really matter to her that one life was lost and another shattered? These people meant nothing to her, and Betsy's fortunes were of academic interest only. Surely she could live with this little discretion, and time would erode its sharp edges?

She knew this was not going to work. Rocket's code might be based on pragmatism, but even in her most flexible moments she couldn't accept that she might stand aside and let such a major injustice go unpunished. So she edged towards compromise; if she were to be at the vanguard of truth – a concept she found rather strange, given the amount of deception she practised each day – then she should pursue the facts on her own. Until she possessed them, and was sure they told the whole story, there was nothing else to be done. She tried to convince herself that all she had were suppositions and theories, that nothing mattered until she had final verification. So much the better if the cops followed her lead and reached the same target.

In the dark bathroom she gained some temporary comfort, but she knew that even the act of returning to bed would reignite all the old uncertainties. She lit another cigarette and thought of Will. He was back at the front of her mind, and all her choices somehow centred on him. Whatever he did, had done and might do, she knew that he was the keystone. She shivered in the chilling anticipation of what that meant.

THIRTY

Michael Medlinger was universally known as Albert. His thick white hair stood up at unbelievable angles, whilst his moustache swooped over his mouth in a luxuriant curve, but his physical similarities to Einstein were as nothing compared to the mental gifts he possessed. Everything he came into contact with became a source of fascination to him, motivating obsessive learning and the acquisition of further knowledge. He had developed complex software programs for the Child Psychology Unit; he had fixed numerous social workers' cars in the parking lot; and he had often brought divine creations from his kitchen to the office.

Unfortunately, many basic social skills had passed him by. His familiarity with the daily regimen of ablutions was fleeting, and his rudeness was legendary; he wore no watch and frequently missed meetings, rarely remembering names and faces without blunt prompting. He inhabited a world that was largely removed from the one in which he operated, and his understanding of custom and convention had led to him being sidelined in the great promotions race. He languished, apparently unconcerned, in an advisory capacity, called upon for his opinions but rarely asked for practical intervention with clients. He spent large parts of his day on a thesis he was writing, the manuscript stored in random bundles scattered across his stifling office.

Albert was thirty-nine; his hair had turned white when he was twenty-two, and he had always given the impression of wisdom gained through longevity. Intimidating and impatient, few had the strength of will to visit him unannounced. But Ellen needed his advice and, knowing that arranging a meeting would prove fruitless, she floated into his office on the off chance that he would be there.

He was sitting at his PC, which was placed squarely in the middle of his desk. From the door Ellen could see the halo of white hair above the monitor; she caught the pungent tang in the air, a combination of sweat, stale food and fossilising dust. She cleared her throat to no effect: he continued to rattle the keys of his computer, his face close to the screen.

'Michael?' she said, somewhat apologetically. One eye appeared at the side of the monitor. It scanned her from top to toe, then moved back behind the computer. 'Hi. I'm Ellen – remember, we met at the Itasca conference?' The keyboard fell silent; then he pushed himself away from the desk and looked at her again, no sign of recognition in his face.

'Yeah?' He sounded bored rather than annoyed by this interruption.

'I need your help.' She moved forward and put her hands on the back of a visitor's chair in front of his desk.

'Join the queue.'

'I don't see one.'

'That's not my problem, lady.'

280

'The name's Ellen, and I need some of your time now. Please?'

'Sit.'

'Thanks. Do you know anything about the Ricky Callahan case – you know, the kid who was abducted?'

'What do I need to know?'

'He lived with his abductors for more than four years, having been taken when he was three. We've now located his natural parents, and we'll be handing him back to them shortly. The man involved in the abduction was killed unlawfully, and his wife is now a suspect in the investigation and is in police custody. The boy has requested that he see this woman – whom he naturally thinks of as his mother – and I need to know whether this is a good idea.'

'For this you need my opinion? You don't have one of your own?'

'Yes, but I'm not sure it's the right one.'

He stretched out his legs and lay back in his chair. He pulled his top lip down so that the moustache completely covered his mouth. Then he smacked his lips.

'On the basis of your thirty-second analysis, I'd say there's no right opinion. I certainly don't have one. It's a moral choice, isn't it, and I don't deal with them. If the kid has some residual attachment to this woman, you could make things better or worse by letting him say goodbye. But, as long as he's given the proper support once he returns to his natural family, I'd say it won't make a whole heap of difference either way. You will, of course, have already considered any legal implications.'

'Such as?'

'If he subsequently refuses to go with his natural parents

– as is his right – then they could possibly sue you. They could claim you took a step which was contrary to his best interests, especially as this woman is the subject of a murder inquiry.'

Ellen had considered this. 'What if I asked their permission first?'

Albert puffed loudly. 'You've got balls of brass, obviously. I know what I would say in their situation.'

'Would it help if I gave you the file to read?'

'Impossible. One – I have no interest. Two – I'm far too busy. And three – I'm not going to make your decisions for you. If you want me to evaluate the child I'll be happy to do so – in about a month's time. Otherwise it sounds as if you're on your own with this one.' He was already pushing on his heels back towards the PC, and Ellen knew he had lost all interest.

'Well, thanks for your help. I really appreciate it.'

'The pleasure's all mine,' he said as he started tapping the keyboard again.

Marla was as good as her word. She arrived at the hotel at lunchtime; Clare told the front desk where she would be and they went to the bar. Will met Marla, kissed her and said he'd catch her later.

'Is everything OK?' Marla asked, nodding towards him as she watched Will walk across the lobby.

'Strained,' Clare said. 'He's a different person. This whole affair has changed him out of all recognition.'

'And you?'

'I'm trying to keep pace with him. He's driven nowadays, not the old Will you knew at all. He's so intense. It can be very frightening.'

'So tell me everything. My God, it's so good to see you guys.'

'And you, Marla. I've missed you, more than you'll ever know. That's been one of the worst things, I suppose – not having anyone to talk to. After my mother died I really had no one. I didn't realise how important she was until it was too late.'

'That's always the way. But what about Will? Don't you talk?'

'Yes, but not in the way I need. He's too close to everything, and he has no idea of the way I feel.'

'Haven't you told him?'

'It's not quite that simple. It seems strange to say this, but I'm really torn apart by Tom coming back. I know we should have him back, and I desperately want him, too, but I can't help feeling that it isn't quite as simple as that. I think it's the old conundrum of whether the heart or the head rules. From what I can gather – and that isn't much – Tom was very well looked after, and was a happy little boy. It hurts like hell to accept that but, if I do, it makes me wonder what we'll do to him once he's back with us. Four years is a long time. It'll be like having a complete stranger in the house, and God knows what it'll do to India. Will doesn't have these doubts. To him, it's an open and shut case. Tom is ours, we're having him back. End of discussion. I feel pathetic even thinking the way I do, and I'm not about to undermine his confidence or show weakness on my part by discussing it with him.'

'It doesn't sound like weakness to me,' Marla said. 'It sounds like common sense. Tom's bound to have problems readjusting, and you're totally right to be concerned. But having those concerns doesn't diminish your love for him, or make you any less committed.'

'I know that. I tell myself exactly the same thing a hundred times a day. But it's better coming from someone else.'

'That's what I'm here for. I've always been a good shoulder to cry on.' Marla grinned at Clare.

'I'm sorry. I didn't mean it to sound like that,' Clare said. 'It's just . . . well, we're so close to having him back now and I feel I should be more uplifted by the whole affair. But I can't shake off this nagging feeling that we're going to change Tom in some way, and that we have to be very careful to make sure it isn't irreparable. I've never said this to anyone before, and I can hardly admit it to myself, but sometimes I think it might have been better if he hadn't been found. So much water's passed under the bridge, and I don't know where to start. Tell me I'm being stupid.'

'You have every right to be confused, and nobody would condemn you for that. But hey, you're forgetting some very important facts. You love Tom – and he loved you. You and Will are model parents in my book. No one could do more for their children. I remember something you told me once about Tom. You said that when he was born you were really shocked by the fact that there wasn't a natural bond between you immediately. All he seemed to do was keep you up all night and cry a lot. You had to work at it before you really loved him. But it happened – and it'll happen again, only this time you've got the benefit of experience. It doesn't seem to me to be so different. No one prepares you for the horrors of having your first kid, and you told me you were constantly worried in case you screwed up. Well, now it's happening all over again –

and I'll bet you deal with it just as well as you did before. But listen to me: the only expert on motherhood who's never had kids!'

'Speaking of which – any news on that front?'

'Well, there is a complication,' Marla sighed. 'Jay's moved out. It's kind of hard to conceive when there's no male member available.'

'Oh, Marla, I am so sorry. When did this happen?'

'A while back. I can give you the time to the nearest minute if you'd like.'

'Why didn't you say anything?'

'What's to say? And anyway, with everything that's going on in your life, it seemed pretty trivial by comparison. Don't worry about me, I'll survive. He's still paying all the bills.'

'What will you do?'

'I fancy the idea of a toy boy, but there are no takers yet. Seriously though, I haven't given it much thought. I sit and cry from time to time. The stupid thing is, part of me wants him back. I guess I just miss the tension. It was thrilling, in a perverted kind of way. Now everything's the same: no fights, no excitement.'

'Whose decision was it?'

'Mutual. He whacked me pretty hard one night, I think out of boredom more than anything else. But I decided I'd had enough of that, so I locked the bedroom door and the next morning we agreed that it was time for a break. I haven't seen him since. He calls, whines down the phone and tells me he still loves me, but I'm being pretty tough and I can't see us getting back together in a hurry.'

'I had no idea.'

'Yeah, I got pretty good at hiding the marks, and he'd got pretty good at hitting me where it wouldn't show. Can you imagine if we'd had kids? It makes me shiver just thinking about it.'

'If it's any consolation, Will went through a very strange period. I mean, he wasn't overtly violent but there was always the threat. He's back on the straight and narrow now, thank God. It was getting to the stage where I was really glad when he was out. I never knew what sort of mood he'd be in, and that was the worst thing.'

'At least with Jay I could guarantee he'd always be pissed about something I'd done or hadn't done. In that respect he was totally consistent: you always knew where you stood with him. Problem was, you didn't want to be standing there.'

'What a life!' Clare said, lifting her glass and drinking. 'Here's to it, and all the men in it.' They drank a toast together and relaxed a little more.

'But you say Will is OK now?' Marla asked.

'He's wound up, naturally, but he seems to have found some new equilibrium. He's even told me a couple of times, completely unprompted, that he loves me and can't live without me, and that is – or was – totally out of character. His main problem was that he couldn't grieve, and he carried round this burden of guilt like some cross. But something happened, I'm not sure what, and he snapped out of it.'

'Dare I ask about sex?' They both giggled girlishly.

'Twelve months ago he had all the sex drive of a king penguin. But now it's much better. I think we're getting rather good at it.'

'Keep practising, that's my advice. Although I'm not

exactly following it myself. I'm afraid it'll heal up if it isn't attended to soon.'

After more laughter and drink Clare leant forward. 'You know, I haven't laughed for a long time. There's not been much to laugh about. You cannot imagine how therapeutic it is. I didn't realise how much I've missed that.'

'You and me both. Look, what are you doing this afternoon? What do you say we have a few more drinks, go and shop till we drop then find a health club to get a sauna and massage, preferably from some hunky male with bulging pecs?'

'I'd like to, but I'm really on stand-by. The social workers could call at any time. I can't really get away.'

'No problem. I've got a mobile phone, and we won't go far. Let's do it.'

Clare drained her glass, put her head on one side and then threw her hands in the air. 'Why the hell not?' she said. 'Life's too short.'

'Good girl. You deserve it, babe. Come to that, so do I.'

THIRTY-ONE

Ellen's stomach churned dangerously as it threatened to reject her breakfast. In the company of Tom she needed to remain calm and unflustered; she knew that he was already anxious enough for both of them, having spent half an hour locked in the lavatory and another twenty minutes deciding on his clothes and brushing and re-brushing his hair. 'Mom will want me to look smart,' he said.

They walked together down the long, dark, institutional corridor towards the secure interview room, holding hands tightly as they harboured their secret thoughts. As they reached the room a policewoman greeted them with a grunt: there was widespread disapproval of Ellen's decision within the station, although there was little they could do to stall it. At a brief court hearing it had finally been agreed that there were no further hurdles to clear: Tom was now in the custody of his natural parents. For reasons that she couldn't really explain, even to herself, Ellen had requested a further twenty-four hours in which to prepare Tom for his transfer and this had been granted. In part this was a selfish request: she was genuinely sad to be losing Tom. But she also wanted him to have an ordered and dignified separation from Betsy; she didn't want him to remember her drawing away in the back of a police car, handcuffed to an officer, with tears in her eyes.

The door was unlocked and Ellen went through it. She had arranged for Betsy to receive some of her own clothes, and she looked prim and neat. She had obviously made a special effort, applying a little make-up, her hair trimmed and washed; to the casual observer she would pass for an innocent, God-fearing woman which, Ellen thought, was exactly how she perceived herself. Betsy's expression, which had been flat when Ellen came in, was transformed when she saw Tom. A special, magical light illuminated her whole face, and years of anguish fell away as she smiled lovingly at her little boy. She got up from the table and walked round to Tom: he rushed to her and hugged her tightly around her thighs. They stayed like this for an eternity whilst Ellen looked on, unable to suppress the lump in her throat.

'Fifteen minutes, OK?' she croaked. Expecting and getting no response, she withdrew and locked the door from the outside.

'Here, come and sit on my lap,' Betsy said as she moved towards the chair. Tom was crying and she needed to hold him against her body. They sat down, Tom curling into her as she put a protective hand around his head. She rocked slowly on the chair and made little clucking noises. 'Now, what's all this about? You don't want to cry, do you?' She wiped the tears from his face with her hand.

'Sorry,' Tom said into her breast.

'So how have they been treating you? Are you eating properly? You feel a little skinny to me. Hey, I can almost feel your ribs.'

'Mom, what's going to happen?' He looked up at her, his dark eyes deliquescent.

'Well, chicken, I guess they've told you that we have to say goodbye for now. You remember I told you that Chuck and I were only looking after you for a while, just until your real mom and pop could come back. Well, now they're here.'

'But I don't want to go with them. I want to stay with you.'

'I know you do, sweetie, but we've all got to be strong. If it's God's will, then we must obey it. You know that. But we'll never forget each other, will we? We'll always remember all the happy times we've had, and when we're feeling really low, just like you are now, we'll think about them and that'll cheer us up. What do you think? I know. Let's play a game. Let's try and think of the best time we ever had. You go first.'

He thought about this as he sniffed away his misery. 'When we went to the zoo, you know? When we saw all the lions and tigers and monkeys, and you bought me cotton candy and popcorn and I got sick in the car. That was the best.'

'That was great, wasn't it?'

'Yeah,' he said dreamily. Then he started to cry again. 'Mom, why do I have to go? Couldn't I stay with you?'

'If it was in my power, I'd let you, of course I would. But these folks have decided that you can't, and we have to live with that.'

'Will you come and see me sometimes?'

'I'd like that, really I would. Maybe one day, when everything's settled down, I can do that. For now though, I want you to be very brave and very good for me. I want

291

you to say to yourself: I can do this, and I will do this. Will you do that for me?'

'I'll try.'

'Good for you. Listen, I have a little something for you. Do you want to see what it is?' He was mildly interested, and she reached into her bag and pulled out a huge bar of Hershey's chocolate. He took it and turned it over and over, as if he'd never seen one before. 'It's your favourite, right?'

'Thanks, Mom.' He held it loosely and rested his head against her once more.

'I think the best time we had was when we went on that vacation. Do you remember that, when we went to Jamaica and stayed in that huge hotel and there were all those pools and lots of things for you to do? That was neat, wasn't it?'

'I only remember I bumped my head.'

'That's right. We were so worried about you. But the next morning you were right as rain and back swimming and running around.' Her throat tightened as she recalled the anxiety and guilt Chuck and she had felt, and how they had sat with him all night and stroked his head. He had slipped and fallen and seemed a little concussed; he had turned pale and vomited all over Chuck as he held him. Betsy could instantly recall every bump and bruise, every graze and cut, every cough and sniffle in his small life with them. She shared every pain and ache he had suffered and still flinched when she thought of them.

Then they were silent, both knowing that a chapter was closing and soon they would only have memories of each other, never to be refreshed by new experience. For Betsy it was similar to amputation, as if a part of her were being removed and she could never replace it. In response she hugged him even tighter, pulling him in so that she could feel his warmth through her blouse and hoping that this closeness would stay with them for ever.

'They want to call me Tom.'

'I know. But it's not such a big deal, is it? What's a name, after all? You know who you are, and so do I. You'll always be Ricky to me.'

'I like being Ricky.'

'And you'll like being Tom, too, I shouldn't wonder. You'll get used to it. And when you're on your own, you can be whoever you like. It can be your little secret, and you never need tell anyone. Only you and I will know.'

'OK.' He nodded. 'I won't tell if you don't.'

'It's a deal.' They fell silent again. Betsy tried to think of nothing and savour this moment of peace and oneness. She wanted to brand him with her ownership, and their quiet, intense embrace was the best way she knew how. She closed her eyes to banish temporal thought; this was a spiritual moment, where their separate lives conjoined and were blessed. She prayed silently and fiercely for courage, for him and her. When she was done, she shook herself back into consciousness and looked down at him.

'Listen. That lady's going to come back in a moment, and this is what we're going to do. We're going to be very brave and we're not going to cry. I'm going to give you a hug and a kiss, then I'm going to turn and face the wall and you're going to walk out that door like a big man and not look back. God will be watching us to make sure we do it right, and He'll get mad if we don't. You have to promise me you'll do that. It's very important, OK?'

'But I might be a bit sad. What do I do then?'

'You squeeze your fists tight and you keep on walking, all the way down the hall and out of here. I'll be thinking of you, and God will be right next to you, even if you can't see Him. Is that a deal?'

'I guess.'

'I've got one last thing to tell you. I know we've never talked about this before, but I know it's been on your mind. You must never, ever tell anyone what happened that day when Chuck hurt his head.'

'But what if someone asks me?'

'You've just to say you've gotten confused because it all happened a long time ago and you were very young. If anyone ever asks you, you just tell them that.'

'But you told me never to tell a lie. You told me you'd whack me good if I did.'

'I know, and this is hard for you to understand because you're only a child and it's all very complicated. But I'm asking you to do this for me, and I promise no harm will come to you if you do as I say. It's so important to me, and I need your help. Will you help me?'

'Sure, Mom. I can keep a secret.'

'I know you can. So let's take a vow that we won't say a word, as God is our witness.'

'OK.'

And then the door opened, and Ellen put her head round it. Betsy stuck to their agreement, despite the implosion she felt inside her. She hugged him, kissed him on both cheeks, tucked the chocolate into his hand and then gently slipped him off her lap. She got up and slowly turned away so that she had her back to him. He lingered by her legs and she could feel his nearness, but she stayed very still and stared at the brickwork as it shimmered and danced in front of her eyes. Ellen was momentarily transfixed until she realised what was happening. She walked over to Tom and took his limp hand; but then he snatched it away from her and turned abruptly on his heel and walked swiftly to the door, breaking into a run as he made it into the corridor. Ellen followed him, a small, lonely figure running hard in a vain attempt to escape from something he would never understand.

PART V

PART THREE

THIRTY-TWO

'Why don't you just fuck off out of my fucking room, you fucking bastard?'

Clare's patience had finally been stretched beyond its natural tolerance and, in spite of her best efforts, she exploded. She advanced on Tom and grabbed him by the shoulders.

'Listen to me, young man,' she shouted into his face. 'You will not talk to me like that, do you hear? Now you'll stay in your room until I say you can come out. And when you do, you'll apologise to me and India.' She pushed him back towards his bed and turned to leave.

'Good,' he cried at her back. 'I don't want to see any of you bastards ever again.' She slammed the door behind her and leant against the wall, listening as Tom continued to hurl volleys of abuse at her. Her face was flushed and she breathed heavily from the exertion of their latest fight, knowing that there was likely to be another one waiting for her when she went to the kitchen.

Week six, and things were getting worse. Clare was not sure which was more wearing: the running war with Tom, which he seemed to be winning, or the skirmishes with Will which resulted from these continual confrontations. At first Tom had been shy, reserved and generally well mannered. He had spent long periods in his room with crayons and paper supplied by Ralph, and came out for meals and other routine activities. He had shown no interest in India, behaving as if she were some alien to whom he needed to give a wide berth. With Will and Clare he had transacted the minimum of conversation, limiting himself to grunts, occasional short sentences and reluctant replies to direct questions. They had taken him out – to the zoo, the cinema, museums and cafés – but he had reacted to everything with the same dead expression. At nights Clare lay awake with all the hopelessness and fear of a new mother; sometimes she could hear him crying and she would go into his room, but he would bury his face in his pillow and spurn her consoling efforts.

The change had occurred when he had found India in his room. She was looking at some of his drawings and he went berserk. He threw her on to the floor and kicked her in the back as she tried to roll away. He had jumped on top of her and scratched her face, drawing blood before running into her room, pulling posters off the wall and shredding books in his fury. Clare had caught him and had held him as tightly as she could as he squirmed and cursed, dragging him back to his room flailing and kicking. They had sat on the bed and she had rocked him until the anger subsided; but from that moment on he was intent on inflicting pain on India at every opportunity. He saw favouritism in everything they did, imagining slights and punishing her for them.

Through all of this Ralph remained an oasis of tranquillity, and Tom was drawn to it. He would go to Ralph's room after a tantrum and they would sit together and study books of art, drawings and paintings that Tom didn't understand but still appreciated. In Ralph's presence Tom acquired an unusual state of grace; he would volunteer his opinion on various pictures, commenting on the scene and the colouring, and Ralph would draw little cartoons for him. Tom was only happy if Ralph accompanied them all on sorties outside the flat, and would beg to be left behind to keep him company should Ralph decide not to go out.

Clare was grateful for any diversion from Tom's wayward moods, and she made great efforts to encourage the friendship he was building with Ralph. She felt that the companionship they offered each other was mutually beneficial, with Ralph taking just as much as he gave. Tom's arrival had seen a great improvement in his mental state: whilst he could still lose touch with reality at a moment's notice, Ralph was more frequently with it, quietly coherent without any noticeable change in his routines or customs. Tom's interest in art had rekindled his own, and he had started to draw occasionally, showing Tom how to use a brush or charcoal or chalks and discussing the merits of various papers and canvas.

Ralph's intervention was not well taken by Will. He wanted to treat Tom like a fragile, rare butterfly, newly emerged from its cocoon, and told Clare that this association with Ralph was unhealthy. Will's relationship with Ralph, which had been decaying before Tom's arrival, was now at an impasse, but Ralph was oblivious to Will's open hostility. In Ralph, Will saw an unnecessary distraction from the task at hand, fearing that his wayward moods and solitary habits would merely encourage Tom to delay assimilation.

The list of topics on which Clare and Will would

disagree was growing daily: schools, clothing, diet and bedtime all became areas over which they wrangled, but their biggest and most intractable war was over discipline. At first it wasn't an issue, as Tom required no guidance on behaviour but, after he had attacked India, Clare began to impose her own code. She was determined to act in an even-handed way, punishing where necessary and trying to show India that there were no special dispensations for Tom. Will could not have been more different: when Tom had spent an afternoon in Will's office, scribbling on papers and reconfiguring the computer, he had received no harsh words from his father. Will had merely shrugged and spent the evening repairing the damage. Will's frustration, when it broke, was reserved for India and Clare. For India to be in the same room as Tom was reason enough for Will to blow his top, blaming her for teasing and inciting him; when Clare tried to intervene, she was accused of undermining Will's authority.

Clare was trapped, caught between conflicts that she couldn't hope to reconcile. In the evenings, when Tom was finally settled, she would stay in the kitchen and clatter pots and pans, listening to the radio as Will and Ralph stared at the television. Hunched over the sink, she would cry as she struggled to come to terms with what faced her. She had known that life would not be easy; when Tom was sleeping on the plane, with his head resting on her lap, she had studied his little features and had imagined all the trouble he might bring with him, but she had never questioned the single purpose and approach she thought she shared with Will. She had never felt the need to talk to Will about what lay ahead, secure in the knowledge that, with his new-found strength and resolution, he would tackle all problems with balance and clarity.

In the few moments when she found herself alone with India she would try to explain, conscious of the need to support Will and yet anxious to allay India's understandable unhappiness. Their conversations often revolved around Will; India seemed reticent to discuss Tom, as if she knew that this was a subject that would inflame her mother and might lead to further misery. Clare would tell her how much they all loved her, and how everyone needed time to settle down. India would listen, feigning comprehension so that she could avoid admission of deeper worries.

Clare now walked towards the kitchen as the noise from Tom's room abated. As she had known he would be, Will was standing there, bristling with fury. She raised her eyebrows and resolved to defuse the row before it had a chance to start.

'Oh God,' she said, 'I just want to fast-forward life. Let's skip the next five years, shall we?'

If she had hoped to disarm him she had failed. 'What the bloody hell was all that about?' he snarled.

'Just another tantrum. I'm sorry – I lost it with him, but he'd really been trying my patience.'

'He must have committed murder, the way you laid into him,' Will replied, no calmer yet.

'Close. He was sitting on India with his knees on her arms. She was screaming, which I suppose you didn't hear, and was in agony. When I came in he flew at me. You heard his language. I'm not prepared to put up with that, and he's got to learn.'

'Everything's his fault, isn't it? There's never any doubt in your mind. It must be so fantastic to know immediately who's innocent and who's guilty. I wish I had some of that.'

His sarcasm was bitter and Clare's anger rose to meet it. 'What do you mean? Tom bullies her all day long, and then you expect me to do nothing about it – is that it? He can be a little shit, and I don't see why we're not supposed to punish him when he is. What's your solution?'

'You don't get it, do you? You think that Tom just has to slot into our lives and make all the adjustments himself. Have you any idea what it must be like for him? He's been starved of love for God knows how long, then he comes home to find that he's constantly berated for everything he does. No wonder he's got problems.'

Cold reason long departed, Clare could not suppress her frustration. 'And what's going to happen if we keep on condoning his behaviour? He's just going to get worse. He's making our lives a misery as it is, and I'm not prepared to allow us all to cave in and let him win.'

'Win?' Will shouted. 'Is that what you think it is, some pissing contest where there are winners and losers? Jesus, you astonish me, you really do. How can you even think that? He's going through a major crisis, and all you can do is call him a little shit. I wonder what your so-called child experts would have to say about that.'

She could see now that Will was ready to hit out: his face was contorted with rage and he was shaking. She put her palms up to demonstrate remorse. 'OK, that was out of order. I'm so tired of all this, and I'm not thinking straight. But he really got to me tonight, and I just couldn't handle it. I'd like some support, that's all. I need you with me, Will. Fighting isn't going to help.'

'And I can only support you if it's mutual. That's what you don't seem to understand. Everything I do is wrong in your eyes, and that's so bloody unfair. India thinks I'm some kind of ogre because of you. You're constantly jumping in to defend her, without knowing the circumstances. What support do you give me?'

'You couldn't be more wrong. India loves you, and I'm always defending you to her. I am so careful about that, but you haven't even bothered to think it through. You've got a blind spot about her – and Tom. You can't even see what's going on.'

This was the moment when he would either capitulate or explode. Clare's muscles tensed involuntarily as she braced herself for whatever happened next. Will breathed heavily and erratically, speech temporarily deserting him as he worked out how to react.

'Fine,' he said at last. 'So, once again, I'm in the wrong. How does it feel to be so bloody perfect? I tell you what, why don't we agree now that you take complete control, seeing as how you appear to have the answers to everything?' Although he said this calmly, he suddenly lurched towards her and she jumped back to the door, pulling her arms up against her torso. But he stopped short of her and merely pushed his face close to hers. 'Is that what you want? Well?' Then he jerked back and pushed her roughly aside as he moved through the doorway to the hall.

'No, Will, you can't run away from this. That's totally unfair. We have to sort this out.'

'There's nothing to sort out. You've already done that, haven't you?' He stormed into his study and slammed the door. Clare remained slumped against the jamb, her heart racing as her eyes watered. When she turned to look into the hall, India was standing there sobbing. 'Mummy?' she cried, and ran to hug Clare's legs.

THIRTY-THREE

'I'm going to die.'

Betsy's voice was weak; tubes ran into her nostrils and another was plugged into her arm. She was attached to a battery of monitors which flickered and bleeped, tracking her relentless decline. Rocket sat on a chair that was squeezed between all this hardware; although she could hear Betsy's frailty, she had no doubt that the iron will was still present, undetected by the technology but prevalent none the less. She felt unable to rebut the claim.

'Is that what the doctors say?'

'What do doctors always say? They try to give you hope when there's none to be had. I have cancer. It's been inside me for years, and now I'm letting it win. It's God's will. I'm ready.' Her breath came in short, rasping bursts; her body seemed already drained of vital signs, and lay in the bed like a living corpse.

'Thanks for seeing me,' Rocket said, trying to avoid a philosophical discourse.

'I thought you might come. It seems right.'

'I don't know exactly how to begin.'

'At the beginning. Where it all began in your mind. That's as good a place as any.' Her voice was softened by the pain and exhaustion of illness, but Betsy retained her level composure. Even in death, Rocket thought, she was unshakeable.

'I thought of everything you said. And I thought about everything I knew. When I added it all up, it didn't make any sense. So I reckoned you might be able to help me a little more, if you're feeling up to it.'

'What is it you want — forgiveness, or guidance? I'm afraid neither is really in my gift.'

'Just information. The others I can deal with sometime else. I need you to tell me what happened.'

'No you don't.' Betsy tried to turn her head to look at Rocket. 'You know, don't you?'

'I think I do, but I can't accept it.'

'And that needs to be part of the equation, does it? Perhaps you're looking at it the wrong way. Acceptance isn't something you can force on yourself. It takes time. It took me time, but I was fortunate to have a special friend to help me. There's so much we don't understand, and we waste too much effort trying to. Much better to let it come to us. Lying here with nothing to do but wait, I've begun to understand a great deal about the order of things. It's cleared my mind, and that's how I know I'm ready.'

'So what do you know now?'

'That there's a plan for everything. Nothing is random, in spite of how it seems. The whole ordeal with Ricky, for instance — that was part of a greater design from which everyone will profit.'

Rocket understood so little of this that her lack of comprehension was almost as if Betsy was speaking in a foreign tongue. She needed an interpreter or subtitles. 'How come?'

'Because we are all, in our different ways, being tested. We're all presented with these choices and we are judged on how we deal with them. It's all about judgement; not ours, but His. You don't see that now, but you will.'

'If you won't – can't – give me what I need, then at least tell me one thing, Betsy. What should be my priority? Do I protect Ricky, or do I go on and search for the truth?' Rocket surprised herself by asking this: had Betsy surreptitiously become a spiritual light in her darkness?

'Can't you do both?'

'I don't see how.'

'One will follow the other. Your problem is that you can't see that yet. But the truth will ultimately offer him more protection. As long as you follow a righteous path, God will protect him.'

'And me?'

'Do you want it? It's there if you do, but you have to ask for it. Can you do that? These are questions I cannot answer for you. You know what I used to say to Chuck, when he had doubts? I used to tell him that everyone has a spirit-level inside them, and only they can know when it's steady. How's yours?'

'I need to find it first, then I'll tell you.'

'There may not be time for that. All I can say to you now is that you go with God's blessing. If you pursue the truth, no matter what the personal cost, you'll have Him at your side.'

'I guessed you'd say that, not that it helps much. But I wanted—'

'I know what you wanted. You wanted it all delivered, nicely wrapped up and presented. But life's not like that.

I can't give you what you want, even if it were in my power to do so.'

'Then what can you give me?'

'I can give you the key, but you have to unlock the gate and follow the right path. That's all I can do.'

'It's a start.'

'Then you'd better listen to what I have to tell you.'

When Betsy had finished her story – an unburdening of her soul that took an hour of unbroken whispered speech – she was shrinking before Rocket's eyes: her voice tailed off and she wavered between the present and another state, where all these matters pressed little on her. Rocket would not have been shocked to see her spirit rise out of her body, such was the sense of an unseen force within the curtained confines of her hospital bed.

Rocket hesitated before she spoke, wanting to be sure that Betsy had really finished. 'Now I understand,' she said. 'Now it's clear. And you can trust me to do the right thing, Betsy. I won't let you down.'

Betsy, eyes closed, smiled. That image stayed with Rocket for the rest of her life.

Dr Frank Beard was a small man, hardly taller than Clare. His dark hair was unfashionably cut, covering his ears and swept across his forehead in a drooping fringe. He might have wrestled with his surname, but had grown a full set anyway, with the first wisps of white hair around the cheeks. He was wearing grey shoes and an ensemble of sports jacket, slacks, striped shirt and paisley tie that had probably looked better on the mannequin in the high street shop where his wife had bought it. He carried a big folder and spoke through his teeth in a nasal, restricted tone.

To get Will to this place – a converted school building in south London that had been annexed by the local hospital – Clare had exercised a full assault of persuasion, coercion, pleading and guilt. She had laid siege to Will, explaining that the benefits of a session with a family psychologist might be small, non-existent even, but where was the harm in trying? Will had talked about psycho mumbo-jumbo and his deep suspicion of professional do-gooders; he had asked why she felt the need for others to interfere in their private business; and he had reminded her forcefully of all the banalities offered by the counsellors in Chicago. But Clare had insisted, staking much on this visit in the hope that it would break the dam and open up new hopes. Eventually he had relented, silently suffering in the minicab as Clare sat between India and Tom in the back seat. He had promised cooperation and nothing more; questions would be answered, but further information not willingly volunteered.

The four of them sat in a circle so that they all faced Dr Beard. His smile was partly hidden by his whiskers, but his eyes glistened with interest and warmth. Tom clutched his comforter and swung his legs under his chair, whilst India looked around at the stark white walls.

'I've read your notes,' Beard said. 'The Americans can be very thorough when they put their minds to it, so I feel I already know something of your circumstances. But perhaps we should start by you telling me what you think the problem is.' Will immediately looked across at Clare and she knew this was a question that only she would answer.

'Basically, we're a little concerned by Tom's behaviour,' she began. 'He seems to be having trouble settling in,

311

and that's causing all of us some headaches. What we really need is some guidance on how to cope with it.' Beard wrote nothing on his pad but nodded encouragingly.

'And what does Tom think about this?' Clare was about to answer, but realised that he was addressing his question directly to Tom.

'Well,' Tom said, 'I guess it's kind of tough for everyone. Sometimes I think no one really likes me, and then I get mad.'

'Do you like anyone?'

'I do when they're being nice to me. But then they get cross – especially Mom – and I don't like them so much.'

'What about your dad? What do you think about him?'

Tom hesitated and looked very quickly at Will before averting his gaze towards the floor. 'He . . . I'm a bit, I don't know, kind of scared of him.'

'Scared of him?' Beard said. 'Why should you be scared of him?'

'I don't know, I guess. I just am.'

'I see. Well, we'll have to work on that one.' Beard seemed undismayed by this observation, and changed tack. 'And what about India? Do you like her?'

'A bit.' Tom looked at Will as he said this, and received a smile.

'Can she be a bit of a pain sometimes?' Beard asked.

'Yeah.'

'And what do you do about that, when she's being a pain?'

'I try to ignore it, but then . . .' Tom stopped, unwilling to say more.

'Do you feel like hitting her sometimes?'

'Yes.'

312

'And what does Dad think about this?'

'I'm probably not as concerned as I should be,' Will said. 'I think it's bound to be hard, and he's experiencing sibling rivalry for the first time. It'll pass.'

'Yup – in about twenty years, in my experience,' Beard said, and they all laughed in relief. 'And what about India? That's a great name, by the way. What do you think about having a brother all of a sudden? Do you like him?'

'A bit,' she said, mimicking Tom.

'It's really difficult, isn't it? I bet there are times you wish it was like the old days, when you had Mum and Dad to yourself.'

'Sometimes.'

Beard wrote something on his pad; Clare was astonished by the way in which he operated, bringing their problems out into the open immediately and forcing them to admit to them. She had expected a much more cautious approach.

'Tell me, Clare, what's the worst aspect of Tom's behaviour? If you had to change one thing, what would it be?'

'The tantrums, without a doubt. After he's got into trouble, he throws some really amazing tantrums, and I just can't deal with them.'

'How does he behave? Is he violent? Does he shout at you in particular?'

'He can be violent, and his language is pretty blue. It's quite distressing.'

'And does he only do this with you?'

'Well, I'm normally the one who has to pick up the pieces,' Clare said, shooting a quick look at Will.

'Ah,' Beard said. 'So Dad stays out of trouble, does he?'

'It's not really that,' Clare said quickly. 'It's just . . . well, I'm more often around to deal with it.'

'Tom,' Beard said, 'who is stricter – Mum or Dad?'

'Mom.'

'And who do you like more? Do you have a favourite?'

'No. I like them the same, I guess. I love Grandpa the best of all.'

'Grandpa – now where is he?' Beard asked.

'He couldn't come today,' Clare said. 'He's not been terribly well recently. But Tom is right – they get on very well.'

'I see.' Beard wrote something else, but pursued it no further. He looked up at India. Clare wanted to answer every question for them, and had to grit her teeth as she listened to their replies.

'Now, India, do you think that Mum and Dad treat you better or worse than Tom?'

'Worse,' India said, looking at Clare as she replied.

'Why do you say that?'

'Because he always gets what he wants, then Mum comes and tells me why.'

'And what do you think, Tom?'

'That's bullshit,' he said loudly. 'She gets a much better deal than me.'

'Do you think they love her more than they love you?'

'Maybe.'

Then Beard smiled and exhaled through his nose with a noisy puff of air. He looked at Clare, aware that she was taking the lead in this discussion. 'Do you and your husband ever disagree on how to deal with Tom's behaviour?'

'Only always,' Clare said.

'And I would imagine that you're stricter than he would be, is that right?'

'Yes.'

'What do you do with Tom when he has a tantrum?'

'I try and stay calm, but it doesn't always work. We get into shouting matches and I end up slamming the door on him.'

'You're right to try and stay calm,' Beard said. 'He has to learn that this behaviour is unacceptable to you, and the way to do that is to give him no attention. If he thinks he's getting a reaction from you he'll continue to do it. I'd suggest you send him to his room and make him stay there until he's ready to behave acceptably. Don't lose your cool, and don't get into an argument. Just be firm and let him know you won't tolerate it.' He looked over at Tom. 'Do you enjoy having these tantrums?' he asked him. 'What do you feel like after them?'

'I feel pretty bad,' Tom said quietly.

'And you know Mum and Dad don't like them?'

'Yes.'

'Do you think you could stop them, if you tried really hard?'

'I don't know. Maybe.'

'I'd like you to try, and so would Mum and Dad. I think everyone would be much happier if you did.' Clare smiled at Tom to reinforce Beard's message, but Tom just looked down at his swinging feet. Beard consulted his notes again. 'Well, there doesn't appear to be much wrong with you as a family. You're trying to deal with your problems, and it sounds to me like you're doing a pretty good job. Dad' – and here he turned to face Will – 'I'd lighten up a little, if you'll pardon the expression. You may be a bit too remote, too distant, but it's nothing serious. If you like, I can have Tom come in again on his own – or India, for that matter – but I think it's probably best if we give it another three months and then you all come back and see me again.'

'That's it?' Will asked.

'What else were you looking for?'

'I don't know. It just seems . . . a little too easy, I suppose.'

'It's not easy, believe me. But you're getting there, and as long as you and Mum can act as a team I don't think there'll be anything insurmountable. One thing I would suggest – and you probably already do this – is that one of you takes over when the other is reaching the end of their tether. That's the kind of support I'm talking about, and it'll help to keep the message consistent.'

They all got up and said their goodbyes, Clare promising to make another appointment. When they were in the taxi – Tom on Will's lap, India on Clare's – they suppressed their desire to discuss what was said. Once home, they went into the kitchen whilst Tom went to Ralph and India watched a video.

'I was totally amazed,' said Clare. 'I never thought it would be like that.'

'No, he was good, wasn't he? He really knew what was going on.'

'So are you convinced now?'

'Let's just say I'm not as sceptical as I was. But I still don't think we'll need another session.'

'If we follow his advice, maybe we won't. But let's not worry about that yet.'

That night, for the first time since he'd been back,

Tom went to bed without a struggle. He hugged Clare round the neck, and was asleep within minutes of his head touching the pillow. Clare noticed this but said nothing to Will. She simply enjoyed the moment, brief as it was, for all it suggested.

THIRTY-FOUR

Rocket could cry. However she totted up the sums of her life – a failed marriage, a lousy credit rating, short of work and drained of energy – she arrived at a negative number. There was nothing to give her any hope. She had looked at Betsy, little more than a transparency between the sheets, and had seen what it was like to have faith, but her own shortcomings were only magnified by such closeness to another's strength. There was nothing uplifting in Betsy's aura: Rocket drew no comfort from her sense of divine justice, and felt no renewal of spirit or purpose, but simply wilted at the prospect of her own future.

As if in pain, she huddled in a cubicle of the bar, smoking and drinking alone. Manny the barman flicked his towel across the counter as he watched her, insulated from the other drinkers by her tortured thoughts. He watched too as an unknown man, dressed in a brown suit that had seen better days, came into the bar and looked around before spotting Rocket and slouching over to her table. She didn't look up as he slid on to the bench opposite her.

'Rocky?' It was Lieutenant Jablonowski. Her eyes moved up from her glass to glance at him briefly.

'Now what would bring you all the way out here?' she

319

said. 'Delivery of an early Christmas gift, perhaps – how touching.'

A waiter came over and took their order for drinks. Jablonowski waited until he was gone before speaking.

'Rocky, I don't need any shit from you, OK? We have some bad news.'

'Tell me something I don't know.'

'Betsy Callahan died last night.' Rocket stopped swirling the melting ice in the bottom of her empty glass; her whole metabolism seemed to stall for a second as she took in the news.

'I knew she was sick,' she said.

'Yeah, well it turns out it was worse than we thought. They say she just faded away, never responded to treatment. But it gives us one hell of a problem. We have a live murder case on our hands and the main suspect has turned up her toes.'

'It's not your case. Why should you worry?'

'Perhaps you didn't notice what I said. The emphasis was on the "we" in that statement. You're up to your neck in all this, and that means I am too. I've been told to bring you in.'

'You've come here to arrest me?'

'That depends. Maybe I didn't find you yet. I won't know until I've talked to you.'

'Is this a new police procedure?' Rocket asked as the drinks arrived.

'Cut the crap, Rocky. Feehan thinks you have something. Sounds like you and he really hit it off. Anyways, he doesn't think you're divulging all you know and he reckons that you might be open to some persuasion. That's why I'm here.'

320

Rocket chewed her lips, then dragged on her cigarette. 'I don't know what he's talking about.'

'Come on, you were at her bedside last weekend and she certainly didn't ask to see you. What did you think you were doing there – offering spiritual guidance? She told you something and it's bugging you. Tell me what it was and we can probably forget I was ever here.'

'There's nothing to tell. She gave me some big spiel about religion and faith and all that good stuff, that was all. Lock me up if you like – it'll be a vast improvement on my current lifestyle.'

'Did she do it, Rocky? Is that what it was – she thought you could keep a secret and she'd feel much better if she confessed?'

She drained half her glass in one go and then looked him in the eye. 'All I can tell you is this.' She paused for effect. 'Betsy Callahan loved that boy like he was her own. She would never have done anything to harm him.'

'And that's what she told you?'

'Pretty much.'

'Then she was wasting your time. I don't know why you're continuing to argue her case. Everything's stacked against her – unless, of course, you know something we don't. The way it looks to me, she had the motive and the opportunity, and they'll prove it eventually.'

'They will?'

'Sure. He was much less certain about this whole business than she was. You said so yourself, remember? The way I see it, she couldn't afford to have him around any more so she axed him – literally.' Jablonowski made a chopping movement, one hand against the other, as he said this.

'And that is your considered opinion of what happened?'

'It'll do for now – unless you know better.'

'Honestly, who am I to challenge the might of New York's finest? I am but a zit on your buttocks.' Rocket waved over to Manny for more drinks.

'I don't think you're taking this quite seriously enough,' Jablonowski said. 'I don't give a flying fuck about the Callahans any more, seeing as they're both six feet under. But, strange as it may seem, I do worry about you. And you're pretty central to everything that's going on. Your name keeps on coming up on all our conference calls with St Pete's and Chicago, and a queue's forming to interview you. They could nail you, and I can't do a damn thing to help you if you don't help yourself.'

Rocket took this in slowly. 'Can we do a deal?'

'It may be too late for deals, Rocky. What have you got?'

'Nothing, I swear to God. That is, nothing yet. But I'm working on it. Give me one week, then I'll do whatever you want.'

'One week is out of the question. Three days, tops. But anyway, why don't you just give it to us? If you've got something, we'll handle it a hell of a lot quicker.'

'Believe me, I'd like nothing better. Let's just say I'm wrestling with a moral dilemma and I haven't worked it out yet.'

'You and morals? Sounds unlikely. You'll have to do better than that.'

'I can't. Just give me three days and I'll call you.'

'And what if I need to call you? My balls are on the line here, Rocky. They could cut them off for this.'

'The thought's appealing,' Rocket said. 'But I'll spare you from that if I can. And as for getting in touch with me, forget it. I'll be far away.'

'Don't go to Mexico, please. It costs us a fortune to get people back from there.'

'Nothing quite as fancy as that.'

'Rocky, I'm warning you. Dick me around on this and you'll be so deep in the shit you'll need an aqualung and flippers. They're not fooling around any more. They want blood, and yours will do.'

'Three days,' Rocket said, and she raised her glass at him.

Will sat in his study and listened. He heard the front door close and waited until he was certain that they were all gone. His preparations demanded complete privacy, and now he had it.

First he made a call to the travel agency. He checked the details of bookings already made and received a confirmation number which he wrote on a slip of paper. He agreed that he would come in to pick up the tickets the following day. Then he filled in a new passport application form with the relevant additions and amendments; he wrote out a cheque and stuffed all the papers into his briefcase. He stopped and looked at the check-list he had written, ticking off all the items on it. He had booked the taxi, which would wait outside the flat. He opened the briefcase once more to look at the bundle of cash and traveller's cheques.

He leaned back in his chair and rubbed his face. He had asked himself the same question over and over during the last few weeks, and he was no closer to changing his

323

mind. This was the best – the only – solution. It was the means of their salvation, and he would be the agent of it. It needed no further explanation. He had begun the final act, and he knew how it would end. He got up, collected his jacket and briefcase, and set off for Petty France.

It was not as serious as they had first thought. Once they had cleaned up the wound it became clear that the cut was not too deep, although it needed butterfly closures over it. What worried them more was concussion, and they tried various techniques to test for it. But Ralph was having an off-day, and Clare had to take the doctor to one side and explain the position.

Ralph had slipped as they were leaving Sainsbury's. Someone had spilt milk on the tiled floor and his foot landed right in it; he lost his balance and tipped over backwards, turning himself as he fell and cracking his forehead as he landed. The blood oozed into the milk to form pretty pink patterns; a circle of onlookers gathered as Clare and a supervisor turned him on to his back and peered into his eyes. He looked totally bemused by what had happened and stared at them both as the blood ran down across his forehead and into his hair. Within minutes an ambulance had arrived and they were rushed to hospital, Clare holding his hand as he lay on the stretcher.

They recommended bedrest and a visit from the GP. Once it had been established that he was ready to go home, Clare could only worry about the shopping she'd left behind at the supermarket: she'd spent over a hundred pounds and was determined to pick it up later. They went home in a minicab, Ralph dozing intermittently and Clare cursing her luck. Will wasn't there when they arrived, and she had great difficulty in getting Ralph undressed and into his pyjamas. She gave him two paracetamol and left his door open; he was soon fast asleep.

Will came home early that afternoon; unusually, the news seemed to upset him. 'Oh Christ, that's all we need,' he said. 'Is he totally bloody incompetent?'

'It could have happened to anybody,' Clare said. 'He was just unlucky.'

'No. We're the unlucky ones.'

'How can you be so callous, Will? The poor old man's just bumped his head and had a real shock. The least you could do is show a bit of sympathy.'

'I don't suppose there's any chance it will have shaken up his brains, is there? He might be more *compos mentis* if it has.'

'Please. Come on, he's not that bad. He's really no trouble at all usually. And he's been brilliant with Tom.'

'And that's another thing,' Will said bitterly. 'Tom will now be closeted with him, stroking his head and doing silly pictures for him. We'll never see him.'

'I don't see anything wrong with that. I think the drawing is very therapeutic for Tom. It's another way of expressing himself, and we should be encouraging it.'

'Probably. But with that old fart I'm not sure it's altogether a good idea.'

Will went to his study before they had a chance to strike up a really good argument. He stayed there until late in the evening, giving the children little attention when they got home from school. But when he came into the kitchen he was almost elated.

'What's for supper?' he asked Clare. 'I'm starving.'

325

'Pasta. Look, I'm a bit worried about Tom. When he saw Ralph he completely flipped. He ran out and shut himself in his room. He says he doesn't want to come out and he's not hungry. He's really upset about it.'

It took Will a few moments to understand this, but the association eventually clicked in his mind. He decided to take a conciliatory approach. 'Shall I go and sit with him?'

'That'd be nice.'

Will went into Tom's room: he was sitting on his bed, knees drawn up to his chest, hand holding the small scrap of material against his mouth. 'What's up?' Will said.

'Is Grandpa all right?'

'He's fine. Just a bump on the head. He'll be as good as new in the morning, I promise.' Will sat down next to him but Tom shifted away from him. 'How's it going at school?'

'I hate it. Everyone's always mad at me. The teachers don't like me.'

'I'm sure that's not right. They say you're getting on really well. And Mum says your reading is fantastic.' Tom shrugged. 'Come on, cheer up. I tell you what, we're going to have a big adventure soon, and you can't be in a bad mood if you want to go.'

'What big adventure?' Tom brightened at the idea.

'That's a secret, and you'll have to keep it. Not even Mum knows about it. But it's going to be really exciting, you'll see.'

'When?'

'That's a secret too. I don't want you to say anything about it, because I want it to be a huge surprise. Can you keep a secret?'

'Yeah. I've kept lots.'

'I know you have.' Will knew, better than most, how good Tom was at keeping secrets.

THIRTY-FIVE

Jablonowski's interference had cost Rocket a lot of money. She had not planned to be buying an airline ticket so soon, but his ultimatum was serious enough for her to break into her money market account. This was her last reserve of cash and she had severe doubts about using it; she tried to apply Betsy's advice to her financial situation, which was now critical, and she consoled herself with the thought that, once this was all over, she would knuckle down and make every effort to revive her flagging business.

The news of Betsy's death had had a strange effect on Rocket. Though she had found her difficult to deal with, and had never connected with the spiritual side, Rocket had rather liked her. She had fashioned herself as a pivot in the ever-changing cycle of events, unyielding in the face of tragedy; of all the players, she alone had stayed the same. This constancy had attracted Rocket like a compass needle to magnetic North: whilst others had lost their way, or changed direction, Betsy remained in place, certain of her bearings and the path she had to follow. Rocket yearned for a similar focus, and Betsy's death pushed her towards it. Once she had cleared her head from the fog of alcohol, she had known what she had to do, and had forced herself to be strong enough to do it.

Betsy had made herself die. This notion was drawn from nothing more than romantic supposition on Rocket's part, but she liked the idea that Betsy, having seen her life fall apart in front of her, had made the conscious decision to meet her maker. It all seemed neat and tidy to Rocket, and that appealed to her as she stood amid the wreckage of her own existence. To have such control over one's own life, to the extent that one could determine the time and place of death, was a concept that Rocket found highly seductive.

She had thrown some clothes into a battered bag in a mad rush to get ready. Finding her passport had proved a trial, but it turned up in a pile of old bills – some still unpaid – and she packed it with the small amount of cash she'd drawn out. She looked around the apartment one last time, overwhelmed by an inexplicable sense that she might not see it again. Everything now looked different to her; her sight had become dislocated by the enormity of the task ahead, so that she felt she was looking at familiar things for the first time. She took one last swig from her beer can and tossed it towards the rubbish bin, missing by some feet; she shrugged and swung round to leave the apartment. As she reached the front door she realised she had left her morning mail unopened, and she scooped the envelopes up and stuffed them into her handbag. It would give her something to do on the trip to the airport.

'What the hell is going on, Will?'

'I don't want to fight any more. God knows we've been through enough together. We must be able to handle things without resorting to another round of arguments and abuse.' Will said this quite calmly as he poured himself a glass of wine. Clare couldn't take her eyes off him; there was another change going on, and she needed to work out what it was.

Without warning he had commanded a premium on reason and order. The crescendo of dissent had vanished and was replaced by a flat, unbroken cessation of hostilities. Clare had reached the stage where she hung on by her nails, unable to think about anything but how she might live through this turmoil. Tom's behaviour was no better, even though she had kept her head and had followed Dr Beard's advice to the letter. But Will had retreated behind a shield: he looked on as she dealt with the tantrums, passed no comment on Tom's companionship with Ralph, and evaded all discussion of their problems with a shrug of his shoulders.

'So that's it?' she replied.

'That's it. Don't knock it. It's the only way forward.'

'I can't work out what's going on in your head. I don't know what you want. Ever since Tom came back we've all been walking on eggshells in case we do something that upsets you. Now you're saying that's all in the past, and you're going to calm down. That's brilliant if it's true. But what's brought this on?'

'A new perspective. That's what I'd call it. I had to get everything sorted out for myself, and now I have. As simple as that.' He clicked his fingers in front of his face to show how easy it had been, but Clare wasn't convinced. He seemed almost manic as he spoke, too pumped up and sparkling for her to be sure.

'So we're all going to be able to relax a bit more now, are we?'

'Absolutely. You see, I think we had a lot of

misconceptions over what life would be like with Tom back in the fold. I know I did. But once I'd had a chance to see what was going on, and analyse it all, I realised that some major changes were necessary on our side – yours and mine. We've tried to put the past back together, and that's been our biggest mistake. Our lives have moved on, and there's no point trying to turn back the clock. We're different people, you, me, and Tom, and we need to look at things with that in mind.'

'I can see that, Will, and I think I understand.'

'We've got to shape our own future now. We can't wait and hope that it will sort itself out. So I'm feeling really positive – excited – about what's in store, because I know what can be done and what needs to be done.'

There was something in Will's tone that suggested he was holding back vital information; all that he said was fine, but Clare worried about the things he left unsaid. She admonished herself for suspecting his motives, but she no longer felt she knew him well enough to take anything at face value. She wondered how much she had changed in his eyes, if at all: was she still the girl he married, or had she matured into someone more, or less, attractive? Whenever she looked at her face in the mirror she saw lines and bags, and her naked body seemed dull and drained. Did he see the same things? He never commented; but he had changed so much that she felt she must have changed too, and he must have noticed it. Was this what he was saying? Was this his way of admitting his knowledge of what she'd become? Was he trying to say something more?

Clare couldn't bring herself to ask. If he had something to say, she would not make it easier for him. 'Is it what you imagined?' she asked, not quite knowing how she expected him to answer.

'What?'

'Having Tom back.'

'To be perfectly honest, I didn't imagine very much. I was so focused on getting him back that I didn't waste much time speculating on how things might turn out.'

'It's like you say – starting all over again.'

'Precisely. It's that famous blank sheet of paper. We're here to fill it in. We can't behave like we did before, because that's all consigned to history and some good memories.'

In spite of herself, Clare asked him the question she most needed to. 'So where does that leave us, Will – you and me?'

'That's what we have to work out, Clare.'

'I know – that's why I'm asking you.'

'Our relationship has changed, you know that as well as I do. We're no longer what we were, to ourselves or each other. That doesn't make it better or worse, it just makes it different.'

'I understand that, but I can't work out what you're saying to me.'

'I'm saying you'll have to give me some time.'

'I don't know if I can deal with that. I need to be sure of you, Will. I need to feel that you're here with me and we're in this together. I don't think that's too much to ask.' She could feel her eyes stinging and blinked to suppress it.

'It's all I can give you – for now, at any rate. I'm here now, and that's the most important thing, isn't it?'

'That doesn't give me much comfort. Is there

something – anything – I can do to make you feel differently?'

'Wait for me. I'm going to get everything sorted out, Clare, I promise you that.'

The problem was, Clare didn't know if she wanted him to.

She had a cup of coffee, stronger than she was used to, and waited. She'd been told he was reliable, and anyway, what choice did she have? Rocket lit another cigarette and looked out of the café window. London was not what she'd expected: for a start, there was a clear blue sky. But the pace of life was quicker than she'd imagined, and there was less to distinguish London people than she'd hoped for. They all pursued their business pretty much as they did in any big American city – perhaps slightly friendlier – and the traffic was just as frantic. Twice she'd narrowly avoided being run down by a bus as she looked the wrong way when crossing the road.

Her bones ached from the flight. But she steeled herself for one last push, one final burst of energy that would lead to catharsis. As she waited for her man she rummaged in her bag and pulled out the letter she'd read again and again since opening her mail the day before. The paper was crumpled and the writing was laboured, obviously formed against a background of much pain. The envelope bore several official stamps and marks, a sign that it had been sent only after inspection.

She read the letter as she would have read a creed, searching for some inner meaning and guidance amongst the few untidily scrawled words. It hurt her to think of how much effort Betsy had put into the letter, and it

334

touched her in secret corners of her soul. Betsy, in a final act of will, had decided to offer her the key to her problem. Perhaps she knew she was about to die and had suffered a bout of contrition; more likely, though, that she couldn't bear to leave without a final, telling testimony of what she knew. In this, as in everything else she had done, Betsy had been thorough but precise, delivering just the right amount of data to leave Rocket in no doubt.

Folding it neatly, Rocket looked up and a man was standing at her table. He was dirty; his skin was rough and grey and his clothes were stained. He frightened her, but she was used to that.

'You Rocket?' he asked in a surprisingly high-pitched voice. She nodded. 'Let's go.'

'Where?'

'You don't think we're going to do it here, do you? The car's parked down the street. You've got the money, I hope?'

'Five hundred. As agreed.'

'There must have been some mistake. The price is seven.'

'I was told five.'

'Then you were misinformed. It's seven – take it or leave it. What's it to be?'

'I'll take it.'

'Sounds like you're desperate. I hope it's worth it.'

'So do I.' Rocket got up and followed the man out of the café and down the street. He stopped at a car and unlocked the rear door.

'Get in,' he said. She looked at him and the car, then did as she was told. There was another man on the back seat who paid her no attention as she sat down. The first man got into the driver's seat and turned himself to face her. He put his hand out. 'The money, please.'

'I think it's customary to pay COD in these transactions,' she said. The man motioned to his friend who pulled out a small package from his jacket. It was well wrapped in black plastic and he handed it to her. From the weight she knew immediately that it was the real thing, so she produced an envelope, counting out the seven hundred before handing it over. The money was re-counted, a nod given in acceptance, and Rocket shoved the parcel deep into her bag.

'Thanks, guys. Nice doing business with you.' She hopped out of the car feeling much more secure; she always liked to carry a gun when she was on unfamiliar territory.

THIRTY-SIX

Her hands were freezing. She had been standing outside the mansion block since six that morning, determined not to miss Clare, and she shuffled from foot to foot in an effort to keep warm. A thin mist hovered over Battersea Park and the sky was dull and cloudy. Rocket watched the front door as a trickle of residents began to emerge: smartly dressed couples burst out into the chilled air and strode off down the road; men and women appeared separately with fat or thin briefcases, wrapped up against the cold; and harassed mothers dragged reluctant children to the bus stop or along the street to their cars.

By eight-thirty Rocket was losing hope. Perhaps they weren't there; perhaps one of the children was ill; perhaps . . . As she considered the possibilities the front door opened and Clare appeared. She was wearing a bright red jacket and a green woollen scarf, and she looked behind her as she held the door open. A little girl came out first, followed by a boy. They were both neat and well scrubbed, and were dressed similarly in grey school uniforms and red sweaters. Each took Clare's hand and the three of them marched off down the street, India skipping whilst Tom kept a steady, measured pace. Rocket watched them recede into the distance. She had no need to follow them, and decided to get herself another cup of coffee.

One hour later she could see the distinctive red jacket returning. Rocket pulled hard on her cigarette, forcing smoke into her lungs and holding it there. Her stomach lurched in anticipation of the meeting; she had no idea how Clare would react. Would she even recognise her? As Clare approached, Rocket dropped the butt on the pavement and ground it out.

Their eyes met before Clare realised, and she looked down to avoid Rocket's stare. 'Clare?' Rocket took a step towards her, but was careful not to invade her space. When Clare looked up again she suddenly understood. 'Rocket. My God, it's you. How are you? What are you doing here?' It all came out in a rush of embarrassment and confusion.

'I needed to talk to you.'

'Fine, but what's wrong with the phone?' Clare said as she smiled.

'This has to be face to face. Is there somewhere we can go?'

'Come on. Will will have gone out by now. God, how long have you been standing here? You look frozen.' They continued to exchange small talk on the way up to the flat. Once inside, Clare put Rocket in the sitting room whilst she made coffee. Rocket began to defrost. She lit a cigarette and searched for an ashtray.

They sipped their coffee in silence, neither fully ready to take the lead. Eventually Rocket started. 'So, how's it all going?'

Clare let out a deep sigh. 'Much as you'd expect. Tom's having trouble settling in, and that's causing a few problems – but nothing terminal, I don't think. We're getting there. What about you?'

'Same old Rocket, I guess. Once the business with Tom was through I pretty much went back to my old life.'

'So what brings you to sunny Battersea? Are you working on a case?'

'Kind of. How's Will?'

'It's strange, really. He's changed a lot, you know. This whole affair screwed him up for a while, and he's still adjusting to it all. But on the whole he's fairly fit.'

'And you?'

'Well, I'm still smiling through it all. You know my mother died, and my father was quite unwell, so he lives with us now. He might make an appearance later. What with one thing and another, I've got plenty to keep me occupied.'

'I'd better come clean,' Rocket said. 'I needed to see you, and not just because I once had an interest in the case. You won't know this, but the woman who took Tom died recently.'

'I can't say I'm particularly sorry to hear that.'

'That's understandable. She and I had an odd kind of relationship. For whatever reason, she chose to confide in me. She was a very strange lady – deeply religious, and absolutely certain of her own convictions. It was scary. But she made it perfectly clear that she never meant any harm to come to Tom, and I believed her. So I suppose I came here to check up on you, to put it bluntly – to see if little Tom was doing OK and you folks were handling it all right.'

'Oh.' Clare made it obvious that she wasn't too impressed with this.

'I know what you're thinking. What right do I have to

do this? And the answer's none. But it's like a pilgrimage, something that has to be done to purge my soul of all the demons. I'm sorry if it offends you.'

'I don't really know what to think. I never realised you were that emotionally involved in the case.'

'Neither did I. But I obviously am, otherwise I wouldn't be here. My life's been shit ever since you took me off the case, and I'm not blaming you for that in any way, but I have to sort myself out and this was my way of doing it.'

Clare listened to this and thought about it. 'Are you going to see Will? Is that part of the process?'

Seeing no good outcome if she told the truth, Rocket had to lie. 'I don't think that's necessary. I'm happier right now. I saw you go off to school with them – they're both fine-looking kids, aren't they? Almost makes me feel broody.'

They laughed at this ridiculous notion; then Clare had an idea. 'Do you want to see Tom's room?'

'That'd be great.' They got up and walked down the hall to the room. Rocket was struck immediately by the contrast between this and the one she had seen all those years ago in Florida.

'It's a bit of a mess, I know,' Clare said, 'but we do tidy it up once a week.' There were posters all over the walls, and books and magazines were scattered over every available surface. On a little desk were a box of water-colours and several tins of crayons and chalks. Rocket went over to look at them. 'Yes, he's heavily into art at the moment. My father was an artist, and he seems to have caught the bug.'

To one side there was a big pile of finished and half-finished drawings and paintings; all brightly coloured, most were obviously copied from a book as the subjects were things that he couldn't have imagined or seen. Rocket leafed casually through the pile.

'Actually, I think some of the things he does are quite good,' Clare said. 'Ralph thinks so, too. And he spends hours in here, or with Ralph, just working away. I think he finds it therapeutic. Come on, let's have another coffee and you can tell me what's hot in New York.'

They went back to the sitting room and Rocket lit another cigarette. She couldn't resist making comparisons between Tom's life here and the brief one he'd enjoyed in Florida. Could she really say which had been better for him? When Clare returned with fresh coffee Rocket was standing by the window with her back to her. She waited until she was sure she could sit down and face Clare.

'Are you all right?' Clare asked. 'You look a little flushed.'

'I'm fine. It's probably the curse!' Rocket wanted to dismiss it all, even knowing she couldn't.

'The things we women go through. Look, I've been thinking. It's really sweet of you to come here. I probably overreacted earlier, and I'm sorry if I did. We've all been under a lot of stress. Is there anything else I can do for you? I mean, I don't want you to have come all this way for nothing.'

Rocket juggled with the possible answers. 'No, no,' she said eventually. 'Really, I've got what I wanted and I won't impose any more. I'll just finish my coffee and that'll be it. You've been so kind, just letting some brassy New Yorker into your home without warning. I'm truly grateful.'

There was a long pause whilst both tried to find something neutral to say. Rocket was uncomfortable in this home, and she wanted to be running down the street so fast that her breathing would block out all other noise. But her instinct was to ask one more question.

'This is a damned cheek,' she said, 'and you can tell me to get lost if you like. But are you happy now? Was it all worth it?'

Clare waited before replying. 'Happiness is relative. If you're asking are we happier than we were before we got him back, then the answer is yes – most definitely. But I don't know what absolute happiness is any more, or if it even exists. I suppose everyone can find something to be miserable about, however charmed their lives appear to be. In the grand scheme of things, I shouldn't imagine we're much more or less contented than anyone else. That's what comes of having a family – you've always got some problem to deal with that eats away inside you. It's just a matter of coping with it, isn't it? That's what life is – coping.' She shrugged to show that she accepted this without much rancour. 'That sounds a bit maudlin, and I don't mean it like that. But you get so tired, so desperately tired, that it's hard to see what you've got and how much you stand to lose if you can't cope any more. It's a grind, but it's going to be worth it. I really believe that.'

'I hope it is, Clare. Nothing would make me happier than to see you guys make it. No one deserves it more.'

'You know, I wish I could have got to know you better. I think you and I have a lot in common.'

'Well, I don't know about that,' Rocket said. 'I don't think I have a fraction of your dedication or perseverance. I'd have folded a long time ago.'

'You learn to deal with it, that's the odd thing. Will and I may have had different methods, but we've both dealt

342

with it in our separate ways. Every day it becomes easier to handle, so that the horrors of yesterday don't seem quite so bad when you wake up. Even when nothing good happens, you just carry on. I suppose it's like your pain threshold – you accept a certain level of pain and, as long as it doesn't get any worse, you find ways to manage it.'

'That sounds far too brave for me. I'm not a pain person.'

'But that's only because you don't know what you can endure. I'd bet you could handle what we had to, if it came to it. And in your job you must have to deal with some pretty dreadful situations.'

'But that's more to do with risk. I reckon I have a little thermostat inside me that tells me how much risk to take and, when I get too much or too little, it sends me a signal. I like risk – you know, the potential for pain – but that's it.'

'Well, I don't enjoy either, but here I am anyway. We make our own fortunes, Rocket. Nothing can change that, unfortunately. We just have to do the best we can.'

There was a quiet sadness to all that Clare had said, and this only intensified Rocket's feeling of dread. She needed to leave and suck in the soggy London air. She also needed to sleep.

'I'm going now,' she said. 'I'm so pleased I came, and I can't ever thank you enough for seeing me. I'll never forget this.' She gathered her bag and got up to go. Clare came over to her and put a hand on her forearm.

'Don't worry about us, Rocket. We're going to be fine.'

'Yeah,' she said, trying desperately to convince herself that they would.

THIRTY-SEVEN

He read the letter again as the blood rushed to his face.

> Will—
> It's time to get this sorted out. We both know too
> much to leave things as they are. Let's talk and see
> if there's some way to solve this problem.
> I'll be waiting at the bandstand in Battersea
> Park at eleven a.m. If you're not there, you'll leave
> me with no choice.   Rocket

Attached to the note was a photocopy of another letter,
and Will had taken some time to assess its importance.

> By now, you should have seen the light. I'm hoping
> you'll take the righteous path, because I no longer
> have the strength. Ricky cannot be exposed to any
> more danger, and it is your duty to protect him.
> Who will come when he calls, if not you?
> You know that he cannot live with that man. Evil
> is in that house and he must be rescued from it. I
> urge you to do what is right. Trust yourself, and
> justice will prevail.
> May God go with you.   Betsy Callahan

Will's first reaction had been to screw the letters up and throw them in the bin. He had sat at his desk and fumed, but the force of those words had drawn him back to them and he retrieved the ball of paper. Having smoothed the pages down, he looked at them again, searching for clues or unwritten signs that might unlock the mystery.

So the little bitch was still in the game. He had blocked her out from his memory, but now she was back with a vengeance. Think, he repeated to himself. What did she want – money? What was her motivation – spite? And where were the police? Was it a trap? He rebuked himself for never having made the effort to understand her; he had used and abused her, but had spent no time assessing what made her tick. He didn't even know why she had agreed to an affair with him. She remained as foreign as the day he'd met her.

He worked through the options he could take. If he saw her, what would it achieve? If he did not, what would she do? Could she be persuaded to stay quiet, by force or otherwise? He was quite prepared for violence: like a silent partner, it slept within him but was ready to support him when all else failed. He knew he could do whatever was required; he called upon the deep reserves of power that lurked inside his soul, and forced his mind to stay in focus. Only one thing mattered now; he must concentrate on that. This was a diversion: it could – and would – be overcome.

Once again he checked the little list of items he'd drawn up, and once again he confirmed that everything was in place. He unlocked his briefcase and scanned the contents, touching each article to verify that it was real. His hands were clammy from the excitement. The long road he had followed was finally at an end; soon there would be nothing left to trouble him, and he would be free.

He looked at his watch: ten-thirty. He had fourteen hours to kill. He looked around the study to see if everything was in order. A small pile of papers and folders lay on the desk, the sum total of his working life. The top of a large metal filing cabinet was clear; the computer diskettes were neatly tagged and stored in a plastic box, and the bookshelves which held manuals, files and reports were neat and clean. There was nothing to do. He stood up and looked out of the window. He didn't want to remember this view, across the busy road to the park; he wanted to erase all memories and come to the future with fresh, uncluttered vision. There was nothing that he wished to record.

He finished his coffee and took the mug into the kitchen. He read a shopping list that Clare had written, a small mundanity which reminded him that her life would have to go on without him. She would still need these essentials regardless of where he was or what he did; she would still exist and function, whatever the circumstances. But that life would be divorced from his, and he would no longer be a part of it. It would roll on regardless, unknown and unseen. This heartened him, to think that he was not arresting the continuum but merely changing it.

He went back to the study and put his jacket on. He slipped the letters into his pocket and went to the front door. He wanted to get out anyway; he needed some fresh air. A walk through the park would do him good.

★ ★ ★

347

She was sitting on the edge of the bandstand. She looked pale, her white skin in stark contrast to the red of her hair. He knew why he had been attracted to her, but felt it no more. He waited behind a bush, composing himself before moving forward. The park's population at this time of day was composed of mothers, nannies and au pairs, all wheeling prams and buggies across the flat wide spaces as they sought to fill the long hours. He could see no sign of anything odd, any indication that she had brought reinforcements. Emboldened, he walked towards her.

Rocket looked up but didn't move. She watched him approach, but made no expression of surprise or alarm. 'You've come, then,' she said as he reached her.

'Nothing better to do.'

'Shall we walk?' She got up before he could answer and he followed her along the path. 'It's been a long time, Will.'

'Not long enough.'

'I think you've lost a bit of weight. It must be all the worry.'

'Can we get to the point? I've no time for small talk.'

'No, that was never your strong point, was it? What I have to say won't take long, I promise. How are your listening skills?'

'It depends on what's being said.'

'Oh, I think you'll find this interesting. Did you read Betsy's letter?'

'I read it. But it didn't make much sense. Am I missing something?'

'I don't think so. I'd guess you understood it perfectly. I know I did. The question is, what am I supposed to do about it?'

'And that's why you're here – to ask me? Sorry, I can't help you.'

'Will, let's play at being grown-ups, shall we? You and I both know what went on. You may be able to live with that, but I can't.' Rocket stopped walking and turned to face him. 'Some lies are white; some are even grey. But this is a pretty black one in my book.'

'Who's lying?'

'Your whole life is a lie. Perhaps you've convinced yourself that what you did was right, but it doesn't alter the fact that you're deceiving everybody, including yourself. At some stage that fact is bound to emerge. You want to know what I think? I think it's unsustainable. You're kidding yourself if you think you can get away with it. Life doesn't work like that.'

'I have no idea what you're talking about. You've lost me.'

'You're right there. I have lost you. In fact, I never found you. You were always remote, even in bed. God knows, I've tried to get a reading on you, but I've failed. You just don't relate to anything or anyone, do you?'

'What do you think you know?'

'Knowledge. Now there's an interesting concept. There's information and there's knowledge. I have information – lots of it – but the knowledge is taking longer to acquire. I thought you might be able to help me there.'

'Maybe I can. We had a crisis in our family. In the old days I might have relied on Clare to sort it out, but it was obvious she couldn't. Her problem's always been that she can't change gear; she's stuck at one speed. So I had to step in and take control, and that's what I did. It's what I'm doing right now. You should try it some time – it feels great. Problems get sorted. Ours did.' He smiled at her. 'Does that help?'

'So how far does your control extend, Will? Does it go as far as determining who will live and who will die?' Rocket tensed her right hand in her pocket, squeezing the handle of the gun.

'That sounds rather melodramatic, even for someone as screwed up as you.'

'Maybe you're right, and I am screwed up. But I haven't lost all sense of perspective. I can still see the difference between good and evil. That's the only thing keeping me sane right now. And I'm asking myself which category you're in.'

'Kind of you to be so concerned about my morals, but there's really no need. I'm doing quite well without your interference, and I'd like it to stay that way.'

'But it can't, can it? Like it or not, your fate and mine appear to be inextricably linked. One of us has got to yield on this, and all bets are off. The outcome's too close to call.'

'I'd have to disagree with that. The smart money's on me. I don't intend to do anything that'll endanger Tom's future, and I wouldn't advise you to, either.'

'So what do you do for an encore? Where's this all leading?'

'That shouldn't concern you. You'll just have to trust to my superior judgement. Go home to your grubby little world of petty thieves and crooks and leave us to get on with our business. You have no place here.' Will turned away and she needed to say something quickly to stop him from leaving.

'Clare said—'

'Clare?' he shouted, swinging on his heel and moving in on her. 'You've spoken to Clare? How dare you? Who the fuck do you think you are?' She recoiled and grasped the gun. His mood had changed so abruptly that she had no time to assess it, merely reacting instinctively to his rage. He grabbed her lapels and shook her, his eyes wild and penetrating. 'Listen to me,' he growled. 'I've put up with this charade for long enough. You have no right, no right at all, to be poking your nose into our affairs. What's done is done, and that's all there is to it. You'd better accept that and keep your mouth shut, do you hear?'

'Or else?' Rocket said in panic. 'What will you do – put an axe through my head? Is that an option, Will?'

He pushed her away roughly and stood with his fists clenched. Then he suddenly relaxed and smiled. 'You really are more stupid than I imagined. You're not worth the effort. I came here because I thought you might have something useful to say, but now I realise that you're just a neurotic little bitch who can't deal with her own life. You're pathetic, you know that?'

Rocket swallowed hard and tried to stay calm. 'Don't do this, Will. You're backing down a dead-end street. Can't you see that? I want to help you, I want to understand what's going on, but you're shutting me out. Please – please. If not for me, then for Tom.'

'What do you know about Tom? You think you can waltz back into our lives, unannounced and uninvited, and dictate terms. Tom's situation has nothing to do with you, and I will not let you break us up. Believe me, I'll do whatever's necessary to stop you. Don't be in any doubt about that.'

'I don't want to break you up, Will. That's the last thing

on my mind, but you're pushing me to the edge. I came here to see what we could do together, not to fight. Sure, you can threaten me and you can frighten me, but I will not be ignored. It's gone way past that.'

He stood very still and looked her up and down. His jaw muscles clenched as he thought about how to play this. 'You're the proverbial bad penny, Rocket, and I want you off my back once and for all. I don't want to harm you unless it's really necessary, and it doesn't need to be if you leave us alone.'

'I can't do that, Will. It's gone too far and I know too much.'

'Then let me help you to change your mind. You seem to be concerned about Tom. His safety depends on how you play this. You mess around, and no one can guarantee what the outcome might be. But if you drop out now, I'll play my part and everything will be fine – including Tom. Isn't that what you want?'

She wanted to pull the gun out and shoot him dead. She could see how this would resolve a lot of problems, even if it created new ones. But the stronger sense was to wait, to see how things might develop now that he knew she was on to him. A part of her reasoned that Tom might indeed be safer and happier were she simply to walk away and pretend it had never happened. Perhaps they could all settle down and she could forget what she had heard from Betsy – and, after all, who would really care?

His final action caught her unawares: he came close and put a hand round the back of her neck and kissed her hard on the lips. 'Goodbye, Rocket Stubblefield,' he said, as he looked deep into her eyes. As he walked away she thought of how easy it would be to gun him down, one shot to the back of the head and walk away. But though her arm twitched as if to pull out the gun, something stopped her, and she couldn't help feeling that her final opportunity had just evaporated.

THIRTY-EIGHT

Even by her own standards, which had fallen dramatically, it seemed pretty daft, but she felt she had no choice. Having lain on the damp bed in her hotel room, incapable of sleep or rational thought, Rocket had decided to stand sentinel outside the Easterbrooks' flat. Late in the afternoon she had taken up position inside the park railings, about twenty-five yards down from the front door of the building; she had brought tins of Coke, baguettes, chocolate and four packets of cigarettes. She had also brought her gun.

She saw Will leaving soon after she arrived; impulsively she wanted to follow him, but she stalled the action and remained where she was. She could see a phone box on the other side of the road, and she came out of the park and crossed over to it. She punched the number and waited.

'Hallo?' a man's voice said, sounding surprised.

'Hallo. Is Clare there?'

'Clare.' He seemed to be no wiser. Then Rocket heard another extension being picked up.

'It's all right, Dad,' Clare said, and Rocket heard the phone being replaced. 'Hallo. This is Clare Easterbrook.'

'Clare, hi. It's Rocket.'

'Oh. I wasn't expecting to hear from you again.'

'No, and I wasn't expecting to call you either. But something came up.'

'Yes?' Clare tried not to sound annoyed, but she obviously was.

'I saw Will.'

'I see. I thought you said that wouldn't be necessary.' She was distinctly icy now.

'I changed my mind. It's a woman's prerogative, remember?'

'And?'

'And this. I got the distinct impression that you and the children may be in serious danger. I tell you, he scared me. And I think he's liable to do something crazy, maybe even fatal. I wanted to warn you.'

'Rocket, you're sounding hysterical. I appreciate your concern, but I think I know Will slightly better than you and I'm sure that no harm is going to come to us. At least, it won't if you would stop meddling. Go back to New York and forget about us. Now, was there anything else?'

Rocket was desperate. She knew how she sounded but couldn't control it. 'Humour me, Clare. Do one thing for me. Go and look for anything unusual in the apartment, any signs that something's different. I've just got this very strong feeling that he's going to turn nasty, or that he has a plan we don't know about.'

'I've just this minute been round the flat, as it happens, and you'll be happy to know that everything's where it should be. With the greatest of respect, I really don't want to talk about this any more. If you get in touch again I'm calling the police. Is that understood?'

356

Rocket gave up. There was nothing more she could do. 'Sorry to have bothered you. Put it down to lack of sleep.'

'Goodbye, Rocket.' Clare cut the line and Rocket stood motionless. A thin sheet of rain started to fall; what the hell, she thought. I might as well get wet here as anywhere else. She went back into the park and leant against the railings.

It was a hunch, no more than that, but right now she trusted them more than anything else. The taxi pulled in at the side of the road at twenty minutes after midnight; its yellow light was extinguished, and Rocket had learnt enough about London to know that meant it was not for hire. She wandered over casually and leant down to look at the driver through his window.

He pulled down the window. 'Sorry, love, this one's booked.'

'I know,' she said. 'It's for Mr Easterbrook, isn't it?' The cabbie looked at his notepad and nodded. 'He asked me to tell you that he'll be a few minutes late and that you're to hang on.'

'A pleasure – the meter's running,' he said, laughing.

Rocket was now high with adrenalin and pushed her luck still further. 'This is going to sound really dumb, but could I sit in the back and wait for him?' She put on her smallest, sexiest voice and it worked: he reached back to open the passenger door for her and she hopped in. Rocket slumped against the hard upholstery and dug her hands into her coat pockets. She was drenched from hours of standing in the drizzle, and her whole body longed for deep, sound, dreamless sleep.

Every minute seemed like an hour. She turned over the chain of events that had brought her to this, preferring to look back than to speculate on how it might turn out. Doing the right thing was uppermost in her mind: hang the consequences, she told herself, and follow your nose. She waited with a mixture of apprehension and naked terror.

At half past twelve the door of the mansion block opened and Will came out. He was carrying two tote bags and he walked straight over to the taxi. The cabbie jumped out to help him with the bags and Will opened the passenger door. Rocket was wedged into the far corner, her feet splayed and both hands holding the gun in front of her. It was pointing straight at Will's head.

'Oh, shit!' the cabbie shouted as he saw her.

'Go and call the police,' Rocket ordered him, never taking her eyes off Will. 'There's going to be an accident.' The cabbie needed no second bidding and disappeared.

Will stayed frozen in his bent position, one hand still on the handles of the tote bag as it lay on the floor in front of Rocket. In the dull interior light of the taxi his face seemed to have collapsed.

'What are you doing?' he said very carefully.

'What does it look like, Will? I'll use it if I have to.'

'That's bullshit, and we both know it.' Although he sounded more certain, he didn't move.

Rocket raised her eyebrows. 'What's in the bag, Will? Planning a little holiday with Tom?'

'You're crazy, Rocket. You'll never get away with this. For God's sake, what's going on here?' He was starting to panic and Rocket could almost smell his fear. She was enjoying it.

358

'I tried reasoning with you but it didn't work. I thought this might do the trick.' She twitched the gun slightly and his eyes focused on it.

'Give it to me and we can sort this whole mess out. We don't need to do this, you know. I'm sure we can do a deal.'

'No more deals, babe. You stay right where you are and we'll wait for the cops, shall we?' She suppressed a shiver and flexed the muscles in her thighs, which were starting to cramp badly. 'What have you done with Clare? Is she OK?'

He let out his breath wildly. 'Christ, she's fine. She's fast asleep. What do you think I am?'

'I don't know, but I wouldn't put anything past you. What about Tom? Is he upstairs?'

'Where else would he be? You're making no sense, Rocket. Please – give it up.' He brought his free hand, which had been resting on the open door handle, in front of him, slowly, palm up, but she shifted her weight and jerked the gun at him.

'Stay where you are, and we'll all be a lot happier.' Then, out of nowhere, Rocket sneezed, an explosion that cracked her in half. As she lurched forward Will saw his chance and jumped back from the door, slamming it shut as he stumbled across the pavement. Rocket's eyes watered heavily and it was several seconds before she could see and assess the situation. She fumbled with the door on her side until it opened and she tumbled out, falling into the road. She picked herself up and could make out Will's silhouette as he ran towards the park; she raised her gun and shouted: 'Stop! For Christ's sake, stop!'

But he didn't. Too tired to chase him, too tired for

rational thought, Rocket abandoned all concepts of right and wrong, good and evil, truth and lies; her whole life seemed dependent on this one moment when all action was frozen and time itself had stopped. Rocket made the decision. She squinted down the barrel of the gun and braced herself.

The first shot hit him square in the side of the thigh. It shattered his femur and he fell heavily, having no time to put out his arms as he crashed to the slippery pavement. She kept the gun trained on him as he rocked himself on the ground; then he began to get up. He grabbed a lamppost for support and pulled himself straight; he was just beginning to move away when she fired again.

This time the bullet winged his shoulder, spinning him round so that he faced her momentarily until he dropped from the force of it. In the orange light she could see the blood on him, could see the ripped and shredded clothes and flesh, and she stood transfixed as Will writhed in agony. Her hands sang with the fizzing pain from the gun's recoil, and her ears were filled with the explosions, blocking the sound of Will's moaning. She dropped the gun and fell against the taxi, sliding down until she was on the tarmac. She retched violently, head thrust between her knees, and waited for someone else to take control.

Devoid of make-up and deprived of rest, Clare's face at last betrayed the years of suffering. She sat on the edge of the sofa as if she might be called away at any moment, but her attention was concentrated on the policeman who sat opposite her.

'At some stage we'll need to take a statement,' he said, 'but that can wait. For now, we just need a few details.'

'I understand,' she said.

Clare sought to hide her confusion and alarm. She had travelled with Will in the ambulance, after the police had broken down her bedroom door to release her, and had waited four hours as they operated and stabilised. She had sat with him, holding his hand and stroking his hair, desperate for some reaction, but he remained unconscious. The surgeon had told her that he would live, even though he'd lost a lot of blood.

As she maintained her silent vigil at Will's bedside, she struggled to reconcile the feelings she had – for him, for Tom, for India, for Ralph and, most difficult of all, for herself. Her overwhelming sense was of release, as if the pressure valve had finally burst: however much she tried, she couldn't resist the compassion she now felt for Will as he hovered close to death. She asked herself how it had come to this, how their lives could have become so complex that only a crisis of this dimension could resolve matters. She blamed herself, reasoning that it was her duty to provide her family with security and peace and that she had failed to do this. Will was a victim of circumstances and must never be put in the same position again. It was up to her to offer him a life free of the agonies he had suffered. Even as she thought of this she knew it would be tough, that there was so much to forgive and forget, but she could see no other course. She needed to know everything, but promised herself that such knowledge would not diminish her determination to pull the family back together.

At eight o'clock the next morning, the police drove her home and she was reunited with India, Tom and Ralph. Outside the building they had closed the road and erected a tent where Will had fallen; all around, interested spectators craned their necks to get a better view as she was led back into the flat.

She went through a ritual of questions and answers with the officer. His tone was soft but insistent. Why was she locked in her room? Did she know where Will was planning to go? Who was Rocket, and why was she there? She forced herself to answer as best she could, even though she doubted her own interpretation of events.

When it seemed they had finished, she asked her own question. 'What happens now?'

He relaxed a little, as if pleased that she should show some interest in his work. 'We've already spoken to the police in New York,' he said. 'This Rocket Stubblefield is quite a character, by all accounts. They're very keen to get their hands on her and we'll be cooperating with them on that, I promise you. Frankly, we'd prefer to get her back into their safekeeping as soon as possible. Once your husband is strong enough we'll need to talk to him about the whole affair. But you have my assurance that Rocket Stubblefield will be properly dealt with.'

'Does Tom need to be involved in this?' Clare asked. 'I really don't want him to suffer any more.'

'I appreciate that, and we'll try to keep him out of it as much as possible, Mrs Easterbrook.'

'Thanks.'

'Is there anything we can do for you?' the policeman asked.

'There is one thing I wanted to ask you,' she said after some thought. 'It's going to sound pretty strange, but I wonder if I could see Miss Stubblefield?'

'Any particular reason?'

'I need to talk to her, so I can get it all straight in my head. I promise I'll behave.'

'That's a pretty irregular request, I have to say. I'll see what I can do.'

'I'd appreciate it,' Clare said. 'It would help a great deal.'

'We're going to leave WPC Henderson with you. She's here to help, so don't be afraid to ask if you need any.'

Clare nodded, her eyes red and misty. 'OK.'

'I'll come back later on, and if you're feeling up to it, we'll talk then.'

'Thanks.' He left, and she didn't know what to do next. The children had been taken to school by neighbours, and Ralph was watching television. She wanted to go back to the hospital; she wanted to close her eyes and wish it all away; but, most of all, she needed to see Rocket.

THIRTY-NINE

'Tell me everything,' Clare said.

The two women sat in an interview room, facing each other across the desk. A policewoman stood guard by the door. The pain in Clare's face was directly reflected back to her in Rocket's.

'You don't need to know everything, Clare. You've suffered enough.'

'I'll be the judge of that. Just get on with it. You can't harm me any more than you've already done.'

'I guess I deserve that,' Rocket said, and lit a cigarette. She blew out smoke and closed her eyes briefly. 'The trouble is, I don't know where to begin. I seem to have said that a lot recently.'

'Why did you do it? Let's start with that, at least.'

'Is this off the record?' Rocket nodded towards the policewoman. Clare caught the officer's eye and the look was enough. The woman left the room and they heard the door lock behind her. 'What I have to tell you is only going to make things worse and, believe me, that's the last thing I want. But if you insist . . .' Rocket waited for Clare to show some emotion, but she merely nodded, a sign that she wanted Rocket to continue. 'Oh shit, let's just do it. Will killed Chuck Callahan.'

There was a strained silence as Clare sat rigid; no muscle moved in her face and her body was equally immobile. She breathed out heavily. 'What makes you say that, Rocket?' she managed to ask.

'There's a lot of history here, Clare. But I'll take full responsibility for that – I'm up to my neck in it anyway. After you dropped me from the case I found I couldn't forget about Tom. And I have to admit that I let personal feelings get in the way of my professional judgement. Whatever – I kept on looking for Tom, and eventually I got lucky. Some contacts of mine picked up his trail in Florida and I went down to check it out. It turned out that they were right – Tom was there, and he was well established with Chuck and Betsy Callahan.'

'So what did you do?'

'I lost control. I was confused and a little mad, so I went to see them. I met with Tom, and I had a long session with them. He was really happy, you know? It wasn't an act, I could see that. In a strange way that made things much worse, because I knew I had to tell you about it but I also feared for Tom. He'd be uprooted yet again, just as he was beginning to get settled.'

'That sounds pretty weak, if I may say so,' Clare retorted bitterly.

'I know, and don't think I haven't struggled with it too. But I was really messed up and I wasn't thinking straight. However, the minute I got back to New York I called Will and told him where he could find them.'

'You didn't contact the police as well? Why the hell not?'

'I felt . . . I felt as if I'd been too involved, and I needed to divorce myself from everything that would follow. Telling

366

Will was all I could allow myself to do. Yes, it was wrong and foolish and I accept that. But I did the best I could at that particular moment.'

'Go on.'

'You know what happened – the police showed up at the house, and found Chuck's body and not a lot else. They went there because Will called them.'

'I don't understand. You're suggesting he killed Chuck, then called the police. Doesn't that strike you as a bit odd?' Clare was showing the first signs of real anger.

'Hear me out, then you'll see why. You know that I spent a lot of time with Betsy after she was arrested. For whatever reason, she felt she could talk to me and I was quite happy to listen, in case what she said helped me to get things straight in my head. When she knew she was going to die she obviously decided to confide in me – and to give me a little test.'

'A test?'

'Oh yes,' Rocket said, lighting another cigarette from the stub of her old one. 'Betsy was very keen on tests, especially moral ones. I think she felt that I'd let her down by telling Will about them, and she wanted to see if I could make amends. She could be pretty weird like that – very religious, pious almost. She handed me enough information to make sure that I'd have no alternative but to take her final test – and, if she wasn't around to witness it, she figured God would be watching me.'

'What information?'

'I don't know exactly what Will did when I gave him their address, but he showed up pretty quick in St Petersburg. Now we're getting to Betsy's part of the story. He hammered on the door and kicked up quite a stink.

They were used to taking serious precautions, so Chuck answered the door only when Betsy and Tom were well out of sight. Will burst in, ranting and raging about Tom and where he was. Chuck must have known that flat denial was out of the question, and he was probably pretty scared. So he told Will that Betsy and Tom had already moved on. He said that they'd left him in the middle of the night and he had no idea where they were – or if they'd ever be back. Meanwhile Betsy and Tom were hiding in the back of the house, listening to this exchange.

'If Chuck thought that this would calm Will down he was much mistaken. Will evidently flew into an even greater rage and started rampaging round the house. Chuck needed to stop him, and tried to, but Will was obviously too strong for him. Betsy said that they kept a small firewood axe in the lounge, just in case. Will got hold of it and used it on Chuck.'

'Betsy saw this?' Clare growled.

'No. But she came into the room just after it had happened. Will was standing there, the axe in his hand, completely incapable of taking in what he had done. Even when he saw her he didn't move or register anything. You didn't know Betsy, but she was tough as nails. You might imagine she'd have collapsed, but she held her nerve. She took the axe from Will and sat him down – with Chuck's body still on the rug, for Christ's sake. She calmly proceeded to tell him that there was a solution to all this, and that he'd better listen real hard. She offered him a deal, although he was in no position to bargain.'

'What kind of deal?' Clare held a stiff, unyielding position on her chair.

'A simple one, really. Betsy said that he could have Tom back, if that's what he really wanted, but that she would go straight to the police and tell them what had just happened. The alternative was that she would keep her silence, and the price for that would be Tom. It was some deal, huh?'

'And you believe this? Aren't you being a little naïve, even by your own standards?'

'Betsy's no killer. The cops had her down for the murder, no question. They saw her as some kind of religious nut, and I figure they'd classified her with the Islamic fundamentalists, you know, capable of anything in pursuit of their beliefs. But her faith was very different, and I think she truly loved Chuck, in her own peculiar way. What's for certain is that she loved Tom to distraction, and she would never do anything to jeopardise his future. Why would she kill Chuck? Sure, she had the opportunity, but where was the motive? That's what the cops have never got a handle on. So yes – I believe it.'

'You still haven't explained why Will made the call.'

'Once he was out of the house and had calmed down, he realised he'd been turned over big time. And he decided to call the police straight away, hoping they'd bust in on Betsy cleaning up the mess and holding the axe in her hand. That way, he'd put her in the frame for Chuck's murder and he'd get Tom back. It was a long shot, but what else did he have?'

'Has Will ever confirmed any of this to you – or is it just all supposition?'

'Not in so many words, I admit. But he did it, that much I know.'

'You think that Will – my husband, whom I have known

all these years – is capable of murder? How dare you say that?'

'We're all capable of murder when it comes down to it. If something matters to us enough, we'll kill to protect it. That's human instinct, Clare. He even said as much to me once when we were talking about Tom.'

'Was that pillow talk, Rocket?' Clare's fatigue-stained eyes looked unwaveringly at Rocket's.

'What do you want me to tell you? How much pain do you need? I don't see the point.'

'Perhaps you think you're the only victim in all of this. Perhaps you feel that everyone else has their lives in perfect order and only poor little Rocket needs to get things sorted out. But I have the same rights as you – in fact, many more when it comes to Will. If you were screwing him I need to know. It would help to explain a lot.'

Rocket sighed and lit another cigarette. 'It was quick and entirely physical. He needed a release and I was available. It meant nothing. I'm sorry it happened, and I know that doesn't make it any easier, but that's all I can say.' Clare was unable to speak, as if this confession had winded her badly. Her head dropped and she stared at her hands on the table. 'Is that enough?' Rocket asked softly.

'What else is there?'

'Loose ends, mostly. I came over here to confront Will. Betsy had driven me to do that at the very least, and the police were also burning my butt. But he showed no remorse. He seemed so different, so frightening, that I suspected something else was going on. That's why I called to warn you. I didn't figure he was going to try and run off with Tom, but that's what he planned to do, wasn't it?'

Clare nodded. 'I found the tickets and passport in his briefcase. If you hadn't stopped him, he'd have gone back into the flat to get Tom. He'd locked me in the bedroom.'

There was another long pause as they both collected their thoughts. Rocket eventually broke it. 'Is this really a complete surprise to you, Clare? Surely you must have known something was going on.'

Rocket could see that Clare was deciding whether and how to answer the question, and she stayed silent to help her. Clare breathed slowly and deeply as she weighed the options.

'You never really know, do you?' Clare said. 'I mean, we never truly know what's going on in someone else's head, however well we think we know them. I thought I could read Will like the back of my hand, but then he changed so much that it was like being married to a stranger. I'm still trying to work it all out, and it isn't easy. If Will intended to run off with Tom he must have believed that they'd be better off away from me. What other explanation is there? I thought we were starting to get things back on track, and that's where I was so wrong. I had no idea that Will was so close to the edge. Of course I knew how desperate he felt, but he never let me get near enough to him to help – he always said I didn't understand. He was certainly right about that.'

'No one's blaming you.'

'No one except me. I just don't know how I could have been so blind to what was going on. What you've told me still doesn't make any sense. His version of events in Florida is certainly very different to yours, and I'll never know what to believe, but I do remember thinking it was odd that he didn't want me to go down there. He said it

371

was too far to travel when I was so pregnant and that he could handle everything. He never mentioned your involvement – he said the police had got a lucky break. Why should I question that? But now, with the benefit of hindsight, I should have realised.' Clare shuddered. 'There were other things, you see.'

'Other things – like what?'

'Ralph, my father. He's a bit senile, you know, and we don't always pay much attention to the things he says. Will started to resent him pretty badly, and I never understood why. But there might be an explanation, and I didn't – wouldn't – work it out. I think Tom called him not long after he was abducted. We'd taught him the number, and Ralph mentioned it much later. That might not be so important, but I have a deeper fear. I think Tom called him after Mr Callahan was murdered.'

'Jesus. What makes you say that?'

'Once I overheard a conversation, a very short one, between Ralph and Will. Ralph said something about Will staying away from him, that he knew all about him because Tom had told him. At the time it meant nothing and I never bothered to pursue it. But now, in the light of what you've told me – well, it adds up, don't you think?'

'You're saying Tom might have seen what happened?'

'Who knows? He was certainly very wary of Will when he came back to us. He even admitted to being scared of him when we went to therapy. But again, that could be for any number of reasons.'

'Have you asked Tom about it?'

Clare shook her head wearily. 'It's one of many things that have been deferred. I couldn't bring myself to ask him about his time with . . . them. And I could talk to my father for a hundred hours and he'd never tell me. His memory's like a bran-tub. You never know what's lurking in there.'

'So where does that leave you? What will you do now?'

Clare looked up and straightened herself. Rocket admired her: she could see Clare literally pulling herself together and restoring her poise. 'I have a family that needs me,' Clare said, 'and I intend to look after them – all of them. That's my role. What you've told me, even were it true, is a story that ultimately has no relevance to our current situation. Right now, we just need to be together and free from any further grief. And I suggest you start worrying about yourself and leave us in peace. You're a very sick woman, and you need a lot of help.'

Perversely, Rocket enjoyed hearing this. It was all that she had hoped for; she had not misjudged Clare. 'Thanks for the advice – I could do with it right now.'

'Do I take it that this conversation is the end of the matter for you as well?'

'You can bet on that. By the time they let me go home, no one's going to give a damn about the Callahans.'

'I appreciate that. I can't say I like you, Rocket, but at least you have some sense of honour.' Clare got up and walked to the door; she knocked loudly and it was unlocked. Rocket watched her leave; then, finally, she felt a new and unusual sense of calm.

Clare stood and watched the flames lick at the airline tickets and Will's new passport. It was a small fire with much significance: she felt that it would help to burn away the sharp pain of her meeting with Rocket, cleansing her of dangerous recrimination. Despite all that Rocket had told her, and all she had worked out for herself, Clare would not be diverted from her chosen path. She only needed to look at Tom and India to convince herself now, more than ever, they deserved the safety and calm that she had promised them. Will was a necessary participant and she would honour her commitments to him, the children and herself. He was wounded and could be – must be – made better, for all their sakes.

When the flames had died she went to sit with Tom and India on the sofa, an arm round each as she pulled them close to her.

'Mum, what's going to happen to Daddy?' India asked. 'Is he going to get better?'

'Oh yes,' Clare said brightly, 'he's going to be as good as new – in fact, better than new. When he comes home from hospital we're going to go on a lovely holiday and we're going to have lots of fun.'

'And we're always going to stay together?' Tom asked.

'Always. We're a family, Tom, and we'll always be together.'

'That's good,' Tom said quietly. They were the sweetest words Clare had ever heard.